PRAISE FOR *MOTHER OF ALL SECRETS*

"*Mother of All Secrets* is a thrilling page-turner and a fierce manifesto about motherhood, powerful women, and what we must be willing to do to protect our children. The plot twists are breathtaking, and I loved staying up late reading this fabulous novel."
—Amanda Eyre Ward, *New York Times* bestselling author of Reese's Book Club pick *The Jetsetters* and *The Lifeguards*

"In *Mother of All Secrets*, Kathleen Willett has crafted an engrossing thriller with both heart and bite. Willett tenderly confronts the realities of postpartum life and the complexities of 'mom friends' while still delivering plenty of dynamic twists."
—Alison Wisdom, author of *We Can Only Save Ourselves* and *The Burning Season*

"This book is my new obsession. I completely devoured Kathleen Willett's addictive thriller *Mother of All Secrets*, which takes the life-upturning experience of new motherhood and brilliantly twists it into a riveting missing person story. Every time you think you know what happened, the book transforms, leaving you chasing the truth as breathlessly as the protagonist. Simmering with righteous anger and revenge under its polished surface, *Mother of All Secrets* deserves to be at the top of every thriller lover's TBR."
—Ashley Winstead, author of *In My Dreams I Hold a Knife* and *The Last Housewife*

ANYTHING
FOR A
FRIEND

ALSO BY KATHLEEN M. WILLETT

Mother of All Secrets

ANYTHING
FOR A
FRIEND

A NOVEL

KATHLEEN M. WILLETT

LAKE UNION
PUBLISHING

Published by Lake Union Publishing, Seattle

www.apub.com

Amazon, the Amazon logo, and Lake Union Publishing are trademarks of Amazon.com, Inc., or its affiliates.

ISBN-13: 9781662513091 (paperback)
ISBN-13: 9781662513107 (digital)

Cover design by Caroline Teagle Johnson
Cover image: ©Yvonne Röder / plainpicture

Printed in the United States of America

Women made such swell friends. Awfully swell.

—Ernest Hemingway, *The Sun Also Rises*

CHAPTER ONE

Monday

The shrill ringing of the landline jolts me from my trance.

I've been staring at my open laptop screen, eyes glazing over, mind drifting from place to place, anywhere except for the words on the document in front of me. Like what to have for dinner tonight. What time Pete's train is arriving back to Montauk from the city. Whether the lunch I made for Kelsey, a cheddar cheese and pickle sandwich, her favorite, made it into her backpack. Whether she would even eat it if it did.

To be honest, the incoming phone call is a welcome intrusion; it gives me an excuse to get up from my desk, which is piled high with nonsensical notes on Post-its and pens without caps. I really ought to get some cute bins and colored file folders to make my new workspace better organized, a little more Pinterest-esque. I need to accept the fact that this is our *home* now and try to spruce it up. Maybe I'm still slightly in denial about the fact that we moved out here to Montauk. For the time being, anyway.

We came out in a hurry in the late spring, when Pete's mom, Helen, took a turn for the worse. She passed peacefully a few days after we got here, as if she'd just been waiting to spend a little more quality time with us, watch a few more *Jeopardy!* episodes with her family by her side.

And since Pete's dad died a few years ago, their retirement home is now ours. After she died, we decided to spend the rest of the summer here; Pete had numerous loose ends to tie up, estate documents to file, a lot of work on the house to do, tons of purging. His parents weren't quite hoarders, but let's just say that dozens of Pete's Little League trophies were proudly displayed on the guest bedroom's shelves, despite the fact that they had moved here from mid-island when Pete was twenty-eight.

We'd originally planned to clean up the house and put it on the market in the fall. But in July, Pete floated the idea of staying out here for the year.

My first reaction was *Absolutely not*. Montauk is beautiful, but I am unequivocally a city person. I love how you can find everything you need within a block or two of where you're standing. I love the restaurants, the concerts, the cheap Thai food. I love not driving. I love our apartment and had no interest in moving into Pete's parents' dated beach house with its fanned blinds and stucco ceilings and lack of air-conditioning.

But Pete was excited about the idea. He's the kind of guy who likely would have preferred to live in a big house in the suburbs, spending weekends washing his car while blasting Tim McGraw. He said if we stayed out here, he could mostly work from home and just commute in for a few days every other week or so. And I can write from anywhere, he reminded me. Besides, it was hard to say no to him when he'd just lost his only remaining parent.

The move wasn't just for him, either. Kelsey had been going through something. It was as if she'd become an entirely different kid overnight. Our sunny little girl had been replaced by a sullen, hostile teenager who skipped classes and smelled like smoke and slammed her bedroom door with brute strength we didn't know she possessed. We weren't sure how much of this was "normal," but we thought a change of scenery might be good for her.

For me, too, if I'm being honest. After all, staying in Montauk would make it easier to avoid some mistakes I'd made—well, one mistake in particular, which our sudden departure had brought a natural and very necessary end to. It was safer here, where I knew I'd never run into said mistake and could just sort of let the dust settle on the whole episode. Midlife crisis, maybe, is what it was. But it's over now, and being in Montauk makes it easier for it to *remain* over.

I hustle upstairs to the kitchen to answer the phone. The sound the landline makes when it rings is urgent, not like the gentle jingle from an iPhone. We don't have a landline in our apartment, and having one now reminds me of being a girl in my parents' kitchen, waiting by the phone for a boy to call and being determined to answer it before my parents could. Twisting the cord around my fingers nervously as I made hushed conversation. Funny how something as simple as a phone ringing can transport you back to a long-forgotten version of yourself.

When I answer the phone, my voice is a croak, and I realize I've barely spoken to anyone all day. I *tried* to talk to Kelsey in the morning when I made her breakfast and drove her to school, but it was a bad morning for her, or what Pete jokingly calls a "black Friday," even if it's not a Friday. "How are you?" I'll ask her on such occasions. "How did you sleep?" And she'll look at me like she simply wishes I were dead. Or she won't look at me at all, as if I'm invisible. A ghost.

"Hello?" I say again into the flesh-colored phone after clearing my throat.

"Carrie," a familiar voice says softly. A jolt of recognition pummels me, but I dismiss it. Because it couldn't be her. It wouldn't be.

"Yes?" I ask, maintaining formality. I'm mistaken about the voice. I must be. It's probably a bill collector, or someone from Kelsey's school, or—someone. But not *her*.

"It's Maya," she says, the shyness in her voice making her sound like a kid.

So it is her.

3

Holy blast from the past.

I swallow what feels like a rock. "Maya!" I exclaim with overly bright enthusiasm, a thin attempt to mask my shock. I am happy to hear from her, of course. She's one of my oldest friends. She was my best friend all throughout college. We were roommates starting freshman year and became inseparable immediately.

But we haven't remained close in the nearly twenty years since college. She moved to the middle of nowhere in the Catskills after we graduated and took a job as an office manager at a tiny accounting firm—an odd choice, given that she was an English major, and most of our classmates were moving to New York or Chicago or Boston, gunning for well-paying or glamorous or at least glamorous-sounding jobs. Maya had considered New York, too, at my urging, but she'd ultimately changed her mind.

She was always better suited for a small town anyway, I suppose. She loved the outdoors and didn't mind solitude (unlike me, who would skip lunch if I had no one to eat with).

And we weren't great about keeping in touch after that, each busy with our own lives. We didn't even go to each other's weddings; she RSVP'd yes to ours but then was sick at the last minute and couldn't make it. And we didn't go to hers because she eloped; she told me she'd gotten married in a brief and perfunctory text. I've never even met her husband.

Maya and I had lunch in the city a couple of times over the years when she was there for one reason or another, but it was clear while making strained conversation over Caesar salads that our friendship had lost its natural rhythm. Once, we met in Rhinebeck for an overnight with the girls, at my suggestion—her daughter, Lola, was just a few months younger than Kelsey, and both girls were around eight at the time—but that didn't go particularly well, either. Lola was very quiet and completely enmeshed in her Beverly Cleary book. When she did engage with Kelsey, it was only to tell her about the chapter she'd just finished. Lola was wearing a Simon & Garfunkel sweatshirt and a black beanie, possessing Maya's exact brand of effortless cool, even at eight. Kelsey had a bedazzled headband and an iCarly sticker attached to her glittery pink rolling suitcase. They weren't exactly two peas.

When I picture our friendship, it has only one setting: Middlebury's green campus. It didn't survive beyond that.

Which is why Maya is the last person I expect to hear from. Especially since she's calling me on the landline of Pete's parents' house. How does she even know we're here? And how did she get this number? I stop myself from asking her. To be honest, if she called my cell phone, I might have let the call pass, waited for her to leave a voice mail, and then called her back later when I was more prepared to talk to her, to avoid being caught off guard like I am now.

I clear my throat again, awkwardly. "It's good to hear your voice. I can't believe it's really you! How is . . . everything?"

"We're . . . we're okay," Maya says hesitantly. "And actually, we're really close to you."

"Hmm?"

"We're in Amagansett."

What the hell are they doing in Amagansett? New York is a big state, and the Catskills are hours and hours from here.

I allow the pause to go on for too long as I process my surprise, so Maya speaks up again. "We'd love to see you if you're free, but I know it's last minute."

"No, of course!" I say brightly, trying to recover. "Of course. I'm home and I'd love to see you, too. You're with Lola and"—I struggle to come up with her husband's name—"Elliot?"

"Just me and Lola," she says, a tightness creeping into her voice. "You're at seventy-one Tyler Road, right?"

I'm taken aback momentarily that she knows our address, but then I remember: Pete, in his excitement about my reluctant acquiescence to stay in Montauk for a year, sent an email blast to all our friends and family with the news of our (temporary) address change. She'd have been on Pete's email list, since they were friends, too; we all went to Middlebury together. She was the one to introduce me to Pete, in fact, albeit inadvertently; they shared a class sophomore year, and I happened to be in that building at the same time for office hours with a professor. I met Pete as he and Maya were walking out together.

And the rest, as they say, is history. Lots of it.

"That's right, you've got it. The house is a bit of a mess, I'm afraid." I think of the dishes in the sink, the unwiped counters. And our fridge is practically empty; I was going to go to the IGA and the fish market today. *What am I going to offer them? And how long are they going to stop by for? Seriously, what the hell is she doing all the way out here?*

"We don't mind. Trust me," she says reassuringly. "We'll be there in about ten minutes."

Ten minutes. Jesus. I'm still unshowered and in my usual unimpressive uniform of leggings and a sweatshirt. Three empty mugs with crusty tea bags sit on my desk downstairs. The breakfast mess is still spread across the kitchen counter, Kelsey's barely touched toast drying on its plate. I've got my work cut out for me.

"Okay! Great! See you in ten! Amazing!" My voice is so strained with false excitement that it hurts my own ears to listen to it. I wonder if Maya can tell.

I really am looking forward to seeing Maya, truly. She means a lot to me. But the idea of having her here in my house makes me twitch. There are reasons we're estranged, after all.

I take a deep breath and brace myself for the flood of memories I know will come when I see her.

CHAPTER TWO

As soon as I hang up with Maya, I run around the kitchen like a maniac, trying to prioritize what to clean, since I clearly can't do it all in ten minutes. Mugs and breakfast dishes join the other dirty dishes in the sink. This house doesn't have a dishwasher, which drives me crazy (Pete claims he likes doing dishes the old-fashioned way, and yet, I don't see him doing them all that often). Mr. Sparkles, Pete's mom's cat—named by Kelsey when she was five—glares at me, not appreciating how quickly I'm moving. "Sorry, Mr. S," I mutter, stepping over him. He views us as unwelcome guests in his house. Me especially.

I run back downstairs to our bedroom (many of the houses in Montauk are "upside-down houses," to maximize the ocean view from the common spaces—a nice idea, but it makes me feel constantly disoriented). I put on a little mascara, despite not even having washed my face yet. I throw a sweater on over my workout top, which is a very meager improvement. I make my bed quickly, too, though there's no reason they would see our bedroom. Besides, given that Maya was my roommate for all four years of college, she likely remembers where I stand with my bed-making habits. I've never really been a star home-maker, in truth. I can cook about five things and would rather do just about anything than vacuum. But hell, I'm a professional young adult fiction writer, a working mother. I don't have to be a domestic rock star, too, right?

Not that the writing is going all that well. Or the mothering. But Maya doesn't need to know that.

I bet Maya makes her bed, though. She always did, meticulously, even in college; her bed looked like it had just gotten turndown service at the Four Seasons when half of our friends didn't even use a top sheet. She's also a good cook—she was the only person to use the dorm kitchen. She'd make pasta for the girls on our hall during finals, bake cookies for all of us to eat during one of our *Real World* binges.

I toss the sham pillows onto our bed and trot back upstairs, wondering how this reunion will go and what we'll talk about. I know so little about her life, and any questions I ask her will only serve to call attention to my lapses in knowledge. I'm 95 percent sure her husband's name is Elliot—I sure hope so, since I already referred to him as such when she called. And they live in the Catskills area, but the town's name is . . . Ridge Something. Ridgewood. No, Stone Ridge. *Making progress, Carrie.* At least I know that Lola is the same age as Kelsey, so I can ask her about her sophomore year and, hopefully, find some common ground there.

Back upstairs, I fold the blanket on the couch, fluff Helen's beloved "Life Is Better at the Beach" pillows, and take one last glance in the mirror above the mantel. Somehow I'm always surprised when a forty-two-year-old woman looks back at me, when I was expecting to see someone much younger.

I can't fix myself up any more than I have, though, because as I'm attempting to smooth down my hair in its bun using its own grease (lovely), the front doorbell rings. I am out of time.

I walk down the stairs to the front door. It takes me a second to budge the front door open; we rarely go in or out this way, usually using the deck off the kitchen as our point of entry and exit from the house.

The front door feels formal, and having to open it for Maya only adds to my nervousness.

Why am I nervous? She's your friend, Carrie. Just try to relax.

I open the stubborn door, and there they are, really here, at my house. Seeing her makes me feel eighteen again.

And not necessarily in a good way.

CHAPTER THREE

"Maya!" I exclaim, opening my arms.

"Carrie," Maya says quietly, a reserved smile on her face. "Thanks for inviting us."

"Inviting" them is not exactly how I would put it, but I know she's just being polite, and perhaps trying to save face, too, since she may feel as weird as I do about her showing up out of the blue like this. I wonder if I would have reached out to her if I'd been in her neck of the woods. It makes me a little sad to admit that I don't think I would have.

Maya's face has barely changed since college; with the exception of some frankly very cute crow's-feet by her eyes, she's hardly aged, and she's as tiny now as she was then, too, both short and slight. The main difference is that her hair is completely ice gray. She wears it well, though, in a chin-length blunt cut, and I'm jealous of the confidence it must take not to run to the salon in a baseball cap every three months like I do.

We lean into each other and hug awkwardly, briefly, our bodies not seeming to fit together—she's nearly a foot shorter than I am, and so birdlike it feels like I could break her if I wanted to. But when I feel her forehead against my cheek, I remember her: the ways she was there for me when I needed her most. How well we really know each other, to our cores. You don't get many friends like that in your life, I don't think. Despite the time and distance between us, Maya is one of those, for me. I know that.

I take a step back. "And Lola! My God! You are—" I catch myself. I know kids hate it when adults talk about how "big" they've gotten. I imagine it's the last thing in the world a teenage girl wants to hear. But she's added at least a foot to her height since I last saw her at our ill-fated sleepover in Rhinebeck. She towers over Maya and is nearly as tall as I am, five foot ten. And skinny, like her mom, with the same shiny dark-brown hair that Maya had when she was younger. "You've grown up a lot in the past few years!" I finish lamely. It's true, though; she looks almost like a different kid than the earthy third grader that Kelsey and I ate french toast with however many years ago that was. Her style is more glam now, with Taylor Swift cat-eyes and shiny leggings.

She looks me squarely in the eyes. "Hi, Carrie," she says, and I bristle slightly at hearing her deploy my first name with such ease. But what the hell would I want her to call me? Mrs. Byrne? It's not even my last name, since I never changed mine to Pete's; I'm still Carrie Colts. I wouldn't want her to call me Ms. Colts, either. No. I'm being ridiculous. Of course she should call me Carrie.

"Come in, come in," I tell them, realizing suddenly how cold it is. It's only November, but the Montauk chill is a more bone-biting type than New York City's, even if the temperatures in both places are practically the same. Other than trotting to and from the car to take Kelsey to school, I haven't been outside all day; I didn't realize how frigid it is. I hope the fleece that Kelsey wore to school is enough. Why didn't I insist she bring a warmer jacket? Then again, it's not like she has to go outside during school. She should be fine. *Stop worrying, Carrie.*

Once we're all inside, I take their coats—an oversize wool peacoat for Maya, a black puffy coat for Lola—and put them on our rack, immediately self-conscious of the piles of shoes at the foot of the stairs, the chipping paint on the banister, and even more so of my athleisure attire and unwashed hair, since Maya looks pretty and polished in black boots, jeans, and a gray sweater. I mumble an apology about the mess and lead them upstairs to the kitchen, where I sit them down at our cleaned-in-the-nick-of-time dining table. "So what can I offer you two? I'm afraid we're a little light on groceries at the moment, but tea or coffee, at least? I could make eggs, toast, if you're hungry?"

"Tea sounds great," Lola says, the assuredness in her voice slightly disarming. She looks around the kitchen appraisingly, immediately making me fret over the state of the house.

"We never really planned to live here," I babble sheepishly, flying around the kitchen as I put on the kettle and fetch mugs from the cupboard—we have exactly three clean ones remaining, mercifully. "This was Pete's parents' place. That's why everything is so . . ." I don't even know the word I'm searching for. The kitchen needs a gut, for sure. The appliances are from the early nineties, at best; the microwave needs double the time indicated on any given item's preparation instructions. The countertops are chipped, yellowing linoleum. The cabinet wood is dark and dated. And don't even get me started on the horrifically creepy unfinished basement that none of us ever go down to except when we blow a fuse. It's the opposite of our beloved apartment, which is now being enjoyed by Craig and Melanie, our renters, a newly married couple who both work at Goldman Sachs. Ugh. *Craig and Melanie.* I think of her using my nice espresso machine, of the two of them having sex in our bed, sitting on our cream-colored couch and watching TV on our flat-screen, and it makes me queasy and envious.

What I'm trying to tell them is that this house doesn't represent me. It doesn't. It's cluttered, haphazard, and aged, and I want to make sure they know that it's not a reflection of who I am now. I suppose it's always that way when you see someone from your past; you want them to see you at your best, thriving. It bothers me that Maya might be getting a very different impression. Although she's not even the one making me feel scrutinized: her teenage daughter is.

But all Lola's done is look around. It's not like she's pointedly handed me a copy of Marie Kondo's new book. I need to stop being so insecure.

"It's nice," Lola says. Maya nods her agreement.

I don't believe them, obviously. "Pete's mom just passed," I continue, rambling nervously. "So we'll probably make some changes. Pete has some projects in mind. And I've already ordered new curtains, paint samples, that kind of thing. We're here for the year, but we aren't sure if we'll sell it or keep it after that." Again, I feel myself flush with shame. *Good thing Pete's mom just died, so we can finally swap out these hideous curtains?* What is wrong with me?

And yet, there's something about the flash of Lola's eyes as she glances around, taking it all in—taking *me* in—that rattles me.

"I like it," says Maya softly. "It's charming. Low key. The perfect beach house," she adds kindly, and I'm reminded of what drew me to her in the first place, back in college—she always knew just what to say to help me calm down. She was the most level person I'd ever known.

Which reminds me that I haven't even asked Maya and Lola how *they* are.

And what's brought them here.

"What's new?" I offer. "How's Elliot?" *Please let his name be Elliot.*

"He's dead," Maya says bluntly, and I spit out my tea.

"I am so sorry," I sputter. "He died? When? How?"

"A few days ago. Heart attack. Very sudden. We're still processing." The clipped nature of her voice lets me know that if she were to go into more detail, she'd likely start crying. And she's trying hard to avoid this. Maya always kept a tight hold on her emotions.

I reach over and grab her hand, which feels strange after all these years, and yet completely natural. We slept six feet apart from each other for years, less than that when we had bunk beds, drifting off simultaneously while watching *Dirty Dancing*. Bodies remember that kind of closeness. "Maya," I whisper, and despite my shock over what she's just revealed, I notice that I like the way her name feels in my mouth. I think I've missed having a reason to say it.

"Thanks," she says, squeezing my hand. Hard. She clears her throat painfully and abruptly releases her grip on me. "That's sort of why we're here. It's hard to be in our house, with all the reminders. And I'm not ready to start thinking about tasks like the funeral, settling finances, that kind of thing. I just needed a beat, and we wanted a change of scenery. Some ocean air. A little time away." She looks briefly at Lola, who glances back at her without expression.

"Of course," I whisper. "That is so awful. Truly. I can't even imagine what you're going through." Goose bumps form on my arms as I try to envision it, Pete dying suddenly and leaving me to raise Kelsey alone. It's unthinkable. "Had he had heart trouble before?" *Why does that matter, Carrie?*

"No," she says softly. "Although it's not as though he kept up with his doctor visits. Maybe if I'd made him see a doctor, he'd have been on some heart medication, and this wouldn't have happened." I want to remind her that men are perfectly capable of getting themselves to the doctor. And then I recall how I lay out Pete's vitamins every morning next to his coffee mug; otherwise he'd never take them.

"It's not your fault," I assure her. "Please don't think like that." I turn to Lola. "It's so hard to lose a parent at your age. My dad died when I was just a little older than you. It wrecked me. I wasn't ready to be without a dad. If anyone's ever ready for that." My dad was a lawyer and former Connecticut senator who died of a heart attack when I was a freshman in college. We weren't *close*, per se, but he was my dad and I loved him, and I was also devastated that he hadn't lived long enough for me to really impress him yet. His pride was hard earned; he wasn't one to just give it away for free.

Maya drove back with me from Middlebury to Connecticut for his funeral, even though we'd only known each other for three months at that point. She said there was no way she was going to let me do that drive alone. We stopped at a Friendly's, and she asked for a McFlurry instead of a Friend-Z, and it was the first time I'd laughed since learning from my mom in a remarkably brief and matter-of-fact conversation that my dad was gone. I still remember how good that laugh felt. And how good the Friend-Z tasted.

"I'm sorry to hear that," Lola says quietly, and I realize with chagrin that in my effort to connect with her, to illustrate that I understand to some degree what she's going through, I've made it about me instead.

"Well, that was a long time ago," I say quickly, embarrassed to receive her sympathy when she's the one experiencing a loss. "But I can imagine how you feel, is all, and I'm so very sorry," I tell her sincerely.

Maya sits up and straightens her back, a reset. "So do you know of any decent bed-and-breakfasts around here? We're planning to stay a few days. Hoping a girls' trip will take our minds off everything, until we're ready to go back and deal." She looks over at Lola again, but this time, Lola's eyes stay fixed on me.

I purse my lips, considering. "Most of the smaller places are closed for the season. There's Gurney's, of course, right down the road, but it's—" I stop myself.

"Insanely expensive, right?" Maya finishes wryly. Money's always been a tricky topic between us. Maya showed up at college with one suitcase, no cell phone, a full scholarship, and a twenty-hour-a-week job at our campus's coffee shop. No family, either—her grandmother had raised her from when she was a toddler and had died the day after Maya's high school graduation. Maya joked to me, after we knew each other a little better, that it was as if it were her grandma's way of saying "My work here is done." Maya had taken the bus (two buses, actually) by herself from Barnstable, Massachusetts, where she grew up, to Middlebury. So not only did she have no money; she also had no support system. Meanwhile, my parents had driven me from Connecticut in their Land Rover, holding hands in the front seat as they usually did, my dad's big hand eclipsing my mom's, a dry news station playing from the radio. Our car was stuffed with half the contents of our local Bed Bath & Beyond. Maya had sat on her bed wide eyed as everything materialized, while I tried to assure her, blushing, that she was welcome to use it all: the microwave, the TV, the speaker. I think we were both always a little uncomfortable with the obvious difference in our circumstances.

Of course, at this point, I have no idea whether she can afford Gurney's; for all I know, she and Elliot were millionaires. Based on the bruised Pontiac that she and Lola showed up in, though, I kind of doubt it.

"We might venture back toward East Hampton or the Springs, then," she says. "Maybe find something around there."

"Stay here," I blurt, before I even realize that the words are on their way out of my mouth.

Maya hesitates. "No, we couldn't. We just wanted to come say hi. I would never ask you to—"

"You didn't ask," I point out. "I'm offering. We have plenty of room." It's true; the house has five bedrooms, and we're only using three of them, since I've taken over the smallest one as my office, while Pete's desk is in our room. Still, I'm surprised at myself; after years of not seeing Maya, having her and her daughter stay with us is quite a leap. But I feel so terrible for them, especially Lola at having lost her dad so suddenly, a grief I remember all too well. Besides, it really is good to see Maya. She's been there for me in ways that no one else has or would have.

Or should have, probably.

And honestly, that's probably why I've sort of kept her at a distance in my adult life. Some of our shared memories, I've worked hard to forget. But nothing that's passed between us should give me reason to be a crappy friend when her husband has just died. Besides, she's the one who showed up here. She *wanted* to see me. I've always felt like she's held a grudge over some of the things that happened our senior year and the summer after it, but maybe she's finally past it.

It's been twenty years, after all.

Though I know I'll never fully move on. I've just gotten good at faking it.

"Are you sure?" she asks. "I mean, it would be so nice to spend some time with you. It's been way too long. But I really don't want to impose."

"I'm positive," I tell her, and she smiles and nods with gratitude, and it is decided.

"Do you have stuff in the car? Should we go get it?" I ask, still not quite believing what's transpired.

"We'll get it later," she says, and she stands up and leans over my chair and wraps me in a hug. She has my arms pinned down, so I can't return the hug; I just pet her arm awkwardly by flapping my wrist. "I can't thank you enough for this," she says, her voice breaking slightly.

I look at Lola over Maya's shoulder, but she's busy surveying the kitchen again. She opens her mouth to sip her tea, and I notice one of her teeth is chipped.

~

1999

"Are you coming to the freshman barbecue?" Carrie asks expectantly. She's applying makeup in front of her vanity. Maya has just entered the room from the showers, towel wrapped tightly around herself, still uncomfortable with the notion of dressing in such close proximity to someone else. Having grown up as an only child to a grandmother who was inclined to keep her distance and having never participated in sports, she isn't accustomed to being half-naked in front of anyone.

Carrie does not seem to have the same problem. She's spent half the afternoon in her bra, trying on outfits as she unpacks.

"Oh, um, yeah, I guess so," Maya says. She's considering skipping it. She knows she should go and try to meet people, but she is also tired and wants some downtime. Plus, apparently the Middlebury library has some kind of a stuffed poodle in its special collection that she wants to go check out. She mentioned it to Carrie and her parents earlier while they unpacked Carrie's things, but Carrie seemed to have no idea what she was talking about. Maya knows that going to the library on the first day is probably dorky, but this poodle sounds so random that she has to see it for herself.

"Well, hurry up! I'm almost ready, and it starts in a few minutes."

"You don't have to wait for me."

"Of course I'm going to wait for you," Carrie says dismissively, as if Maya's suggestion is absurd. "We'll go together. What are you going to wear?"

Maya opens one of her drawers. It only took her about ten minutes to unpack, since all she's brought is one duffel bag with her clothes and toiletries, and her bedding. "Um, jean shorts and a shirt, probably."

Carrie walks over to her own closet and pulls out an orange tube dress. "This would look amazing on you. You're so tiny."

"Oh no, that's okay," Maya says quickly. She knows that Carrie is just being nice because she has to, since they're roommates.

Though she does kind of love the dress. She's never worn or even imagined wearing anything like it before. Her grandma took her shopping exclusively at Walmart, and she's always stuck to the most basic possible items: white T-shirts, jeans. Clothes that conjure the power of invisibility she's grown accustomed to.

"No, seriously," Carrie pushes. "It's too short on me anyway. I look super slutty in it. But on you, it will be totally classy. Perfect for the barbecue. Seriously! Try it on!" Carrie tosses it on Maya's bed, still on its hanger.

Maya smiles hesitantly and slips it on over her head, carefully and strategically keeping her towel on her body as she slides the dress down. She steps in front of the full-length mirror that Carrie's dad nailed to her closet door before he and Carrie's mom delivered their final goodbye lecture about how they were paying a lot of money for this school and that Carrie had better believe they'd find out if she was skipping any classes. Maya had noticed how Carrie's face reddened during this conversation. "I like it," Maya says softly.

"Um, no shit. You look amazing. You are for sure wearing that. You can just keep it." Carrie turns back to her dresser mirror.

Maya looks at Carrie uncertainly. "Are you sure?"

"Uh-huh," Carrie mumbles, her mouth open. She's applying lip gloss and can't really talk.

"Thanks. I'll wear it today, but you can take it back whenever you want."

Carrie snaps her lip gloss shut and shakes her head no, ownership of the dress already relinquished. She moves on to eye makeup.

"Want me to do your eyes, too? I just learned wings," Carrie says proudly, walking toward Maya brandishing an eyeliner pen like a weapon.

CHAPTER FOUR

When Pete gets home from the city late in the afternoon, his presence fills both me and the house with a warm relief. It's been only a few hours with Maya and Lola here, and already, I'm questioning my decision to invite them to stay. Our conversations have been stilted, and whenever they've retreated to their rooms, I've been scared to make any noise in case they're napping. What was I thinking, really? Maya and I haven't spoken in years. A long coffee with her would have been taxing. Having her with me twenty-four seven for—God, we didn't really settle on a length of time, did we?—feels like a *lot*.

"Mayaaa!" Pete says as he walks upstairs into the living room, as if her visit has been a long-anticipated bright spot on our calendar. "So good to see you, but hey, I am *so* sorry about Elliot. How awful. Jesus. We're here for you." She stands up from the couch and he wraps her in a hug, and it strikes me that Pete is the best hugger on the planet. There isn't a more secure place to be than in his arms. Once again, I find myself feeling selfishly grateful that his mother's death dragged us out of the city, because it also forced me to end something that never should have started in the first place. If not for Pete's mother passing away, who knows how long I'd have let it go on for? And what if Pete ever found out? Light-red spots form on my neck at the thought of it. He can never, *ever* know.

Pete is handling Maya's sudden visit much more gracefully than Kelsey is. When I picked her up from school and gently told her we had guests, my old friend Maya from college and her daughter ("you remember, Lola, right? From that bed-and-breakfast sleepover, years ago?"), she glared at me and said, "Seriously? *Who?*" with that cruel sass that only teenagers can deliver. I explained to her that Elliot had died suddenly and that it is important to help friends when they need it.

"Whatever, Mother Teresa," she huffed, looking out the window. "Just keep them out of my room."

I'm still not used to the new Kelsey. Up until a year ago, Kelsey was happy to have dinner with us each night, to come to yoga classes with me on the weekends. She'd tell us about her day in great detail: a corny joke her math teacher had made, an impactful sociology assignment about whether minimum wage was actually livable, something off-key the principal had said over the loudspeaker without realizing it was still on. Kelsey didn't even mind when I chaperoned class trips. Hell, she'd sit with me on the bus ride home. I remember the parents of her middle school friends trying to commiserate with me about how tough middle school girls were—the moodiness, the snark—and me feeling like I didn't have much to offer them in return. I thought we'd gotten lucky with Kelsey. Or, if I'm being honest, I thought we'd done such a damn good job parenting her (A-plus for us!) that our girl was simply *better* than the other kids. I'm embarrassed at my own smugness now.

Then during her freshman year, she ditched all her old friends and started hanging out with new ones. She all but stopped talking to me. She blocked Pete and me from following her on Instagram. She came home smelling like both kinds of smoke. Her grades started slipping. And in the spring, it all came to a head when she and her new friends pulled the fire alarm at their school. Since it wasn't a planned drill, everyone thought there was a real fire, and the exit was more chaotic than usual. A junior named Eva fell down the stairs and broke her wrist.

The girls were caught on school surveillance setting off the alarm. The evidence was as cut and dried as it comes.

They were suspended for a week, and the school made it clear to us that had this not been the first offense, the girls would have been punished more severely for this "thoughtless and completely unacceptable" transgression. The parents of the injured junior likely could have sued us, too, but apparently their own son had gotten in some trouble himself when he was in high school, so they had empathy for our position.

Kelsey, for her part, showed little remorse. "We just wanted a break from class," she'd say with a shrug every time we asked her what she'd been thinking. "We didn't think anyone would get *hurt*. God. It's just a fire alarm. It's not like we robbed a bank." As if that were anywhere close to a sufficient apology, or even an explanation.

We spoke to the parents of the other girls who'd participated in the prank, who were as horrified as we were. We went to a family therapist to talk about Kelsey's recent behavioral changes, and she basically told us to make sure that Kelsey knew we were there for her. That she was pushing us, and we needed to show her we were unbreakable. That we still loved her, *no matter what*. Which was obviously true. But despite how frequently we reminded her of this, and how often we asked her what was *really* going on with her, she wouldn't budge.

My mother lovingly reminded me that I was "a nightmare" when I was that age, shuddering with the recollection of teenage me as she sipped her gin and tonic and fingered an enormous diamond earring. My parents expected me to be perfect since *they* were perfect, pillars of the community climbing the ladder of life in the exact way that people were meant to. So even my most minor infractions, like my B pluses and the pack of American Spirits they found under my mattress, were met with grave disappointment. Since my dad was in the public eye, they loved reminding me of my responsibility to represent our family well. But it was clear to me even when I was little that my sister (a Stanford grad who now works in politics herself) was the better daughter, so in a way it felt simpler for me to just accept my role as the one destined to fall short.

I've tried so hard not to put that kind of pressure on Kelsey, to really let her explore and feel free of expectations so that she wouldn't have to rebel, but somewhere along the way, we still went wrong. I miss my little girl. And I'm scared she won't find her way back.

Kelsey didn't take our decision to stay in Montauk well, of course: she referred to herself as a "hostage" when we told her we weren't returning to the city for the time being, that we'd spend the year here and enroll her at East Hampton High. She made sure to tell us in no uncertain terms that we were the worst parents in the world and that she hated us. And yet, she *has* seemed better in Montauk. She's been eating normal meals (in the city, she went an entire month eating nothing but Cinnamon Toast Crunch), reading more books, and going for long walks with Pete, whom she seems to hate considerably less than me. She's been moody and bored and resentful, but her unhappiness hasn't felt quite as terrifying as it was in the months prior.

After Kelsey said a brief and unenthusiastic hello to Maya and Lola, she started to retreat to her room, but I gave her a look, and she rolled her eyes and sat on the couch dutifully. And even though I knew she was staying begrudgingly, I was relieved not to have to be alone with them anymore, having struggled to make conversation all afternoon. Other than having teenage daughters, Maya and I have little in common at this point in our lives. It was the same way in college, actually—we were sort of an odd pair, two mismatched socks. She was quiet, I was chatty; she was neat, I was messy; she was short, I was tall; she was a straight A student, I was—well, not. But at the time, our friendship felt to me like the most natural thing in the world.

"And Lola!" Pete exclaims. "You've gotten so big!" Okay, he apparently didn't get the memo that we don't say stuff like that to teenagers. "Hey, so sorry about your dad," he adds kindly, placing a warm hand on her shoulder. Unlike Maya, Lola didn't stand up from the couch when

Pete came upstairs, and that's because Mr. Sparkles the cat is lying on her lap, purring. It's very unusual for him to be so affectionate, but he's taken an immediate shine to her.

"Thanks," she says drily, and exchanges a quick glance with Kelsey, who smiles at her, a smile that says *Sorry about my clueless dad.* But it's a *smile.* A real, spontaneous smile. I haven't seen Kelsey smile like that for . . . a long time. It's a beautiful sight.

"You've got a fan, huh?" Pete tries to pet Mr. Sparkles's ears, and the cat cuffs him. Pete withdraws his hand and raises it, surrender-style. "You're the first of all of us to win him over."

"Animals like me," Lola responds matter-of-factly.

"Sorry to just barge in on you like this," Maya says to Pete, blushing slightly.

"Barge in? Please. We're so happy to have you guys. Carrie's probably told you that we don't exactly have a lot of friends out here yet, so it'll be nice to have the company." He walks to the fridge to get himself a beer, unaware of the *Why did you tell her that* glare I'm shooting into the back of his head. I don't need Maya knowing that I'm a friendless loser out here. Though if she's going to be staying with us, she'll see for herself soon enough that I don't exactly have a buzzing social life. Even though we technically live here now, the locals still look at us as city people, summer folk, outsiders of the tight-knit community. At home, I've got lots of friends and calendar entries beginning with "Drinks with," but here in Montauk, the only adult I talk to is Pete. The other moms at East Hampton High don't even acknowledge my existence at drop-off or pickup as they all get out of their cars to talk with each other. Unfortunately, I suspect that Kelsey is having a similarly tough time making friends, based on the fact that she spends every weekend watching nineties horror movies on her bed, and that every time we try to ask her if she's met anyone new, she basically tells us to screw off.

Pete turns around from the fridge, holding up his bottle of beer, and says, "Does anyone else want one of these?"

"I think I'll have wine," I say, suddenly itching for a glass, even though it's only 4:45 p.m. In the city, I barely drank at all, maybe a couple of glasses a week, but in Montauk, it's becoming dangerously easy to view 5:00 p.m. as wine o'clock, a reward for getting through another gray, lonely, unproductive day.

I pour myself a generous glass of chablis, and one for Maya, too, though she stops me midpour: "That's plenty for me," she says quietly, and suddenly I am self-conscious about my enormous glass. She never was a big drinker, even in college, when most people's lives revolved around getting drunk at parties. Her parents were addicts, which was why they were unable to raise her themselves. It had made her understandably careful.

"I'm going to start making dinner," I say decisively. "Is everyone okay with spaghetti?" *I hope so, because it's pretty much the only option, since I didn't shop today.* It would be easier to just pick up dinner from a restaurant, but I feel embarrassed not to cook on their first night here. Not that I'm really *cooking*—it's boxed pasta and the easiest tomato sauce ever—but at least I can use some oregano and basil from my little herb garden on the deck. And I think I have some salvageable lettuce and cucumbers in the fridge for a salad. A homemade dressing with lemon and olive oil and grainy mustard. It won't dazzle anyone, but it'll be serviceable.

"Spaghetti sounds great," Maya says. "I'll help you cook."

Please don't, I think as I say, "Great! Thanks."

"Can I see your room?" Lola asks Kelsey, nodding in her direction.

Kelsey looks taken aback but says "Sure" with a shrug, and they stand up from the couch and walk downstairs together, Mr. Sparkles trailing them. Pete flashes me a pleased expression, and I try my best to mirror it.

CHAPTER FIVE

"This pasta is amazing," Pete says emphatically, nodding appreciatively as he sucks in a noodle. "Even better than usual."

I try to stop myself from grimacing. Maya all but took over the sauce, doing things I never have, like adding sugar and a cheese rind from an old wedge of Parmesan she'd found in the fridge. I tried to convince her to leave me to it, to go lie down for a few minutes or peruse Helen's collection of Mary Higgins Clark books while the girls were occupied in Kelsey's room, but she wouldn't hear of it. "It's the least I can do," she insisted.

I take another small bite of pasta. It is undeniably a vast improvement to the sauce I usually make.

"Carrie's herbs really take it to the next level," Maya says graciously, though she must know that the leveled-up sauce is because of her, not me. "How long have you been gardening? I had no idea you had a green thumb."

"No, I really don't," I say quickly, though in truth I am rather proud of my little garden. "Just something I started since we've got the space out here. It's all easy, low-maintenance herbs. Foolproof, which is perfect for me. Really, I just use it as an excuse not to write!" I laugh, and then instantly regret bringing up my fledgling career.

"I loved your last book," Maya says sweetly. "It may have been my favorite of all of them. The guidance counselor character was hilarious!"

My heart warms. "You read my books? That's—that's so nice. Thank you." It really does mean a lot to me. And I'm glad she seems to think that I'm some glamorous, successful author, when that isn't quite the reality; only my first book, about a girl who sets out to reverse all her regrets before graduating high school, has sold respectably, but even that one didn't earn out of its advance, and the other two haven't come close. The one I'm working on now has potential, but writing it feels like pushing a double stroller up a hill. Each sentence has been a struggle. And I'm fairly certain my publisher only signed off on this one as a courtesy, a polite last chance.

"Kelsey, you must be really proud of your mom, the big author," Maya says to her.

"Her books aren't really my style," Kelsey says dismissively, and I feel myself flush. The irony of writing YA fiction and having so little understanding of the young adult living in my home is not lost on me. Plus, it's one thing for Kelsey to be mean to me in private, but in front of guests is a little humiliating. Besides, she *said* she liked my first two books. Back when she used to like *me*. It's only the latest one that she's refused to even glance at. "All of your main characters are so self-centered," she said to me once recently, and though I know they aren't *me*, it felt like she was talking about me.

Maya nods slowly at her and then turns back to me. "Well, it's great you found your way back to writing. I know it's what you always wanted. I was surprised when you left *People*." For several years after college, I worked at *People* magazine, climbing my way from administrative assistant to editorial assistant to, eventually, associate staff writer. But the hours were ridiculous and the pay meager, and after I had Kelsey (young, so young, but it's what Pete wanted and I owed him, even if he didn't realize I did), I needed something more practical, so I got a job running the Writing Center at the Fairley School, a fancy Upper East Side all-girls private school. Besides, the *People* gig had started to wear on me; it was the kind of job that sounded cool, which, when I took it, was the most important thing to me. But the older I got, the less I cared about celebrity breakups. And yet, when I took the job at Fairley, it still felt like some kind of defeat, a dream going up in smoke.

"So you're working on another book?" Maya asks, gracefully putting a small bite of pasta in her mouth.

"Well, trying to, but I've been slacking. For some reason, I'm having trouble getting into it." I shrug as if it's no big deal, when the truth is that I'm one failed novel away from unemployment and a complete crisis of identity.

"Well, I hope our being here won't distract you," Maya says, looking slightly concerned. "You mentioned some house projects? I'd be happy to help with anything you have in mind. You know I love organizing." I can remember vividly Maya's laminated notes in college, her color-coded desk files in our dorm room, whereas my desk always looked like a bomb had gone off and sent papers flying. Sort of like how my desk downstairs looks now.

I have a system, though. I swear I do.

"We're not about to put you to work!" Pete protests with a laugh. "You're here to relax. You've suffered a huge loss. Come on. You need to rest. Both of you. And you've come to the right place. There really is something therapeutic about Montauk. Something in the air that just . . ." He drifts off and looks at me, waiting for me to corroborate his romantic view.

"It's really nice," I chime in lamely.

"Well, we're grateful for a break," Maya says. "It's so hard being in that house. Both of us just see Elliot everywhere."

Pete and I look at Lola sympathetically, but she's busily twirling a bite of pasta onto her fork. When she feels us eyeing her, she looks up.

"Yeah, it was awful," she says, nodding vigorously. "I found him at the bottom of the stairs. At first, I thought he was just sleeping, but the way his body was kind of slumped—and when I got closer, he looked so white." Kelsey is staring at her wide eyed, as am I. Maya didn't mention that Lola was the one to find Elliot.

"That's probably more detail than necessary," Maya admonishes lightly, and Lola shrugs, looks back at her pasta, and says nothing more.

"Poor kid," Pete murmurs; even he can't come up with anything to brighten the somber mood that Lola's recollection has created.

My phone buzzes, and I'm glad for a distraction from this awkward moment. I fish it out of my back pocket to check it quickly (technically, we have a no-phones-at-dinner rule, though Pete and I are practically as bad about adhering to it as Kelsey is).

I nearly drop my phone into my spaghetti when I see who the text is from: Lara G., Hazel's Mom.

It's not really Lara. There is no Lara, and no Hazel. At least, not that I know. That's just what I put Kyle's number in as, in case Pete ever saw a text come through from him.

Kyle is the name of my midlife crisis, and part of the reason I agreed to hide out here in Montauk.

I shove my phone back in my pocket without looking at the text. It's been a couple of weeks since I've heard from him; every time I get a long stretch without contact, it starts to feel like I'm in the clear. That I've successfully disentangled myself.

So this newest text from him feels like a major setback, like I'm being pulled back into quicksand.

"Everything okay?" Maya asks. Pete glances at me with curiosity. My face must have betrayed me.

"Fine," I tell them. "Gap sale, in case anyone's interested."

Maya nods at me, her eyes flickering lightly. I can tell she doesn't believe me.

She really does know me too well.

~

1999

When Maya gets back to the dorm room she shares with Carrie, having finished her five-to-eleven-p.m. shift at the campus coffee shop, she is exhausted.

Working twenty hours a week plus keeping up with her classes and schoolwork is starting to take a toll on her; she's lost weight and is only sleeping about five hours a night. She has no choice but to keep grinding, though, if she wants to keep her scholarship.

Carrie isn't there when Maya gets home, which is something of a relief. Maya likes Carrie, likes living with her, but Carrie is always so talkative, and Maya doesn't have it in her to make conversation tonight. She just wants to collapse on her bed and lie there for a few minutes before attempting to do a little more schoolwork.

She dozes off almost immediately but wakes up when Carrie comes back into the room. Stumbles into the room is more like it. Carrie has clearly been drinking, even though it's a Tuesday night.

"What time is it?" Maya asks groggily.

"No idea," Carrie whispers, though her whisper is as loud as her regular volume. "So sorry to wake you."

"No problem. I wasn't really sleeping, I just closed my eyes for a minute." Maya glances at the clock; it's nearly 1:00 a.m. Shit. She was supposed to be doing her World Religions reading; her class meets at 8:00 a.m.

"Here you go," Carrie says, handing over a box.

"What is this?"

"It's a mini pizza," Carrie slurs, still whispering theatrically even though Maya is clearly awake. "I just picked it up on my way home. The snack bar was about to close, and I wasn't sure whether you'd have had dinner since you had work tonight."

"You—you got me a pizza?" Maya is confused, as if the words Carrie has said and the words that she's now repeated are in another language, and the box she's holding is a curious object she doesn't recognize.

"Yeah? In case you were hungry. I don't know. Just toss it if you don't want it." Carrie yawns.

"Thank you," Maya says, suddenly realizing that she is starving. Not only did she not have dinner, but she didn't eat lunch, either. All she ate all day was a dry corn muffin. She starts shoveling warm pizza into her mouth, and it might just be the best thing she's ever tasted. "Thank you so much."

"Of course." Carrie flashes her a thumbs-up, strips to her bra and underwear, and folds herself into her bed without even going to the bathroom to brush her teeth. She passes out within seconds.

Is this what Maya has been missing out on all this time? She never bothered trying to make friends before, instead accepting her role as the weird girl. It was easier than fighting it—plus, she knew it was way above her grandmother's pay grade to worry about hosting playdates and sleepovers. The last thing Maya wanted to do was make more trouble for her grandmother than she already had by being born and then abandoned.

But having a friend was nice. Really nice.

"Thank you so much," Maya repeats, though she knows Carrie is unconscious.

CHAPTER SIX

After dinner, Maya and I wash the dishes while Pete entertains the girls with a new drone camera that he just got ("Pete and his toys," I whisper to Maya with an eye roll before immediately feeling guilty complaining about my very alive and very faithful husband). When Maya and I are done, we join them on the couch. I cut up a few brownies from Round Swamp market, plate them, and put the plate on the coffee table. Pete opens a Juicy IPA mini growler from Montauk Brewing Company and splits it into three glasses for me, him, and Maya. I put on a Taylor Swift album, one of the moodier ones—hopefully something that both the adults and the kids can enjoy. It feels nice, all of us talking in the living room—and it's certainly the longest that Kelsey has voluntarily hung out with us in a long time.

"So I know you and my mom were roommates. What was it like the first time you met?" Lola looks at me intently, biting into a brownie. Kelsey is turned away from me, looking at her phone, but I can tell from a slight perk of her ear that she's interested in hearing the answer to Lola's question, too.

"Honestly, I think I blacked it out because I was so nervous," I say with a laugh. But it's true. "Walking into my dorm room for the first time with my parents, seeing Maya—seeing your mom—sitting on her bed reading a book, already unpacked—it's sort of a blur. I was literally sweating through my shirt with anxiety."

"What were you so nervous about?" Lola asks curiously. Maya, too, is considering my face carefully, waiting for my response.

I'm not sure how to answer. Why *was* I so nervous? I'd had friends in high school, of course. Officially, I suppose I'd even been "popular." But I had to work so hard for it, it felt ridiculous, not to mention exhausting. I never felt at ease, socially, when I was young; it's also why I drank more than I should have at parties, leaning on alcohol to make me feel more confident, interesting, and attractive than I ever would have otherwise. Maya turned out to be the first friend to whom I felt comfortable showing my real self: faults, insecurities, and all.

Though eventually, I showed too much.

"Well, I guess I was primarily worried that she wouldn't like me. That she'd be, like, ten times cooler than I was and have, like, I don't know, a guitar and tattoos and a modeling contract. All I knew about her was that her name was Maya Matthews—sounds *very* cool, right? And here I was still sleeping with a stuffed animal at college."

Maya laughs. "Aw, Skeet! I remember him. Do you still have him?"

I look at her with mock horror. "Duh! I'd never abandon Skeet. I don't sleep with him anymore, though," I add quickly. "He's in Kelsey's room."

"I have no idea where he is," Kelsey says with disinterest, and for a second, my heart goes heavy with irrational concern for my worn stuffed elephant.

Lola nods at me expectantly, prompting me to go on.

"I mean, I was also worried that I'd be assigned to a roommate who was, like, an axe murderer or S&M enthusiast. But no, my primary concern was that whoever my roommate was would think I was totally lame. And don't get me wrong—your mother *is* cooler than me, and smarter, and more well read, and a better cook, et cetera. I had to wear her down a little to get her to be my friend. I pretty much begged her to come with me to things for the first couple of weeks. But eventually, she realized she couldn't get rid of me that easily!"

Except, it turned out, she could. Because after what happened our senior year, it was easier for me to go through my life if I didn't have to look at her, knowing that she knew the very worst things about me. Our friendship was one of the casualties of my selfishness.

I try to shake it off, laughing and nudging Maya playfully, but she's looking at me with narrowed, incredulous eyes.

She shakes her head slowly. "That's not how I remember it at all. I remember that you were so confident—it was as if you owned the school and knew everyone on our hall, even on our first day. You walked into every event as if you had organized it yourself. I thought you were doing me a favor by letting me tag along with you. I was sure that your mom had told you to be nice to me or something."

I shake my head back at her. Vigorously. "No way. That couldn't be further from the truth. I was terrified to go to anything alone, so I clung to you. And you were cool as a cucumber about all of it. You were totally unfazed. Most of the time, people didn't even realize you were a freshman!"

Maya is quiet and looks thoughtful for a second. "Is that true? I guess it was just that I had made my peace with the idea of being a loner, because that's what I was used to. But you changed that course by deciding to take me under your wing."

I don't want to argue with Maya, but the idea of anyone thinking that I had *wings* during freshman year at Middlebury—it's just unfathomable. I barely had arms. What I did have was plenty of stress dreams about being naked in class. In the wrong class. And paranoia that my professors hated me. And fears of tripping up the library stairs while upperclassmen pointed and laughed at me. And an always-nagging inkling that everyone thought I'd only been admitted to Middlebury because of my dad (which, frankly, was probably true). *Wings?* Not even close.

Maya looks at Kelsey, who's now listening openly. "Your mother is being gracious. And modest. She was always adored at school. Everywhere she went."

"I really don't think so, but you were, too," I insist. "And regardless of how it came to be—'chosen family,' right? That's what we always said."

"Right," Maya says, a dreamy expression clouding her face. "Chosen family."

Pete laughs. "All I know is you two were attached at the hip. Sometimes I had a hard time remembering which one was my girlfriend."

Maya swats Pete playfully and rolls her eyes at him. I take a long sip of my IPA, hoping we can let this drop. Kelsey looks back at her phone. But Lola continues to look at me with intrigue.

CHAPTER SEVEN

Tuesday

In the morning, I am exhausted, having tossed and turned all night thinking of the text I received from Kyle during dinner. I can't believe you aren't going to talk to me was all he said in the text. It wasn't *that* ominous. But knowing that he's still thinking about us, that he's angry with me, is unsettling. I wish he'd just let it go, the way I have.

I wish it never happened in the first place. I still can't believe I'm capable of hurting my husband as much as I have. A husband who has never been anything but loyal and supportive, even after I unceremoniously dumped him at the end of our senior year, only to come crawling back six months later, when I became sufficiently appalled by my dating experiences and realized how good I'd had it. A husband who respectfully accepted my decision not to have any more kids when he'd have loved a litter of them. A husband who agreed to live in the city even though he'd prefer to raise a family with a yard and a swing set and a grill.

And yet, as understanding as he was, I'm not sure that Pete ever really grasped that the reason I couldn't retreat to the suburbs was because I was afraid of disappearing among the SUVs and trees, becoming a background decoration in my own life. I'm not sure he understood that, as much as I loved Kelsey (infinitely, immeasurably, irrevocably), I couldn't have another child because I couldn't stand to have motherhood be yet another area where I performed mediocrely, and I thought that maybe if we had just one, I could manage to keep my head above water and actually do a decent job with her. And I *know* he didn't understand the fury of sitting in the "Mother's Relief" room having milk squeezed out of my breasts, feeling anything but relief and instead worrying about the baby's nap schedule and her happiness and the laundry and doctor appointments and groceries, fully aware that at that moment he wasn't worrying about any of those things. Resentment built slowly enough that I didn't even know it was there, until I did.

And perhaps that's why I did what I did with Kyle; I was always searching for some version of myself that existed outside the margins of my roles as wife and mother. Trying to salvage some shreds of the me who had existed before I trained myself to want the *right* things. I had the aching feeling that whoever that person might have been had eluded me long ago.

Of course, none of that is an excuse for how poorly I've treated Pete. I mean, how can I resent *him*, after what I've done? And I wish I just meant recently.

Whatever I was looking for, I was searching in the exact wrong place. An affair isn't a productive step on the path to self-discovery, or self-recovery, or whatever. It's a cheap, shiny Band-Aid to hide but not heal untreated old wounds. I know that now—a little late, as usual.

Kyle could have been anyone; there was nothing about him specifically that lit me up, in retrospect. He was good looking and charming, sure, but mostly he just happened to be the one in the right place at the right time. Or the wrong place at the wrong time. I mean it literally. Every morning on my way back from walking Kelsey to school, we'd pass each other. Every single morning. Between 8:16 and 8:20. Between Eighty-Sixth and Eighty-Eighth Streets, on Columbus Avenue. Like clockwork.

At first, it was just glancing. Then the glances became discreet smiles—innocent enough because we were just sort of laughing to ourselves over the fact of seeing each other every morning in the exact same place. It was fun and sexy having an inside joke with a handsome stranger. There was something so intimate about it.

The looks that passed between us grew longer and more unabashed. He raised his coffee cup at me once, a passing cheers. He winked at me once, too, and I felt myself grow hot underneath my raincoat. The sidewalk where we'd passed each other felt like it might burst into flame. It reminded me of seeing a high school crush in the hallway. It fueled me; I hadn't realized how much I'd missed that feeling. I started putting on lipstick and mascara before leaving the house.

Around mid-October, Kelsey told me that she didn't want me to walk her anymore, because she was going to start walking to school with a friend who lived in a building across the street from us. I made excuses to continue leaving the apartment around the same time—to go write at PlantShed or Starbucks, even though I'd recently converted our third bedroom into a beautiful office for myself. Pete left for work earlier than Kelsey left for school, so he wasn't around to bat an eye at my odd preference to schlep my laptop to a coffee counter rather than just work in the comfort of my own home.

And then one day when I was sitting at PlantShed, laptop open, fiddling absently with a new book idea, there was my alluring stranger: not just passing me on the street this time, but walking over to my table. He sat down across from me wordlessly.

"Hi!" I exclaimed breathlessly, the proximity of him nearly knocking the wind out of me.

"Hi there," he said, and he passed me a croissant in a bag with his number on it. "Kyle," he added quietly. His eyes were incredibly blue up close, and I could only stand to look at them for a second.

"Carrie," I managed.

"Finally," he said, and grinned.

"Finally," I agreed.

I liked how new I was in his eyes. To him, I could be anyone I wanted. I could be the kind of woman who was simple and free, with an unstained past. Frankly, I also liked that he wasn't going to ask me what was for dinner.

Pete and I were *fine*. We were always fine. More than fine. It wasn't some dried-up, loveless marriage that existed just for Kelsey's sake. Not at all. We went to concerts, binged Netflix shows while eating sushi and drinking wine, laughed at memes we'd sent each other, hugged often. And yet, I think we sometimes went months without really looking at one another. And whenever I complained about this to a girlfriend, the response was always, "But that's marriage, right?" Was it really supposed to be? And was I really supposed to be okay with that?

But despite occasionally yearning for a different life, I also knew how empty mine would be without Pete and Kelsey.

And maybe that was part of the problem. A part of me was always aware that I didn't deserve the happiness I had. Because of decisions I'd made all those years ago.

It's funny: back then, I'd been so focused on making sure no one else learned my secret that I didn't realize the one thing that mattered: that *I'd* always know it and be stuck with it.

I waited five days before texting Kyle (or Lara G., Hazel's Mom, as I'd put his number in as, blanching at the sneakiness of it) and stared at myself in the mirror for nearly an hour before sending the text, asking myself if I really wanted to do this.

And then I reminded myself that I'd been a screwup ever since I was a kid, so I might as well hit send.

It's Carrie. So now you have my number, too.

He immediately sent back a smiley face, and I recoiled slightly at the cheesiness of a middle-aged man using an emoji. I think I knew even then that it would end poorly, but I'd already made my decision; it was too late to back out now. It's funny, now, thinking how familiar that feeling was to me, that I wasn't allowed to change my mind. That I'd already started something, and I'd just have to see it through, even if I realized it wasn't the right course.

We met up later that week, at a small hotel in the neighborhood that would become our regular spot. We agreed we'd never go to each other's apartments. As if that somehow made what we were doing okay.

Kyle and I would take turns paying for the hotel room, and we'd meet in the mornings, when our kids were at school and spouses were at work. It wasn't just sex; we'd have coffee, talk. It felt like a new friendship, or like the exhilarating early stages of dating. It was fun, at first. It was also careless, in retrospect, and a miracle that we didn't get caught; I know so many people in the neighborhood. But I had an excuse at the ready in case I ever did run into anyone while I was heading into the hotel; Kyle works at a talent agency, so I was going to say I was meeting with an agent who wanted to work with me on selling the film rights to one of my books. Granted, Kyle was a sports agent, but his company did have a film division. So the lie might have checked out if I'd ever had to use it, which, mercifully, I didn't.

By March, though, I was starting to feel a little trapped. I liked Kyle, but it was becoming clear to me that the thing I liked most about him was the fact that he liked me, a trait that I'd been carrying with me since childhood. We didn't really have many of the same interests, and from our conversations I'd gathered that, like Pete, he was the "fun parent," while his wife filled out all the school forms and bought all the birthday presents. Knowing this annoyed me and made me feel guilty for abetting his betrayal of her.

Especially when he brought up leaving her. Actual logistics. He started talking about how he'd budget for alimony, the kind of apartment he could afford. How he'd try a mediator before contacting a divorce lawyer. How his kids would probably love having Kelsey as an older sister. The trapped feeling I was starting to experience turned into full-on panicking. I'd never been planning on divorcing Pete, not for one second.

Pete's mom's sudden decline, and our subsequent move to Montauk, gave me what felt like a Get Out of Jail Free card. *(Thank you, Helen. And I'm very sorry for cheating on your son.)*

I didn't exactly *ghost* Kyle, but my communication with him became sparse, and eventually nonexistent. I simply told him we were going to Montauk, and I wasn't sure when we'd be back.

And then after a few weeks, I stopped returning his texts.

Okay. Maybe that's ghosting. But the affair had run its course. What more was there to say?

Sometimes I wonder how I live with myself, how I kiss Pete good night as if nothing happened. But I've become well practiced at keeping the truth from him. This wasn't the only omission, and it wasn't the biggest one, either. And maybe that's sort of why I started the affair, too— I'd built our relationship on a foundation of secrets. It felt like slipping on an old, familiar cardigan that I'd forgotten about. Like returning to myself. Even if I don't particularly like her, I can't escape her.

And I don't deserve to. I deserve to be reminded of who I really am, and the deception I'm capable of. Even if it stings.

I coax myself out of bed and splash my face with cold water and then rub some face oil haphazardly over my cheeks and forehead, briefly raising my eyebrows so I can see how my forehead wrinkles look today. I throw on leggings and a sweatshirt and go upstairs to the kitchen, where Pete is making pancakes. It's just past seven o'clock, but Maya and Lola are already awake, sitting at the table with Kelsey, and the kitchen feels busy, crowded, like we're the Brady Bunch or something. I'm a little embarrassed, suddenly, about my attire; everyone else is properly dressed. Even Kelsey, who frequently wears sweats to school, is in jeans and a black top. Black, Lola's preferred clothing color. Interesting.

"Morning, all," I say, trying to sound cheerful, and I walk over to the counter to get coffee. Pete swats my butt lightly with a spatula. Maya is drinking a coffee of her own, and Lola is painting her nails at our kitchen table without using a paper towel under her hands. She looks up at me, and the brush drops a spot of polish onto the table. Kelsey, naturally, does not acknowledge me.

"I'm definitely going to the store today," I announce more loudly than I intended to as I stir almond milk into my coffee. "Does anyone need anything?"

"Our bathroom is running low on shampoo," Lola responds almost immediately. *Our bathroom.* I cringe inwardly and glance at Pete, who is pouring pancake batter onto a pan, seeming not the least bit fazed. Maya, meanwhile, shoots Lola a warning glance, and I immediately soften; she's just a teenager. She's a slightly different breed than Kelsey, who is broody rather than brash, but they're cut from the same cloth. And I feel for Maya, who is obviously embarrassed by Lola's demand.

"Shampoo, got it." I give her a dorky thumbs-up. "Oh, almost time to go, Kels. You ready for school?"

Lola looks up from her nails with interest. "Can I come, too? To school?"

Maya, Kelsey, and I each look at Lola with surprise. Mr. Sparkles, who is stretched out contentedly on Lola's lap, meows territorially as if to say, *You're not going anywhere.*

"Um," I say awkwardly.

"No, Lola," Maya says firmly. "We're here to catch our breath. The point is for you to take a little break from school, you know?"

"What am I supposed to do all day?" Lola whines. "I want to be with kids my own age." She gives Maya full-on puppy dog eyes, and sucker that I am, my heart goes out to her; I remember too well that when my dad died, the worst thing for me was what everyone said I needed, which was to take it slow and *rest.* Whenever I was still, I just started wallowing. And it was Maya who got me out of bed on mornings when I felt too heavy with grief to drag myself to class. It was Maya who insisted on keeping me company and watching movies when I said I didn't want to go out. It was Maya who encouraged me to leave our dorm room, to get some fresh air, go take a yoga class at the campus wellness center. And she was right—it helped.

"We'll find stuff to do," Maya assures her. "It's Montauk. It's beautiful. We can play mini golf and go for ice cream." Maya suddenly looks so nostalgic and hopeful that it hurts me a little.

"I'm not five," Lola says, looking at her with a very familiar teenage brand of disdain.

"I'm sure the school doesn't allow visitors anyway," Maya says, a little more curtly. Lola crosses her arms petulantly.

"It's probably fine," I offer timidly. "The school is pretty casual about stuff like that. It's not like New York City, where you have to show a student ID and go through a metal detector. I can just go into the office and tell them we have a family friend visiting, make sure it's okay for Lola to shadow Kelsey through her classes. And since they're in the same grade anyway . . ." I trail off, the look Maya's giving me making me suddenly uncertain as to whether I've completely overstepped. Lola, for her part, looks thrilled.

"You don't mind, do you, Kels?" says Pete, nodding his head toward her expectantly.

Kelsey frowns at me and Pete, but when she looks at Lola, her face softens. "No," she says quietly. "It's fine. I don't mind."

"It's *really* not necessary," Maya says. "Lola, we can go to the beach today. Maybe even find a place to get manicures."

"It's freezing out, and my nails are already painted, Mother, as you can see," Lola says with sarcastic sweetness, lifting her hands for Maya. I find it odd that Maya is protesting; I'd be thrilled if Kelsey were clamoring for extra school. But she likely wants to keep Lola close, given what they've just been through.

Maya locks eyes with Lola for a lingering second and then turns her gaze back to me, shrugging with a small, defeated smile. "Okay, I guess so," she says. "Sure. If you're certain the school will be okay with it, and Kelsey, if you really don't mind hosting Lola. It's very generous of you."

"No problem," Kelsey mumbles, draining her water.

"Great! It's settled. We'll need to pack you a lunch, too, then," I say, turning to Lola. "I made Kelsey a—"

"Do you have mozzarella and tomato?" she asks, cutting me off. "That's my favorite. I'd never even tried it until—" She stops abruptly. "Until a few years ago," she finishes, looking at Maya uncertainly.

I'm taken aback again. "Um, no, sorry. I can pick some up today, though."

"Do you like mozzarella, too?" she asks me, suddenly seeming younger than fifteen. It's such a disarmingly innocent question.

"Um, yes, I do. Love it, in fact. I mean, who doesn't like pizza, right?"

"Me too," she says happily. "I love pizza, too." My eyes settle briefly again on her chipped tooth. I wonder what happened. "Do you have basil? That's good in tomato mozzarella sandwiches, too."

Maya nudges Lola and says, "Okay, sweetheart. That's probably enough with the grocery order. Remember, we're guests here."

"Sorry," Lola says softly, blushing slightly.

"No problem. I have basil in my little garden. So we're set on the basil front." *The basil front? Get a grip, Carrie.*

Pete kisses Kelsey's head, and she grimaces. "All right, ladies, I have a call that I'm going to take downstairs. Have a great day at school, everyone!" He retreats down the steps. Maya and I get up at the exact same time to get more coffee.

"After you," I tell her.

"No, please, go ahead," she says, and I accidentally fill my cup too full, leaving a measly few sips' worth behind for her.

CHAPTER EIGHT

Once I've gotten Lola squared away with a cream cheese and jelly sandwich, pita chips, and an orange in a brown paper bag, the four of us walk out to the car together. Mr. Sparkles gazes mournfully from the window after us at Lola, tail twitching with displeasure that the one person he's liked since Helen died is leaving him.

"Hi, Ida," I call out dutifully to our elderly neighbor, who is smoking a cigarette while she waters her porch plants. From what I can tell, she despises us, seeming to carry the opinion that, as city people, we don't have a claim to Montauk. Or she might hold a grudge since Pete's mom once called the police on her adult son, who lives in her basement. Pete's mom said she'd caught him spying, lurking around her property with binoculars. Granted, Helen had an active imagination in her final years, but Ida's son does seem like a creep. I've seen him a handful of times, and he has a distinct leering quality—and the thin strands of hair on his otherwise-bald head, combined with his habit of wearing nothing but boxers outside, make me a little queasy. Ida grunts and jerks her hand, but it looks more like a dismissal than a greeting. She turns to glance suspiciously at Maya and Lola, and I think I catch her rolling her eyes, as if to say, *Great, there are even more of you now?*

"She's friendly," Maya whispers wryly as we close the car doors.

"Oh yeah, some of the locals don't exactly love us city folk. They're a bit territorial over their space. I can hardly blame them, though. It is beautiful." It really is. Even the commute to East Hampton High is stunning, the stretch of beach visible from over the side of the highway. And every summer, the locals have to deal with city people arriving in droves, acting like they've discovered it, taking up all the parking, littering beer bottles on the pristine beaches, ignoring bonfire rules, treating restaurant staff who live there year-round like second-class citizens. It must be infuriating.

"It is stunning," Maya murmurs, gazing off toward the gray ocean.

"So what's the school like?" Lola asks Kelsey excitedly. I, too, listen eagerly for Kelsey's answer; we can barely get her to talk about school. I know what classes she's taking and the names of her teachers, and I've heard her mention one friend, Rachel, but otherwise, I know very little about what the hours between 8:00 a.m. and 2:50 p.m. are like for her. It makes me feel like a complete failure as a parent. When Kelsey was little, I always imagined that when she was a teenager, and an adult, she and I would be best friends—we'd go for runs together, invent random Crock-Pot concoctions, watch *Party of Five*, eat pizza in bed while we talked through boy (or girl) trouble she was having. I so badly want her to start talking to me again, to start *loving* me again, or even liking me, but I also don't want to push her further away by bugging her all the time. It's a delicate and rather painful balance.

"Um," Kelsey says. "I don't know. It's okay. It's like a high school from a teen movie or something. Jocks at one table, music kids at another, that kind of thing. It's a lot bigger than my old school. The teachers are pretty nice. Especially to us kids who actually show up for class." *Well, at least Kelsey counts herself among that group. That's a win.*

"It sounds perfect," Lola says with a dreamy sigh. I glance in the rearview mirror and see Kelsey give her an amused look.

When we get to the high school, I park in the lot instead of just driving up front to the curb and dropping Kelsey off like I usually do. "I'll go in and make sure it's okay for Lola to join you," I explain. Kelsey looks aghast at the prospect of me walking into school with her.

"I'll walk in ahead of you," I assure her. "And I'll wear sunglasses and a hat, so no one will see that we look alike." I'm trying to be funny. She doesn't laugh.

The girls really do keep their distance from me, huddling in a corner of the office while I approach the reception desk. The school secretary, Ms. Hammel, who appears to be in her eighties and whose retro-looking nameplate gives me reason to believe she's worked at East Hampton High for a very, very long time, looks Lola over and nods. "Here's your visitor badge," she says, handing Lola a lanyard with a laminated card tied to it. "Please keep it on all day. And sign in here," she adds gruffly, gesturing toward a clipboard on the counter.

Kelsey gives me a half wave as she walks away with Lola, who calls, "Thanks, Carrie!" behind her. As I watch Kelsey and Lola walk down the hall toward Kelsey's homeroom, I see Lola link arms with Kelsey; to my surprise, Kelsey bends her elbow to more comfortably welcome Lola's arm into the crook of her own. And I know I should be happy to see Kelsey be friendly with another girl her age; it should be a relief to know that maybe she's simply saving her worst for me, and when she's around other people, she's okay. But for some reason, it makes me squirm to see her and Lola lope down the hall arm in arm.

When I get back to the parking lot, Maya is biting her nails, a habit I remember vividly from college. I'd assumed she'd outgrow it; it's such a girlish tic, and seeing her do it now makes me feel like the two of us are about to hit up the breakfast buffet at the dining hall before class, some index cards with biology terms spread before us, me talking about which parties we should attend this weekend while Maya tells me to focus.

It feels like yesterday and a lifetime ago all at once.

"They're all set!" I tell Maya cheerfully. "Maybe it'll be good for Lola to have a busy day. And this way, you can get a break, too." She nods halfheartedly, looking less than convinced. I pull out of the parking lot and head back onto the main road. "Plus, honestly, I'm glad that

Kelsey will have the company. I've been worried about her here. I don't think she's really made many friends at East Hampton High. She's very unhappy about being here."

"To be honest," Maya ventures slowly, "I was surprised when I got Pete's email blast with your change of address. You were always New York or nowhere. What made you decide to move here?" I can feel her looking at me as I focus on the road ahead. I hesitate, unsure of how much more I want to tell her about Kelsey's issues.

But hell. She's the mom of a teenager, too. I'm sure she'll understand. I give her an abridged version of Kelsey's changes in behavior and friendships and the fire alarm.

I sigh heavily, feeling the weight of it all as I talk. "The thing is that I always felt like I was letting my parents down because I didn't like the things they thought I should be interested in. And I wanted Kelsey to have more freedom than that. To get to be her own person. But given what happened—I think I may have done exactly what my parents did, after all. Put too many expectations on her, or pressure, something. Why else would she have felt the need to act out?"

Maya nods thoughtfully. "I don't think that kids' behavior is always a barometer of our parenting. I mean, look, she felt safe enough to make a big mistake, right? She knew you'd love her no matter what. Kids always test boundaries. It's how they learn." She laughs suddenly, unexpectedly, and I'm surprised to see a tear slide out of her eye when I glance at her. "When Lola was twelve, she rolled tea into printer paper and tried to smoke it in her bathroom." She laughs out loud again, almost hysterically, and another tear slides out. "She almost burned our house down." She's laughing even harder now, and I laugh with her, though I don't find it quite as hilarious as she seems to.

When she collects herself, she says, "Kelsey's a sweetheart, Carrie. It's a phase."

"I know you're right. It's just hard to take how much she hates me. I'm like enemy number one to her."

Maya shakes her head. "She doesn't hate you. How could she? She'll come back to you. All you can do is wait and welcome her when she does. Girls always come back to their mothers." Her face drops slightly, and then she recovers, returning her expression to neutral. A whiff of a shared, rotting memory passes between us, and I try to pretend I don't notice it.

My phone buzzes from the media console. I'm grateful for the interruption until I glance at it and immediately feel my neck flush. *Lara G., Hazel's Mom.*

Again.

I can feel Maya glance at it, too.

I grab my phone to silence it while still trying to keep my eyes on the road, and I accidentally open the text instead. *Shit.*

Usually, his texts are relatively innocuous, like the one he sent last night. Sometimes he'll say, "Still thinking about you," or even, "I miss you."

The text today is a little different.

You really are a bitch. I wince and gasp involuntarily. Three little dots tell me he isn't done, but I stick my phone under my leg, praying Maya didn't see.

"Everything okay?" Maya asks quietly. I'm driving too close to the left, and very slowly, completely distracted by what I've just read.

"Yes. Totally fine." But my voice cracks sharply as if I'm an adolescent boy, and I don't think anyone would believe me, let alone Maya, who knows all my tells. I try to change the subject, quickly. "So what are you going to do today? I need to get some work done, but maybe we could go for a beach walk together later before we pick the girls up?"

"Sounds great." I can feel her looking at me carefully. "Are you sure you're okay?"

"I'm positive." *How much did she see? I need to cover my bases.* "Yeah, this woman, Lara . . . I was supposed to serve on a committee at Trewell, Kelsey's school in the city. She hasn't found someone else to fill the position." *Lame. Lame. So lame.* "She's a little miffed, that's all." I shrug, trying to appear blasé.

I glance at Maya, who's staring straight ahead and raising an eyebrow. "Kind of rude of her to be mad at you for something as insignificant as the PTA, no? Especially when you came out here because of a death in the family. Plus, it's November—she's really still pissed about it?"

I nod, hearing exactly how weak my lie was as she talks through it. "Well, that's New York City for you. People are super intense." *A PTA emergency? Why couldn't I have come up with something better?*

Maybe it's that lying to Maya about my affair feels sort of pointless. She already knows that I have plenty to be ashamed of.

"Well, even if it's over something stupid, it must be upsetting," Maya says. "I know how much it means to you that everyone likes you."

I blink hard at that and say nothing, knowing that, as usual, Maya is right.

~

2000

Carrie barrels into the tiny dorm room, mascara dripping down her face. "I failed," she wails miserably, and flops down on her unmade bed.

Maya turns to face her but does not get out of her desk chair. The first few times, she rushed to her side to rub her back, but now, she knows to take a beat first. "Failed?" she asks. "You studied so much. You were ready. I'm sure you did better than you think."

"You don't understand." Carrie moans into her pillow. "I studied all the wrong stuff. Like, all. I mean, there were three hundred freaking slides—I tried to memorize all of them, but that wasn't working, so I just focused on, like, a sampling from each time period. And apparently, I chose the wrong sampling to focus on. Every. Single. Time." Carrie pushes herself up on her arms, slides off her bed droopily, and walks over to Maya's desk. She pulls

a tissue from her tissue box and blows her nose loudly. She tosses the tissue into Maya's trash bin but misses and doesn't notice. She walks back over to her bed, throwing herself on top of it once more.

Maya picks the tissue up and places it in the bin. "I'm sure the professor will assign partial credit where she can," she says softly. "And again, it can't be as bad as you think. Sometimes I think I did poorly on a test, and—"

"And it turns out you aced it, because you're literally the smartest person in all of your classes, and school is easy for you," Carrie says, her face smooshed into her pillow.

Maya knows she isn't the smartest person in her classes. She's no smarter than Carrie. The difference between them is that Maya would have memorized all the slides. Not just a "sampling." She wants to remind Carrie that she's there on a full scholarship, which means that she can't let her grades slip below a 3.4, or the scholarship will be revoked. That often she feels like her very life depends on completing her schoolwork.

She doesn't say any of this. She never does. Instead, she just says, "I'm sorry, Car. I bet you can ask for extra credit, if you need to." And you'll get it, she thinks to herself. You always do.

CHAPTER NINE

For most of the morning, Maya keeps to her room, and I'd be lying if I said it wasn't a relief. I really am glad she's here (well, glad-ish), but I don't need to spend every waking second with her. I surprise myself with a really productive morning of writing, finally, and when I leave to go to the grocery store, I decide not to knock on her door to ask her if she wants to come, just in case she's napping. That's what I tell myself, anyway. The truth is that the idea of solo errands after one day with a full house sounds like a mini vacation.

I'm especially in need of some time alone to resettle myself after reading Kyle's texts. He sent another one after you really are a bitch that said you don't get to just pretend that this never happened. Bile rose in my throat when I read that. Kyle always seemed so funny, so light, so harmless. Like Pete, in fact. God, why did I have an affair in the first place, if the person I was having an affair with wasn't very much unlike my own husband? Truly, what is the matter with me?

But these texts he's sending have exposed another side to him that I wasn't aware of before. I didn't respond—what could I even say?—but now I'm realizing that my ghosting strategy is not going as well as I'd hoped. I briefly consider blocking his number, but then I wouldn't even know if he was still texting, and that feels even riskier to me. As much as I don't want to continue receiving his texts, I can better monitor the situation if I know, to some extent, what's going through his head.

I try my best to shake it off. I put the groceries away when I get home (Lola's shampoo, tomatoes, and mozzarella included in my haul, of course) and go back downstairs to start collecting laundry to do a load. I go into Kelsey's room to get hers and pause for a moment to breathe in the scent of her. I'm reminded of that quote about mothering older kids from Celeste Ng's *Everything I Never Told You*: "It was like training yourself to live on the smell of an apple alone, when what you really wanted to do was devour it, to sink your teeth into it and consume it, seeds, core, and all." It was excruciating not being able to hug Kelsey when I wanted to, not being able to talk to her, to laugh with her. And I have no idea whether "respecting her space" is really the right approach. I have no idea whether making her come to Montauk for the year was the right thing, either. Despite having fifteen years of practice as a mother, sometimes I feel ill equipped to be the one making these decisions about another person's life. I always try to put myself in her shoes, to remember how I felt at her age, but then I have to remind myself that Kelsey isn't a miniature version of me; she's very much her own person. And I feel like I don't know that person very well at the moment.

My own mother always seemed so poised and unflappable to me, so sure that she knew best and that her rules were the right ones. But I wonder if it's just a facade all mothers wear, when in reality, none of us know what we're doing, not when our kids are babies, toddlers, teenagers, and adults. We just pretend we do and hope it turns out okay.

I collect Kelsey's dirty items from the floor. Plaid pajama bottoms. White cotton underwear. A gray T-shirt. It wasn't that long ago that her clothes used to be all sparkles, unicorns, rainbows. She wouldn't wear anything that wasn't bedazzled in some way. Now, she dresses to blend into the crowd.

There is some evidence in her room of the old Kelsey, though. I gently touch the Beauty and the Beast globe that sits on her desk, a clear plastic orb with a red rose preserved inside it. She got it at a plant store when she was seven, soon after we'd seen *Beauty and the Beast* on ice. She was convinced the rose was the very same one from the Beast's castle. I like knowing that this was one of the things she made sure to bring to Montauk with her when we told her we'd be spending the year here, rather than putting it in storage in our apartment building's basement. It gives me hope that the little girl who got so excited when Belle came out on skates holding her stack of books is still inside the morose teenager who now inhabits this room.

I'm throwing laundry into the machine when Maya comes out of her room, and I can tell she's been crying. Her eyes are swollen, and her cheeks are dry from tear salt.

"Oh, Maya," I say lamely, lurching toward her like a bear. I hug her clumsily, wishing I could say or do anything to make her feel better. I don't bother to ask if she's okay—it's clear she isn't. And how could she be? She's just lost her husband. She returns my hug briefly, then pulls away from me and tries to smile, but it's totally unconvincing. "Are you hungry?" I ask her. "I went to the store."

She shakes her head, even though I know she hasn't eaten anything since breakfast. "I'm okay for now. Time to go get the girls?" She glances at the clock anxiously. She must be eager to see Lola. I still feel a little guilty for enabling Lola's attending school with Kelsey when I knew that Maya was uncomfortable with it. I shouldn't have interfered. But I really did think it would help to get Lola's mind off things.

"Yup! Let's do it," I tell her. I run upstairs to the kitchen and fill my thermos with tea for the drive, and one for Maya, too. When we walk to the car, I notice Ida's son sitting on their front patio, drinking a Red Stripe—a little early for beer on a Tuesday, but I'm hardly surprised. His eyes never leave Maya as we walk. A chill goes down my spine. At least he's fully dressed this time, though.

"Did you work things out with your friend?" Maya asks as we start driving. My brows furrow with confusion until I realize what she's talking about. The nonexistent Lara G. and our completely fictional PTA spat.

I bob my head vigorously. "Oh. Yeah, it's fine. I honestly don't really care if she's mad."

Maya looks surprised. "I'm impressed to see you so impervious to people's opinions. It's good you've evolved."

"Ha. Thanks," I say with a small laugh, wincing slightly at her words because I know how true they are. I've always been too desperate for people's approval. And had it not been for a crippling fear of disappointing people, there are some things in my life I might have done very differently. As Maya is aware.

I'm eager to change the subject. "If you want to talk about Elliot, we can, you know," I tell her lightly. "I know so little about him. I'm sad that I never got the chance to meet him. What was he like?"

Maya takes a deep breath and braces herself. I can see that it's difficult for her to talk about him.

"He was . . ." She hesitates. "He was a good man," she finishes with effort. "He wasn't perfect—and neither was our relationship—but what relationship is? When I met him a couple years after we graduated, I was pretty closed off." I can feel her looking at me meaningfully, but I do my best to ignore it, to let it deflect. "Anyway, I always felt like he sort of saved me, pulled me out of my funk. He was funny and sweet and took good care of me. He was just sort of a low-stress, positive guy."

"Like Pete," I offer.

Maya looks at me out of the side of her eye. "Kind of. Yes. Anyway, and then we had Lola, and as you know, having a child definitely puts a strain on a relationship, but it also makes you realize how precious your life together is." Maya pauses, searching for words. "What can I say? It was a marriage. It had some holes, but it was very wearable. You know?" *Do I ever,* I think to myself.

"Anyway . . ." Maya sighs, rubbing her forehead briefly. "He worked for a local real estate company. We're near Woodstock, so there's a good market over there. His office was close to the school that Lola went—the school she *goes* to," she corrects herself loudly, "so he would pick her up for lunch dates sometimes. He was a good dad, and she really loved him. But the thing is . . ." She hesitates, her voice growing weak. "We had a fight the night he died, and I don't think I'll ever forgive myself for it."

I feel my heart pull. My dad died on a Monday. I always called home on Sundays, but that Sunday, I'd been invited to a holiday party at the football house—a date party, my first—and I was so excited about it, especially since I was only a freshman. I'd been so consumed with getting ready, finding the perfect outfit, and pregaming with my friends (Maya included, though from what I remember she wasn't going herself) that I'd forgotten to call. I missed my last opportunity to talk to him, to assure him that I was doing (relatively) well in my classes and staying out of trouble. It was hard to forgive myself for forgetting to make that call.

"I'm sure he knew you loved him," I tell Maya. "Despite the fight. Guilt will only make your grief worse. Don't do that to yourself." She nods at me and looks ahead at the winding highway, steeling herself as her eyes fill. "How's Lola doing with it?" I ask.

"Hard to tell," she says, and doesn't elaborate. I can't help but agree with her; the girl in my kitchen professing her love for mozzarella and tomato sandwiches and begging to go to school doesn't exactly seem like she's in the throes of loss. Though I know that everyone copes differently, and at different times, too. It happened very recently, so it may not have fully hit her yet.

When we pull up to the school, Kelsey and Lola are waiting outside on the curb, and Kelsey is laughing.

Laughing.

They climb into the back seat, and Lola is whispering something to Kelsey. She stops as they get settled in their seats.

"How was school, guys?" I venture cautiously. I exchange a glance with Maya, who looks equally intrigued.

"Delightful," says Lola, a hint of cheeky sarcasm in her voice. With her plum lipstick and tight black pants, she looks like she just came from a nightclub, not school.

"Was it similar to your school, Lola?" I ask. I'm ashamed to admit that I'm more comfortable asking Lola questions than I am my own daughter, for fear of the inevitable sharp retort. No matter how many times she tells me to screw off, it still hurts to hear it.

"Hmm, tough to compare," she says. Maya shoots her a look in the rearview mirror. "But yeah, kind of," she adds, apparently catching her mother's drift that she should be more polite.

The girls go back to whispering, and when we get home, they immediately retreat to Kelsey's room and close the door behind them.

CHAPTER TEN

Later that night, after dinner, I am lying in bed trying to read a thriller about an ex-con turned housekeeper, but I can't focus on the words. I can hear Pete brushing his teeth for a ridiculously long time, just as he does every night. He's done this for as long as I've been with him. He said his dentist as a kid told him to brush for four minutes twice a day, and he's just never questioned it, though I'm sure he must have misheard. "Too late for me to change now," he always says with a shrug when I tease him about it.

For dinner, I'd picked up pizza and greek salad from Blade and Salt for all of us. I should have cooked, especially since I'd gone grocery shopping, but the thought of being shown up by Maya once again in my own kitchen really didn't appeal to me. Maybe having her around is bringing back memories from college, of Maya being on time to every class, showered and neatly dressed, making the dean's list despite having to balance her job on top of her schoolwork . . . and me, wearing the same pair of yoga pants every day, being late to every class that started before 11:00 a.m., earning only two As the entire four years, sleeping in a bed with pretzel crumbs and a stray laptop cord strewn across my comforter. I suppose that Maya's always made me hyperaware of my many shortcomings.

After we'd picked them up from school, Kelsey and Lola spent the entire afternoon in Kelsey's room together. When I knocked on the door to ask what kind of pizza they wanted, Kelsey shooed me away quickly, telling me that Lola was helping with her English homework, but not before I saw Lola on Kelsey's bed holding her Beauty and the Beast globe and a pile of lipsticks—my lipsticks—in her lap. Oh well. Not like I have much occasion to wear lipstick these days, anyway, given our lackluster social life in Montauk. Still, it was odd for Kelsey to show an interest in my makeup. She never had before. When I casually asked what they were reading in English, Kelsey yelled, "*The Glass CASTLE,* by Jeannette WALLS!" And then she slammed the door. Lovely.

Pete comes out of the bathroom, finally done with his teeth, and flops down on the bed, rolling over to face me. "Should we watch something?" he asks, gesturing toward the TV.

I ignore the question. "Don't you think it's weird how close Kelsey and Lola seem to be already?"

He rolls onto his back and looks up at the ceiling, considering, then turns to face me again. "Weird? I mean, I guess it's surprising, since Kelsey hasn't been all that . . . cordial lately, but that's just to us. It's nice that she'll have a friend here, if only for a few days. Plus, in a way, she's known Lola since she was little, so maybe she just feels more comfortable with her than with the kids at East Hampton High. It's a relief to see her pal around with another kid her age."

I put my book down across my chest. "But Kelsey didn't even *like* Lola that time we got together. When we stayed at the bed-and-breakfast in the Hudson Valley, Maya and I could hardly get the two of them to exchange a word. And now they're, what, best friends all of a sudden?" I twist my two fingers together to illustrate my point. "I think it's strange."

Pete gives me his skeptical *You're being silly* look. "Maybe they have more in common now. I think it's good for her, having Lola around."

"I know you're right," I tell him, turning my feet around in circles and cracking my ankles, trying to relax. "I think I'm just having a hard time adjusting to having houseguests after barely talking to anyone but you for the past six months. And, to be honest," I add, lowering my voice even more, "I'm a little weirded out by the fact that Maya hasn't said anything about how long they're planning to be here. I know I'm the one who invited them, but, like . . . I didn't really mean for it to be indefinite?" I know I'm being completely ungracious, but I've always felt safe venting to Pete, showing him my true self.

Most of it, anyway.

"Babe, I hear what you're saying, but it's only been two days. Not even. They won't be here forever. I know you haven't been close with Maya in a while, but she's one of your oldest friends, and she needs people around her right now. Her husband *died*, Car." He looks at me pointedly.

My heart sinks in my chest. I know how selfish I sound, even to my own very nonjudgmental husband. "You're right," I tell him. "I don't know what's wrong with me. Sorry. I'm just on edge. I've got a deadline coming up, and I think I'm just a little stressed out having guests on top of that."

"It's a lot to get used to," he says, nodding understandingly. But I don't think he does understand, because he doesn't seem the least put out by hosting. He goes about his business as usual, holing up in our room to work, coming up for lunch when he feels like it. All evening during dinner, he was charming and unbothered as ever, pouring wine, asking Lola questions about her life, telling her stories about Maya in college, like how she used to smuggle trays from the coffee shop for us to use as sleds when it snowed, and how she was a flip-cup champion, except that she'd only do the flipping part and make someone else chug her beer for her ("Often me!" Pete added).

"Maybe you just need to adjust your thinking," he tells me softly. "It's an opportunity to reconnect with someone who used to be your best friend. And it's still your house—just do your thing! You don't need to remold your life because they're here. You don't have to play Martha Stewart. Just let them look after themselves." He squeezes my arm reassuringly. "And as far as Kelsey goes, I really do think it's good for her. We don't know Lola that well, but she has to be better than the hooligans she was hanging out with in the city." Pete and I tend to blame Kelsey's new friends for the changes in her and then the prank, though I've often wondered if their families privately talk about Kelsey in the same way. I'm sure they do.

"You're right," I say to Pete, promising myself silently that I'll take a chill pill and just try to enjoy their visit, however long it might last. It *would* be nice to get close with Maya again. Even though I had plenty of friends in the city, they were pretty superficial friendships compared to what Maya and I once shared. And I have exactly *zero* friends in Montauk, so I should appreciate having someone to chat with, walk with, run errands with for a few days, or a week, or whatever.

Maybe the increased socialization would even help me with my writing. Perhaps my lack of inspiration is happening in part because I've been spending too much time alone. Having Maya and Lola around could be a good thing for *all* of us. Not just Kelsey.

And even if I don't *enjoy* hosting, exactly, I should still try to be more like Pete. A generous person who cares about others and comes to the aid of friends without griping.

A fresh pang of guilt washes over me as I think about Pete's virtues.

I lean toward Pete and kiss him, and he holds me in the kiss. He rolls closer toward me, and I can feel the heat from his body. "We'll have to be quiet," I whisper.

"I can't promise that," he whispers back with a lewd grin.

I kiss him hard and try not to think about the texts on my phone from Lara G., Hazel's Mom, as well as ancient buried secrets, known only by someone who's now sleeping down the hall.

CHAPTER ELEVEN

Wednesday

In the morning, I wake up feeling rested and resolved to stop stressing out so much, and just enjoy Maya's stay, as Pete suggested. And to be there for her. It's the least I can do.

While Pete showers, I put on my workout clothes, but then over my leggings, I put on my coziest socks. It's an outfit that says, *I might work out, but I make no promises*. I head upstairs to the kitchen with purpose: I'm going to make up for my lack of cooking dinner last night by making omelets for everyone for breakfast, with Boursin cheese and fresh herbs from my garden.

When I get to the kitchen, Maya is already there, and she's just finished brewing a pot of coffee. I usually make my coffee with half decaffeinated beans and half regular. I'm sure she hasn't done that. I try to suppress the wave of irritation that I feel pass through me and remind myself that I am going to be an unfailingly gracious and easygoing host. Even if it kills me.

"Thanks for making coffee," I say as brightly as I can, though I know the extra caffeine will make me twitchy and dry mouthed.

"No problem," she says sweetly. "How'd you sleep?"

"Really well," I tell her. "You?"

"Not bad," she says. "The air here is amazing. The proximity to the ocean—I don't know. It's so restorative for me." I know what she means, and I know Pete agrees, but for me, truthfully, being this close to the ocean makes me feel like I could easily fall off the edge of the earth, and no one would even notice. It makes me feel obsolete, irrelevant somehow. Small. They call Montauk the End because it's the easternmost tip of Long Island, but sometimes it feels like the end of the earth to me.

"Totally," I tell her, and open a cupboard to get a mug to drink the overly strong coffee she's made.

But the mugs aren't there. Instead, the cupboard is filled with pantry items—pastas, sauces, oils, spices.

"Um?" I say helplessly. I suddenly feel completely disoriented, dizzy, like I might fall down. Like I'm not even inside my own body.

"Oh! I hope you don't mind that I reshuffled a few things," Maya says, breezing past me toward a different cupboard. She opens it and hands me a mug. "No offense, but the organizational scheme of this kitchen made no sense. The mugs should be near the coffee maker, right? And this cupboard here," she says, gesturing to the one that formerly housed mugs, "is meant for food items. That's why it's so big." She shrugs casually. "This way, you can stock more stuff, if you want to. Clear bins would be good, too, so that you could formally separate everything by category instead of just lumping it all in there. I tried to lay the groundwork for that." I can see that she's put canned goods in one section, nut butters in another, and so forth.

Her proud smile quickly drops when she sees the dumbfounded expression on my face. "Oh shoot, Carrie. I'm sorry—it's just, you said you didn't really like this kitchen. You said that this place didn't feel like home yet. You know I love organizing, so I just—thought I could help." I try to smile back at her, to reassure her that it's fine, that it's great, but my mouth feels weighed down. When did she even complete this little project? We all turned in around the same time last night, ten o'clock, and it's not even seven o'clock now.

As if she can read my thoughts, she says, "I couldn't sleep last night. I figured I could do something useful with my time instead of just lying in bed thinking about . . ." She trails off, and the guilty feeling returns to my stomach. She's mourning. She's just trying to keep busy. Why am I being such a jerk about her kind gesture?

Pete saunters into the kitchen, not a care in the world. I still haven't said a word to Maya.

"I really am so sorry if I've overstepped," Maya says carefully, glancing nervously at Pete behind me. "You're so generous to have us stay here, and I love tackling little projects. You don't mind, do you? You should be focusing on what you do best—writing! And, I mean, Carrie, you were always hopeless with this stuff. Remember how you used to not even fold your clothes before putting them back into drawers? You said it was your 'system'?" Maya laughs affectionately. I know what she's talking about, but I was only eighteen, for God's sake. Obviously, I fold my clothes now. Somewhat.

Maya was eighteen then, too, of course, yet her drawers were always meticulous: color-grouped T-shirts folded crisply and stacked tight. At her desk, notes and binders were neatly shelved. Under her bed were snacks in labeled containers.

Much like how my cupboards are on their way to looking now.

Pete looks at me quizzically, and I snap to life. "No, no. Please. Sorry, I'm just moving slowly this morning. Of course it's okay. I mean, people pay good money to have their kitchens organized! Besides, it wasn't even *my* system; it was Pete's mom's. I wasn't attached to the way it was set up. So thank you. Truly. This really is much better. Better— feng shui, or whatever?" I try to laugh. "It's a big improvement."

Maya's face brightens with immediate relief. "Okay, phew! You had me worried there for a second. So, want me to show you what else I moved around? Don't worry, it's not that much. And I do have a purge pile, expired products and such, but I wanted to show it to you first, to make sure I'm not tossing anything you want to keep." She opens the other door of the cupboard that was *clearly* supposed to be the pantry, and now I see that she hasn't only categorized the foods; she's also labeled the shelves. *Did she bring her own label maker?* We certainly don't own one that I know of. BREAKFAST FOODS. SWEETS. NUTS AND SUNDRIES. *What the hell is a "sundry"?*

"This looks so much better!" Pete says, and for a brief second, I plot his murder.

I try to bring my shoulders away from my neck and focus on getting myself sorted with coffee. As I'm doing so, the girls shuffle into the kitchen. They are both dressed; Kelsey is once again slightly more done up than usual in high-waisted jeans and a black V-neck. I think I know the reason she's dressing up, and that reason is holding Mr. Sparkles and kissing his wet nose, dressed in leather leggings, a cropped black sweater, and Gwen Stefani topknots. Maya doesn't bat an eye at Lola's choice of clothes, and to be fair, I suppose this *is* how a lot of girls dress now—I've seen *Euphoria*, too.

"Cool if I go to school again today?" Lola looks at Maya innocently. Maya holds her gaze, and something unspoken passes between them.

"I thought we agreed it would just be for one day," Maya says, her lips tight.

"Well, the lady in the office gave me a pass for the week. See?" She holds out her visitor pass proudly, with WEEK OF 11/7 clearly printed on it, and waves it toward Maya.

"I don't mind," Kelsey says quickly. She really seems to like Lola.

Maya pauses. "Okay then," she says tersely.

I look closely at Kelsey and notice that she has bags under her eyes, her soft cheeks even paler than usual. "Did you get enough sleep?" I ask her.

"It's my fault," says Lola apologetically. "I kept her up too late talking. Just trying to get a sense of what goes on around here. Like, school gossip," she adds, clarifying.

I give Pete another look, like, *Are you sure this friendship is really such a great thing?* He gives me back a look that says *Calm down.* The silent conversations of married people.

"Okay, well, early bedtime all around tonight, I guess," I say. Kelsey rolls her eyes at me, and Lola smirks at her. I get the eggs out, the Boursin cheese. The items in the refrigerator have mercifully not been moved around by Maya—yet. Who knows what she has planned for the day. "Can I make you girls an omelet?"

"I'd love one, Carrie," Lola says, and I grimace slightly without meaning to. I don't know why it feels so strange for her to call me Carrie.

She nudges Kelsey, who hasn't responded, and says, "Omelet, Kels?" *Kels?*

And Kelsey, despite having resisted breakfast for over a year, says, "Sure. Sounds good."

I try to act like her response is completely normal, so as not to ruin the moment. "Pete? Maya?"

"Yes please, thanks," says Maya.

"Sounds great, Care Bear," says Pete, and Kelsey mutters "Oh my God" under her breath while Maya laughs lightly at hearing my ancient nickname.

"Care Bear?" Lola asks, looking back and forth between the two of us. "What's that about?"

Pete grins at her. "Well, you know, 'cause her name is Carrie. And, like, the Care Bears." He looks at Lola pointedly, and Lola stares back at him blankly. "Care Bears?" he says incredulously. "Those little fluffy pastel-colored bears who, like, did good deeds for people? It was a TV show."

"I've never heard of it," Lola says uncertainly. "I like the nickname, though."

Pete whirls to look at Maya in a playfully accusatory manner. "Matthews, you never gave your child a Care Bear? Why are you depriving her of a simple childhood treasure like a Care Bear?"

Maya looks back at him, an odd, ruminative expression on her face, eyes a bit glassy. "I guess I never did, no. She didn't watch a lot of TV when she was little. And she was always more into dolls than stuffed animals. Even though I never pushed dolls on her." Maya's expression is pleasantly nostalgic, but then a flash of pain flits over her face. She's likely remembering that the partner who helped her raise Lola is gone.

"I'll be right back," I say softly, trying to pivot all of us away from the heaviness of the moment. "Gonna grab some herbs from the deck to make these omelets a little more Parisian. Nothing but the best for our favorite guests!" I say, trying to adopt some of Pete's casual cheer, though it sounds forced and almost sarcastic coming out of my mouth.

I wrench open the sliding door. When I step out onto our deck, a blast of cold, thick air goes right through my insubstantial workout shirt. I can't remember the last sunny day we had here. And it's not even technically winter yet. But it sure feels like it.

I walk toward the row of herbs, planning to yank some parsley and thyme for the omelets.

But the stems are completely bare.

As if they've been skinned.

As if there were never any herbs there at all.

I check each one to make sure I'm not mistaken. But there isn't a single leaf left in my entire bed planter.

My heart starts beating rapidly. *What the hell happened to my garden?*

I try to take a deep breath. It's not that big of a deal. It's strange, sure, but I don't exactly know what I'm doing as a gardener. It may have gotten too cold for the plants to survive. I may have overwatered them. Or underwatered them. Or they haven't been getting enough sunlight.

It could have been anything, really.

But they were fine two days ago. And if it's no big deal, why do I suddenly feel light-headed?

I walk slowly back into the kitchen. Pete looks at my face, and his own immediately drops with concern. "What's wrong?"

I shrug, an effort to fight tears that I know are trying to come. How embarrassing it would be to cry in front of everyone over some freaking herbs. "My herbs seem to have flown the coop," I say. Pete looks relieved; my face must have implied that it's something far more serious.

But it feels serious to me. I liked my herb garden.

Maya looks at me, perplexed. "That's too bad! Do you think an animal could have gotten into them somehow?"

"Could be," I say, nodding pensively, processing. But an animal would have made a bigger mess of the pots and the dirt, I'd imagine. There was no mess—just neatly stripped stems.

"Maybe Ida finally decided to take revenge on us for existing," Pete says wryly. He's trying to use humor to defuse my upset. But I can't help but wonder if our neighbor Ida *might* have done something like that—she really seems to hate us. Or, even more likely, her weird son, who was staring over at our property just yesterday while drinking his midday beer.

I shrug again and try to plaster on a smile. "Maya's probably right. It was likely an animal. Or it could be weather related. I'll do some googling. Find out if this can be caused by external conditions," I tell them. *Shake it off, Carrie.* "It's no big deal. Cheese omelets still taste good, right?"

"Actually, we should get going," Kelsey says. "I have to get something from my locker before class."

"Oh. Okay. Well, let me grab some granola bars from"—I reach into the wrong cupboard before correcting myself—"over here," I tell her. "And just give me one minute. I still need to make you both lunches to bring."

"I already made us TBMs last night," Lola says, stopping me in my tracks. "They're bagged in the fridge, ready to go."

"TBMs?" I stammer, stunned.

"Tomato basil mozzarella sandwiches?" The word "duh" is implied in her tone, even though she doesn't say it. I'm silent. "It was no problem," Lola adds, as if my feeling indebted is the reason for my incredulousness.

Basil. Did Lola use the basil from my garden? She must have because I didn't buy other basil. Was Lola the last person in my garden? Could she have . . . ?

There's no way. Why would she have done that? Whatever happened to the herbs must have occurred sometime between when she took the basil and this morning. She'd have no reason to mess with my herbs. And it wasn't just the basil that was destroyed—everything was.

"I made one for you, too," Lola adds offhandedly.

"I'm sorry?" I'm sure I misheard.

"You said you liked mozzarella. So I made one for you, too. It's in the fridge, wrapped in foil with your name on it."

"That's . . ." I search for the words. Random? Strange? "So nice. Incredibly sweet." Better. "Thank you, Lola. Thank you so much!"

She blushes furiously. "It's just a sandwich." Kelsey is standing next to her, looking at the ground with what might be vague annoyance on her face.

Pete gives me a look as if to say, *See? She's a great kid.*

"Okay. Well. Thank you again. I can't wait to eat it. Shall we?" I look at Maya, expecting that she'll want to come with me.

But her eyes are on Pete, and it takes her a second to realize that I'm waiting for her response. "Actually," she says, shaking her head, "do you mind dropping them without me? I can make breakfast for the three of us while you're gone. And I need to make a call to our accountant. Go over some estate-related paperwork and next steps," she says grimly, turning her eyes downward.

"Of course, absolutely," I assure her hurriedly.

As I walk out the deck door with the girls, who are whispering to each other as they walk ahead of me, I glance back to the kitchen and see Maya mixing eggs in a bowl, Pete standing behind her and laughing at something she's said.

~

2000

Maya raises her hand—timidly, even though she knows what she's going to say is valid. Much more so than what Kelly Van Kirk just said, which was that the characters in The Sun Also Rises *used alcohol as a coping mechanism for their trauma and drank "way too much." Obviously, Kelly.*

"Maya," Professor Mulrooney says, nodding at her encouragingly.

"I feel like . . ." She groans inwardly at herself. Why did she start that way when she knows exactly what she wants to say? She begins again. "It's a novel about a group of friends, but they aren't really friends with each other."

Professor Mulrooney looks intrigued. "No? They're together the whole book, traipsing around Europe. Codependent and inseparable. It may not be a healthy friendship, but it's a friendship, nonetheless, is it not?"

"I don't think so," Maya says lightly. "They're too polite *to be real friends, for one thing. They're bizarrely formal, even the ones who aren't aristocratic. They never tell each other how they really feel. And they didn't choose each other, either. They're just in the same place at the same time, and have some similar experiences, and they can't handle being alone, so therefore they think they should be friends. But Jake has a more meaningful interaction with a statue than he does with a breathing character in the entire book."*

"Interesting, Maya. So what is Hemingway's point here? Would the characters be better off opening up to each other and trying to form a more authentic connection? Could they handle it?"

Maya thinks for a second. "This novel is like a self-preservation guide-book. The characters have already been hurt so much both physically and mentally by the time they meet each other that they can't risk further pain. And if they were to really lean on each other, that pain would inevitably come. People always disappoint each other, and they're smart enough to know that. The bill always comes, like Jake says."

Pete, beside Maya, whistles softly, causing the class to laugh lightly, breaking the tension. Mulrooney laughs, too.

"That's a great place for us to end today, I think. I'm interested to see if anyone will have a differing view following the fishing scene in the upcoming section, whether Jake and Bill start to build a more genuine friendship, or if they're still stunted. Let's make sure we start there next time. Can someone remind me?"

Kelly raises her hand and gives Mulrooney a simpering look as she makes a note of it in her pink planner. The students start packing up and chatting easily about homework and parties and lunch plans, as if the discussion never happened. Already, everyone's moved on from Hemingway.

"Damn, Matthews! You've really got some thoughts on this book, huh!" Pete nudges Maya playfully, and Maya's heart skips a beat. Every time he touches her, that happens. When their elbows graze during class, she's sure that the table they share might spontaneously combust from the energy between them. And he must feel it, too. She can't be the only one.

It's been three months of sitting next to each other in class, walking across campus together afterward, occasionally studying together in the library at night. He winks at her when they see each other in the dining hall, and it's all she can do not to faint. He is the reason that she's borrowed Carrie's mascara every day for the last sixty-seven days, despite having gone the first eighteen years of her life without wearing any makeup at all.

"I really like this book," she says with a shrug, trying to sound casual. But the truth is she's so invested in Jake's plight that she's had to stop herself from reading too far ahead of the class, lest she accidentally allude to something the rest of them haven't read yet. Not that she's concerned about spoiling it for them; based on their contributions to discussions, she's fairly certain that half of them aren't even reading it, opting for SparkNotes instead. Hell, that's what Carrie did when she took this class during spring semester last year.

"Maya!" a familiar voice calls as they're approaching the doors to exit, and Pete and Maya both turn around. It's Carrie. What is she doing here? They've never run into each other in this building before.

Carrie comes running up to them, slightly out of breath, blonde hair in a nest atop her head, wearing her usual uniform of sweats and a jean jacket. "Hey," she says, grinning. "I was just meeting with a professor. Negotiating an extension," she adds with a sheepish shrug. Of course, *Maya thinks.*

Carrie glances at Pete and then lets her eyes settle on him more squarely. "Hi," she says. "I'm Carrie."

Maya looks at Pete looking at Carrie; his eyes are reflecting the light in her hair, and the dimple that Maya spends way too much time thinking about has appeared above his jawline. No, *she thinks, simply,* no. Please, no. No.

CHAPTER TWELVE

When I get home from dropping the girls off at school (it's bizarre how quickly they've become "the girls," as if we've always had two daughters), I enter the kitchen through the deck and can't stop myself from investigating my herbs again, half expecting that they'll have magically reappeared, like they were just hiding or something, turtles who'd temporarily retreated into their shells. I examine the stems and roots gingerly, so as not to hurt them, as if they could be ruined twice. It really does look like they've been stripped—by a hand, or a knife, or a pair of scissors. Like how someone curls a ribbon for a gift. I linger on the deck, take out my phone, and start googling. The pictures of plants and gardens that were mauled by animals look much messier, as I suspected they would. And the weather we've been having, while cold and gray, should have been plenty warm enough to accommodate these specific herbs, which are supposed to thrive in winter.

I put my phone back in my pocket. It was just a stupid herb garden. A pet project. A distraction from boredom, guilt, stress.

But I was proud of those damn herbs. Of successfully ignoring the voice in my head that told me not to bother with a garden, I'd only botch it.

Pete comes out of the kitchen and onto the deck while I'm still busy inspecting the garden. "They'll grow back," he says, squeezing my shoulders hard with his strong hands. I melt under his touch, and he massages my shoulders for about a minute in silence. "We made you an omelet," he says finally. *We.* I don't know why hearing him describe himself and Maya as "we" rubs me a little roughly. There was never anything between Pete and Maya—they were always just good friends. She never seemed to have a crush on *anyone* in college. And I learned not to press her on guys; she got very defensive every time I asked if there was anyone she was into. But she knew him before I did, and they were more similar than Pete and I were, too—both look-on-the-bright-side sort of go-getters (hence the twitch-inducing reorganizing of my cabinets), whereas I was a bit more of the "sleep until 1:00 p.m. on weekends" variety.

Pete kisses me on the head and then goes back to the kitchen and down the stairs to disappear into our bedroom and start his workday. With Maya in town picking up some toiletries, as Pete's informed me, I am blessedly alone. I go back into the house and start my daily laundry collection, once again venturing into Kelsey's room. It's even messier than usual; she and Lola appear to have taken practically every single dress out of her closet and have predictably neglected to hang any of them back up. Maybe Lola wanted to try on some of Kelsey's clothes, which would make sense, given they're the exact same height and size. I search for the part of myself that should be pleased that my daughter has a new friend, but something about the sight of her and Lola walking down the hall arm in arm still vexes me.

Splayed out on the bed is *The Glass Castle.* Kelsey must have forgotten it; my stomach lurches for her, hoping she won't be unprepared for class. I grab the book and flip through it absently. I read over some of Kelsey's annotations, written out neatly on different colored Post-its that stick out from the pages:

"Walls chooses to start the novel with fire to introduce the family dynamic as something that may seem exhilarating but is in fact suffocating and dangerous."

"While Jeannette's mom is initially characterized as charming and exciting, the moment Jeannette finds her under the covers eating chocolate, she's exposed as the selfish, emotionally immature woman she really is."

"Jeannette's geode collection symbolizes her loyalty to her father, since he is so interested in mining. When she has to leave it behind because he tells her there's no room for it, it may seem like she's submitting to him as usual, but she's actually relinquishing her unrealistic adoration of him, privately knocking him off the pedestal she'd kept him on."

Damn, I think to myself, slightly stunned by Kelsey's insights. As impressed as I am, I'm also a little sad. There's so much inside my girl's head that I know nothing about. To be unknown by one's own mother strikes me as one of the saddest things in the world. I vow silently to rectify it, no matter how long it takes and how much Kelsey resists.

I place the book back on the bed, careful to keep Kelsey's place, and when I do, I feel something hard beneath it. I slide my hand under Kelsey's comforter to see what it is, and when I bring my hand out, I'm holding my own college yearbook.

What the hell is Kelsey doing with my yearbook? Where did she even find it? It's been buried in the garage, as far as I know, within the few storage boxes we've always kept here. I start flipping through that, too, and see that she's carelessly dog-eared some pages with no regard for the expensive, glossy paper. The selections seem random; some of the folded pages have pictures of me or Pete on them, Maya, too, but some don't. I keep flipping to pages that feel bent or altered until I'm near the end, in the portraits section. I find the *C*s: Sarah Calworth, Matthew Chisholm, Carrie Colts.

Except there's no photo above my name. It's been cut out.

Much like my herbs from their bed.

My chest swells with annoyed indignation. Granted, I haven't looked at my yearbook in years. But still, it's an important keepsake. And now it's ruined.

And where the hell is my picture? Why would she have done this?

I'll have to talk to her about it when she gets home from school. I'm sure I can predict how well that conversation is going to go.

I exit Kelsey's room, forgetting to bring her laundry with me.

Upstairs in the kitchen, Maya is back from town, putting away groceries.

"Hey!" I say, too brightly, trying to shake off my irritation about the yearbook. "How was town?"

"It was good," she says. "The people here are so nice." *Of course they already love you,* I think to myself enviously. Everyone likes Maya. And yet, I've been here six months and still haven't gotten the host at the Dock restaurant, where we pick up dinner at least once a week, to so much as smile at me.

"I grabbed some herbs for you at Round Swamp," she adds lightly. "I know they won't be the same as the ones from your garden, but hopefully they'll be good enough for now—just until you can grow new ones." She looks at me sympathetically, and again I feel ridiculous that this woman who has just lost her *husband* is concerned about my distress over my stupid herbs.

"Thanks," I tell her. "Thank you," I add again, hoping she can hear the sincerity of the gratitude in my voice. It really was a nice gesture. She must have picked up on the fact that I was more upset than I was trying to let on. I think about what Pete said. How having Maya here is a chance for us to reconnect, for me to be there for her. How I should be grateful for this time with my old friend, even if it was sort of unexpected.

"Hey, so, do you want to hang out tonight?" I ask her, fidgeting my fingers. *Smooth, Carrie.* "I feel like we haven't really had a chance to properly catch up since you guys have been here. I've got a really good bottle of cabernet with our names on it," I tell her. Though I know the cabernet will be more for me than for her. Maya was always fairly close lipped about her parents in college, but she said enough for me to know that the reason they couldn't raise her was because of drugs and alcohol, and she had no intention of going down the same path.

"That sounds great. I would love that," she says, almost shyly, as if I've asked her on a date.

"Okay, sweet!" I chirp. *Why am I being so awkward about this?* "All right, I'm going to go back downstairs to my office and try to get some work done. Need anything?"

"No, I'm good," she says. "Want me to pick the girls up this afternoon, to give you a break? I know the way to school now. It would be no problem. And you dropped them off, so it's my turn anyway."

I hesitate slightly. It feels strange to hand what's now one of the only benchmarks of my day over to Maya. But at the same time, it *would* be nice to have the whole day to write, to exercise, to get some things done around the house, without my 2:00 departure creeping up on me faster than I expect it to, as it always does.

"That would be great," I say. "Thanks. You can take our car. I just filled it up." And then I blush furiously, hating myself for implying that Maya can't afford gas. She nods lightly, and I trot downstairs quickly to skirt my embarrassment.

CHAPTER THIRTEEN

I come upstairs from my office when I hear Maya and the girls get home. Kelsey and Lola are talking quietly, staring into the open fridge. Lola turns to look at me as I walk toward them.

"You didn't eat the sandwich," she says accusingly, and it takes me a second to remember what she's talking about.

Crap. The tomato and mozzarella sandwich she made me. I've been working and completely forgot about it; I stuffed a Luna bar from my desk drawer into my mouth about an hour ago.

"I was just going to eat it now!" I'm lying, but she looks satisfied, and she hands it to me from the fridge. I unwrap it from the tinfoil and take a big bite.

"So good," I tell her. "Thanks again." She glows. It really is good, and even though I thought I wasn't hungry, suddenly I'm starving.

"You're welcome," Lola says, grinning like a Cheshire cat. She nudges Kelsey, and the girls slink downstairs, holding seltzers and a bag of popcorn they've just microwaved, Mr. Sparkles weaving in and out of Lola's legs. "How was your day at school?" I call after them.

Kelsey ignores me, but Lola sings out, "Amazing!" I guess I'll have to wait to ask Kelsey about the yearbook. The surge of anger I felt earlier has already passed. I really don't care about the yearbook. I still want to know why she did it, though.

Even though "the girls" have been home for only a few minutes, Maya has already spread out in the kitchen and is preparing dinner. Herbs weren't the only thing she picked up at Round Swamp market; I can see that she also got salmon, arugula, parmesan, potatoes, and crusty french bread. "Is there anything I can help with?" I ask her pathetically, as if it's me who's the guest.

"Nope," she says. "The least I can do is make some meals, since you've so generously agreed to host us. Besides, cooking is like therapy to me."

I nod at her, feeling gangly and clumsy and in the way. It's strange to be rendered so pointless in my own kitchen, my own *life*: she's made breakfast for my husband and picked up my child, and now she's cooking dinner in the kitchen that she organized.

I know I should just enjoy the help that Maya's offering. It's not like I love driving to East Hampton twice a day, every day, to take Kelsey to and from school; I've complained about it plenty of times to Pete. My kitchen cabinets are way tidier now that Maya has had her way with them. I've actually gotten some decent writing done and might finally be on the right track with my manuscript. I've done two Peloton core workouts. And it's good to have a break from cooking dinner. It should be, at least. I don't really like cooking.

Unlike Maya, who apparently just *loves* it.

Ease up, Carrie. She's just trying to keep busy as a way of distracting herself from her loss.

I loaf around the kitchen for a few more minutes before finally setting the table awkwardly, even though it's only 4:00 p.m., feeling like I've been relegated to a job that a six-year-old could complete.

Finishing my sole task in about thirty seconds, I clear my throat. "Okay, well, if you're sure you don't need any help, I guess I'll work until dinner," I say to Maya. It's obvious she doesn't need any help; she's already rinsed the salmon and is now doctoring it up with olive oil, lemon, and seasonings.

"Go!" she agrees encouragingly, and preheats the oven.

When I walk downstairs, the door to our bedroom is open. Usually, Pete keeps it shut when he's in there working; he has a lot of calls during the day and wants to mute any background noise. Since it's open, I poke my head in, and I see that Lola is standing behind him at his desk. He's showing her something on his computer. Then he turns to look up at her from his chair. She's standing so close to him that his face practically touches her shoulder when he turns his head up. She laughs at whatever it is he's said, and points to something on his screen.

I am frozen at the door watching them until Kelsey interrupts all of us. "Mom, what are you doing?" she asks, irritation dripping from her voice. She's in the doorway of her own room, directly across from where I'm standing.

Pete turns when he hears Kelsey's voice, then sees me standing in the doorway. "Hey, ladies," he calls. "Lola here was just asking me some questions about work. I think she's the first woman in this house to ever show an interest in what I do!" He laughs good naturedly. "I was showing her my Excel skills. Pretty impressive, right?" he says to her, standing up and offering his closed fist for a bump.

"Not bad," she says, meeting his fist with her own.

"'Not bad'? Come on, I'm an Excel *artist*. I'm the Dave Grohl of Microsoft Excel. I don't just crunch the numbers; I make them dance!" Pete exclaims with another laugh.

"Oh my God, Dad," Kelsey says, cringing. She's standing beside me now.

"What was so funny?" I ask. I can't help myself.

"Funny?" Pete asks quizzically.

"You two were laughing."

"Oh, I don't know. I probably made a hilarious joke about how to differentiate the tabs or input an algorithm or something," he says affably. In his hoodie, he looks like he could be a college student. Perks of working from home. But really, he still possesses the same boyish good looks he had when we met at Middlebury. Most of his hair, too. Why do men age so much more slowly than women? Is it because they worry less?

"I was laughing about how nerdy it is that he's so excited about his Excel spreadsheets," Lola adds jokingly.

"Nerdy? Or inspiring?" Pete asks, a lopsided grin on his face.

Kelsey hasn't taken her eyes off Lola. "Did you still want to show me how you do your eyeliner?" she asks in a small voice.

"Sure," Lola responds, and I feel a swell of relief in my chest that Lola didn't reject her invitation. The girls disappear into Kelsey's room once more.

Pete leans back in his desk chair and looks up at me. "All okay?" he asks. I am looking at him funny, and he can tell.

"Fine," I tell him, but it comes out sounding like a question.

He looks down at his iPhone. "I have a call," he says. "It'll be done before dinner." I take the hint and leave the room, shutting the door behind me. As I retreat to my office and sink into Helen's well-worn desk chair that makes my lower back scream if I sit in it for too long, I wonder what this pit in my stomach is about. They were just looking at Pete's work stuff. With the door open. She's a teenage girl, for God's sake. There wasn't anything unsavory happening whatsoever. I know that, beyond the shadow of a doubt.

And yet, as I sit in my office attempting to work, the sight of the two of them laughing at Pete's computer screen keeps flitting through my head, making me uneasy.

CHAPTER FOURTEEN

At five thirty, Maya calls down the stairs to summon us for dinner. When I open my office door, I can already smell it—butter and citrus and fish—and when I get upstairs, it looks even better than it smells. It's a more elaborate meal than I've prepared in months, I realize guiltily.

I go to the fridge and take out a cold bottle of chablis, pouring three glasses. I make mine slightly bigger and take a few large sips to even them back out before I put them at our place settings. I feel like I need the head start.

Pete ambles up the stairs a minute or two after me. He turns to Maya, who's whisking a salad dressing with a fork. "Maya, it smells amazing in here."

"It's just salmon," says Maya, waving her hand modestly. "Lola's favorite," she adds pensively. "She loved it even when she was only one year old. She would just gobble it up with her fingers." Her eyes glaze for a second with the memory before she snaps back to. "I've got everyone plated already, so just grab your plates and have a seat, and I'll pass around the dressing!" It feels incredibly odd to be hosted by someone else at my own house. And I always dress the salad so that I can toss it. Besides, we usually plate ourselves. Kelsey is a selective eater.

But to my surprise, when we sit down, Kelsey starts eagerly shoveling Maya's rosemary potatoes into her mouth. So maybe it's just *my* cooking that she's picky about.

"How was school today, girls?" I ask, finding myself keen to veer the conversation away from how wonderful Maya's cooking is (though truly, it is delicious).

"Great," Lola says. She's eating her salad but hasn't yet touched her salmon. "Well, math was pretty boring," she adds. "But the other classes were really cool. Better than I imagined. Better than at my school, I mean." Maya gives her a warning look.

"How big is your school?" I ask her.

She looks at Maya instead of me. "Oh, like the classes? Um, around twenty-five?"

"That's right. About a hundred in each grade," Maya adds. "There are two local middle schools, which combine for high school. Still, pretty small. Where we live is a big summer town, but the population thins out in the off season. A lot like Montauk, I guess."

I nod at them. "Oh, that reminds me, Kelsey, I think you left your copy of *The Glass Castle* here today. I saw it in your room when I was getting your laundry." *Along with my mangled yearbook,* I think.

"Stay out of my room," Kelsey mutters in response.

Do your own laundry, then, I almost retort. But I remind myself that I'm her mother. I'm the adult. Being snarky toward her certainly won't help us. "Hopefully you didn't need it. Looks like you had some annotations in there that may have been useful for class."

"You read my homework?" Kelsey asks with annoyance. "Stalk much?"

I clear my throat, having already lost my nerve but determined to press on. "Um, I also saw my old yearbook in your room?"

Kelsey and Lola exchange a brief look. "Yeah, we were looking through it yesterday. I needed an old picture of you for a family tree project we're doing in history," Kelsey says hurriedly, pushing another bite of food into her mouth.

"Oh, okay. Well, next time, just ask me, okay? There's no need to cut pictures out of my yearbook. I could have given you an old photo." Pete raises his eyebrow at me, but I can't tell whether his expression is saying, *Whoa, she really did that?* or if it's saying, *Leave her alone—who cares about the yearbook?* It bothers me that I can't discern the difference.

"You look the same, you know," Lola says, studying me carefully. Her gaze is so focused that I find myself needing to look away after I've met her eyes.

"Oh, you're very sweet, but I don't know about that."

"No, really."

"I think your mother here is the one who hasn't aged." Lola looks at me for another second before transferring her gaze to Maya.

"I guess you're right," she says.

Maya insists on cleaning up after dinner, even though the rule in our house has always been that whoever cooks doesn't have to clean. Kelsey and Lola bring their plates to the sink; I notice that Lola's piece of salmon hasn't been touched.

"Do you want to save that for tomorrow?" I ask her.

"No, that's okay. If anyone else wants it, though, they're welcome to have it."

Maya doesn't turn around from the sink as I wrap Lola's piece of salmon in foil, a little surprised that she passed up her favorite food.

Kelsey and Lola slink toward the stairs. "I wish we could stay and chat, but there's a smoky-eye demo happening on TikTok in five minutes, and it's much more fun to catch it live," Lola says. She grins, and for a second her chipped tooth gives her an eerie, jack-o'-lantern-like quality. Kelsey nods her agreement eagerly despite the fact that I've never known her to watch a makeup tutorial. Then again, there's lots I don't know about her, I'm realizing.

Pete grabs my hand and kisses it. "I have to do a few more minutes of work," he says. "Cool if I leave you two?"

"Of course," I tell him, and he kisses me again.

"You two are as cute as ever," Maya says, a hitch in her voice making this sound not quite like a compliment. Pete grins at her, apparently not catching it. But I pull away from him, suddenly uncomfortable.

~

2001

Another creak. Maya rolls over and puts her pillow over her head. She considers, for what feels like the thousandth time in the past hour, leaving the room to go sleep on the couch in the communal space in the hallway.

But then they would know she's been awake the whole time, which would be horrifically awkward. Why did she feign sleep when they came in? She should have just said hello and then taken a graceful leave when they stumbled through the door, drunk and pawing at each other. But if she left now, Carrie would be all apologetic and worried that Maya is mad, and Maya would end up consoling her, even though Carrie is the one currently having sex with someone (not just someone, but Pete), while Maya is three feet beneath her in the bottom bunk. God damn these bunk beds. Why couldn't they have had two twin beds like they did freshman year?

Maya silently laments the fact that she's still bothered by Pete and Carrie being together. She's tried so hard to extinguish whatever little sparks of feelings for him were beginning to form.

For a while, in high school, Maya wondered if there was something wrong with her. She had no interest whatsoever in any of the boys she'd grown up with—but that was likely because they reminded her too much of her dad, or what she remembered (more likely, imagined) of him—a Boston sports fanatic with wiry muscles who was quick to anger and quicker to consume any drink or drug available to him. She had no desire to date, if that's what you could even call what the other girls at school were doing with these boys. She thought maybe she was just missing the romantic love chip, and though that made her a little sad, it was also a relief. So many problems could be avoided by not falling in love—especially with the wrong person, as her mother had done, according to her grandma, who blamed Maya's dad for everything that had happened with her parents.

But then she met Pete and she knew that that part of her did *exist. Her reaction to him—to the thoughtful things he said in class, to his warm smile, to the fact that he held every door open for her—was as much physical as it was emotional. When he was around, her heart beat faster. Her adrenaline spiked. She lost her appetite. Her—vagina fluttered? Can vaginas* flutter? *It's all very new. And worrisome. She's here to focus on school, not get caught up with a boy. Or get her heart broken. Between classes and work, she doesn't have time to date, and she definitely doesn't have time to nurse a broken heart.*

Fortunately, Carrie snagged Pete before Maya could fall too deeply. Lucky, right? Better, all around. As soon as it became clear that Carrie and Pete were going to be an item, Maya started working even harder than she already had been to squash her crush on him. Maya has always considered herself a master of control over her actions and feelings—even as a toddler, she was so careful never to upset her mom or make her life more difficult in any way. She understood implicitly that if her mom barked that it was time to put her shoes on, then that meant it was time to put her shoes on, even if those shoes were two sizes too small, and a color she hated, and sandals when it was December. She would earn her mother's love with compliance.

And then, when her mom dropped her off at her grandma's for the last time, she was determined to make her grandma's life easier and better, too. She would not be abandoned again. She would curate a version of herself that no one would ever want to leave.

And her grandma did love her, as best she could, which was enough for Maya. It worked. So Maya is now well practiced at not letting her emotions "get the better of her." She is in charge of *them, and not vice versa. And if it's time to turn whatever feelings she once had for Pete off, it shouldn't be a problem. She's shoved down and swallowed feelings millions of times before. Every day of her entire life, really. She'll just stop thinking about him. Period.*

But it's difficult not to think about him when he and Carrie are having sex three feet above her.

"You're amazing," Pete whispers, breathing heavily, and Carrie squeals quietly, and finally, they are still. Maya's pretty sure Carrie faked it—granted, Maya has never had an orgasm before, so what does she know?—but it was the same squeal Carrie makes when she stretches upon waking in the morning, and Maya has to imagine that orgasms are more intense than a morning stretch.

"You are, too," Carrie whispers back, giggling.

"No, I'm serious. I'm so glad I met you."

You're welcome for the introduction, *Maya muses bitterly, and then tries to shake the thought out of her head. She doesn't want to begrudge them the happiness they've found with each other. Carrie has always been kind to Maya, and Maya knows how much Carrie cares about her. It's more overt than Maya has ever experienced. Maya's grandma loved her, yes, but her love was muted, reserved. They probably only hugged a couple of dozen times, on birthdays and holidays and such, the loosest and limpest and briefest of hugs, followed by her grandma's gruff "Love ya, hon." Carrie, on the other hand, throws her arms around Maya every time they see each other on the quad, even if it's only been two hours since they've last been together. She knows Maya's schedule by heart, and typically does her homework at the coffee shop during Maya's shifts, just so they can be in close proximity. It is nice to be liked so openly, so abundantly. Especially by someone like Carrie, who could be friends with anyone she wants to.*

So it wouldn't be fair for Maya to start hating Carrie just because she's having sex with the guy Maya likes in the bed above hers, right? They'll probably break up in a few months, anyway. Which is not to say that Maya could still date Pete in the future. She knows she could never "do that to Carrie." (Girls and their stupid rules. Maya has never had close girlfriends, but she's learning quickly.) In any case, at least when they break up, Maya won't have to see them together every day. The discomfort Maya is experiencing is temporary. It certainly isn't worth ruining the closest friendship she's ever had over.

Maya puts her pillow over her head and tries to go to sleep, even though the motion from the bed above suggests they might be starting again.

CHAPTER FIFTEEN

"Do you want to drink this outside?" I ask Maya, gesturing to the bottle of California cabernet I've put aside for us. "It's cold, but we can bring blankets." I am intent on making good on my promise to spend some real, quality catch-up time with her tonight. The girls are holed up in Kelsey's room, and Pete hasn't resurfaced from his "few minutes" of work. I have a feeling ESPN and a cold can of Juicy IPA are involved in this alleged work.

"That sounds lovely," she says, and suddenly I feel like we're in college again: walking around campus after the first snowfall and marveling at the beauty of it, dancing our hearts out to mediocre cover bands in off-campus basements, bringing each other hot chocolate when we knew the other one was in the library studying, sleeping in each other's beds after a bad day or just because we'd passed out after watching a movie curled up together.

We used to be so close. Like sisters. I always thought we were the kind of friends who could get through anything. Then again, the fights we'd had before that had always been about silly things—one of us never taking out the trash in our room (me), borrowing each other's tampons and clothes without asking (me again; come to think of it, I never got mad at her, because she never did anything inconsiderate).

But after that summer, we didn't know how to talk to each other anymore, how to be with each other. The elephant in the room was too big; it threatened to suffocate both of us.

Which is why I was so surprised when she showed up at my door with her daughter two days ago. I didn't think she thought of me like that anymore—a lifeline. But I *want* to be that for her, the way she was for me back then. Maybe we've both been through enough by now that what happened that summer can stop wedging itself between us. And I *am* excited about reuniting with her. It's oddly comforting to be in the presence of someone who knows something about you that literally no one else does.

If a little unnerving, too.

I'm already a little buzzed from the chablis I had at dinner, but I pour us both a huge glass of wine anyway, even though I know Maya will never finish hers. We pull on beanies, grab our wineglasses and a blanket each, walk outside onto the deck, and sink into the well-worn deck sofa, arranging our blankets on top of us. The stars are twinkling above us, and we spend a second or two taking them in. "Cheers," I say, turning my face back down to look at her. "I am so glad you're here. Lola's amazing."

Maya's eyes well. "She really is. Thanks. So is Kelsey."

"Hey, what happened to her tooth, by the way?" It's none of my business, but I'm suddenly curious.

Maya looks momentarily confused before recentering herself. "Oh. It happened when she was little, and it's so small the dentist said it wasn't really worth fixing." She pauses, and I continue to look at her, waiting for her to elaborate. "She banged it on a bunk bed," she finally offers.

"It's very cute. Sort of like her own signature Madonna gap or something."

"Hmm. Yeah, sort of." *Okay, Carrie. Talking to her about her daughter's dental history is not the bonding experience you were striving for.*

"I'm really so sorry for what you're going through, Maya," I tell her sincerely.

She nods. "So am I. It's a relief to be here, though. To not have to think about—what I left behind." She takes a deep breath and shakes her head. "I can't let myself think about it."

"I'm sure it's devastating." I pause, and when she says nothing, I keep going. I'm determined to make her open up. "I mean, you planned to grow old with this person, and then out of nowhere, he just dies of a heart attack. It's awful, Maya. And after you and Lola leave, I want you to know that we'll do anything we can to help you get back on your feet. We'll visit. And if you need help with logistics—funeral, anything—we can help with that, too."

"Thanks," she says, but there's something halting in her voice. She starts to speak again, but then falters and buries her face in her hands.

"Maya," I say softly, rubbing her back.

"It really was my fault," she whispers, clutching her full wineglass tightly.

"Maya, no, it wasn't," I say softly but emphatically. "He had a heart attack. No fight could have caused that. And besides, all couples argue. You can't beat yourself up for it. There's no way you could have known that whatever conversation you had before he died would be your last."

"I lied to you, Carrie," she breathes, her voice barely audible. "It wasn't a heart attack."

Goose bumps immediately appear on my arms. "Oh. How did he die, then?" I am trying to sound even-keeled, but my head and heart have both started to race. Why would she have lied about how Elliot died?

She takes a long sip of her wine, finally, and I do the same. "See, he'd always had a bit of a thing with drinking—nothing too extreme, just beers after work. And more on the weekends. Kind of weird I ended up with an alcoholic, right? Like my parents?" I am thinking it, too, though of course I would never be the one to say it.

"But he was a different type of alcoholic than they were. He never got angry, always made it to work on time, always seemed fine, you know? I never even really realized that he *was* an alcoholic. But he'd finally decided, on his own, that he was tired of waking up hungover. And he wanted to be more present for Lola. I admired what he was doing and supported him completely." Suddenly, I'm a little embarrassed about all the wine I've been slugging tonight.

"It was harder for him than I thought it would be, though. But he was really committed. He'd do workouts at odd hours, stay at his office late, to distract himself, I guess. He started meditating all the time. Drinking weird green juices. And I was so proud of him for getting sober, but at the same time—it was difficult to be on the journey with him, if that makes sense." She looks searchingly into my eyes.

"It does. I can completely understand that." I really can. For a year or two, Pete became obsessed with biking and spent full days biking around upstate New York, leaving me to care for Kelsey on my own, who was around five at the time. I was excited for him that he had a new passion, especially one that was good for his health and well-being, but it was infuriating at the same time to be on solo parenting duty for most of the weekend.

"So I was frustrated with him to begin with, and one night—*that* night—I blew up at him over the stupidest thing." She takes her forehead in her hands and shakes her head, fighting the pain of the remembrance. "For weeks, we'd been planning to get rid of this old armoire that had belonged to his parents. It was a total eyesore. Bulk-disposal day where we live is Wednesday. So we had to get it to the dump by Tuesday night. Obviously, I couldn't get it onto his truck myself. He'd promised me he'd finally take care of it, but here we were, on Tuesday night, and he was still at work. I didn't want to wait another week with this thing on our lawn, so I called him and insisted he come home from work to help me with it, which he did. And I was so"—she shakes her head with self-disgust—"I was so snippy with him about it. So annoyed that he hadn't done it the other times I'd asked." I nod at her, unsure of where this is going.

"So he went to the dump to drop off the stupid armoire. And then I guess after that, despite all the progress he'd made, he went to a bar." It clicks, suddenly. Maya nods at me, seeing me understand. "And then later I got the call that his car was wrapped around a tree." She rubs her temples. "I was so relieved that Lola was at a sleepover so that she wasn't with me when I got the call. She was at a sleepover. She was." Maya's eyes go vacant, and she grabs her knees and starts rocking back and forth. She looks like a child soothing herself. I put my arm around her to steady her.

My mind flashes briefly to something that Lola said when they first arrived. She said she was the one to find him. She described seeing his body at the bottom of the stairs. "Slumped." I'm fairly certain she used that word. So specific.

And apparently, she was lying.

As if Maya can read my thoughts, she says hurriedly, "I told Lola to tell you it was a heart attack. I didn't want you thinking that I was married to a reprobate or something. He was a good person. But I can't help but feel ashamed. It's like I'm not allowed to mourn or something. Because he died doing something so reckless, so selfish, that could have hurt other people, too. And I didn't want that to be your first impression of me, after all these years." That, I can relate to. I remember how mad I was when Pete told Maya how we have no friends here. And driving drunk is a much bigger stain than simply being unpopular.

To be honest, though, I'm a little perturbed that Maya told Lola to lie. I don't think I'd feel comfortable encouraging Kelsey to lie about anything, not at this age, when their moral fibers are still being formed. It'd be such a confusing request from a parent. Especially about something so big—and when she's in such a fragile place mentally, having just lost her father.

Even more unsettling to me, Lola seemed to do quite well with the lie, going so far as to offer details about the shape of his body at the bottom of the stairs. A rather adept liar, perhaps. A practiced one.

And I would know, wouldn't I? Months of "breakfast meetings" and "barre classes" and "writing sessions at a coffee shop" were actually hotel dates with Kyle. So apparently Lola and I have something in common.

I bring myself back to the conversation. Lola's overactive and morbid imagination isn't the most important thing right now. The important thing is that Maya is letting me in, telling me something real. She needs me. And I have a chance to be a supportive friend.

A better one than I've historically been.

"That's terrible, Maya," I say, rubbing her back again. "I am so, so sorry. I can certainly see why that makes processing his death even more difficult. And I understand why you weren't eager to share it. But of course it doesn't make me think any less of you, or of Elliot. Nobody is perfect. I know that better than anyone," I add dryly.

"Well, you and Pete actually *are* perfect," she says, correcting me lightly. "You two are as happy as you were in college."

"*No* relationship is perfect," I tell her insistently, my voice low. I go to refill our glasses, but only mine needs refilling. I do so, even though I already feel drunker than I intended to get.

"What do you mean?" she probes. I hesitate. "You know you can tell me anything. But of course if you aren't comfortable, I respect your privacy." She looks hurt, though. And the last thing I want to do is hurt her when she's already at such a low. And when she's just shared something with me that was difficult for her.

I shouldn't tell her. I know I shouldn't. It's safer if no one knows. And yet, there is something so tempting about unloading. It's so exhausting being all alone with this secret, this guilt. Letting someone in on it might feel cathartic. Besides, Maya already knows even more reprehensible things about me, even darker secrets. What could it hurt if she knew this, too? She's the only person who's truly seen me at my absolute worst, and she's still here, sitting beside me drinking wine under the stars.

I take a long breath and chase it with another gulp of wine, immediately feeling the acid from the wine wick the moisture from my mouth. "Right before we came out here, to care for Pete's mom—there was someone else." I almost gasp as I say it, surprised at myself for admitting it.

To Maya's credit, if she's appalled, her face doesn't betray her. She nods evenly, prompting me to go on. And fueled by wine, I do. "His name was Kyle. It didn't last that long—a few months. I think it was some sort of a midlife crisis. And it's over now, of course. I regret it, deeply. But—it happened."

She takes a beat. "I'm assuming Pete doesn't know?"

I shake my head quickly. "No, definitely not. And I hope he never finds out. I don't want to hurt him. And I know I'll never do anything like that again. It's out of my system. I don't know what I was thinking, truly."

"None of us are perfect," she says simply, echoing my own words, putting her hand over mine.

"Especially not me," I murmur, and I'm surprised to feel a lump in my throat when I say it. "As you well know."

It's the closest we've ever come to talking about that summer. It feels like we're venturing into territory we have not yet been to.

She clears her throat. "Did you ever tell Pete about that?"

I shake my head vehemently. "No. Never. And I never will." I glance out toward the ocean, and I instead see Ida's son sitting on their front steps, looking up at us as he sips a beer. He gets up and walks inside the second he sees me looking at him.

Maya nods slowly. "Well, look around. Look at your life. It's all worked out for you. It always seems to." Her tone is kind, and yet, a chill runs down my spine as she says it. I take another sip of wine and wonder if I've just made a huge mistake by letting her in on yet another of my secrets.

~

2001

Someone backs into Maya from behind, jostling her and causing her beer to spill over onto her hands. Yes, she may be partially to blame, for carrying around a full beer all night. Maya was self-conscious about not drinking at first; she worried that people would think she was a bore, or a narc, and that she'd have no friends. But Carrie has always casually and discreetly handed Maya cups of Pepsi only, instead of Pepsi and rum, during their dorm-room pregames. And it didn't take Maya too long to realize that no one was paying attention to what she was or wasn't drinking, because people were mostly worried about themselves and what people might be thinking of them. If everyone understood this, they could all save themselves a lot of unnecessary worrying.

So she always fills up a beer when she first gets to a party, drinks a few sips of it throughout the night, and that's that. Funnily enough, she actually likes the taste of beer, at least when it's fresh out of the keg and still cold. But she knows that developing a penchant for alcohol is the absolute last thing she needs. She has too much studying to do to be hungover, and the fact that addiction is in her blood scares her.

This particular party is winding down; a handful of people are dangling from the front steps smoking cigarettes, a few are circled around the kitchen table sharing a bong, but otherwise, it's not nearly as crowded as it was a few hours ago. There was another party at the lacrosse team's house that many of this party's guests (though "guests" seems too civilized a word to describe attendees of an event that serves no food, with bathrooms that are leaking urine into the living room) migrated to earlier on. Maya wanted to leave earlier, too, in part because one of the guys who lives at this house is in her precalc class and has called her Megan the entire semester while breathing down her neck trying to cheat off her quizzes. Nick is his name. Maya knows his name, even if he doesn't know hers. He's a philosophy major and has spent most of his time in precalc pontificating on the futility of being forced to learn math when our time on earth is meant to be pleasurable.

But Carrie wasn't ready to go when Maya suggested it, which is strange, since Pete is at the lacrosse house, and Carrie and Pete have been dating solidly for about three months. "I'm just about to get on the pong table," Carrie whined when Maya said they should head out. "I've been waiting for an hour. I can't leave now. Just a little while longer." Maya reluctantly agreed.

Now, Carrie is nowhere to be found, and the friends they came with, Ashley and Kaitlin, are long gone as well, rather unsurprisingly, given that it's two in the morning. Maya wonders for a second if Carrie has left without her, but that would be so unlike her. That's a rule they made for each other in the beginning of their freshman year, when one of the girls in their hall was assaulted at a football party after all her friends had left without her; the next morning, as the girls comforted her in their common area while she sobbed, and encouraged her to tell campus security (she didn't), they heard half a dozen other stories of assaults or close calls, and this was only November. It's a rule they've held on tightly to. Never leave the other one alone at a party. Never make the other one walk home alone. Neither of them has ever broken this promise.

Maya tiptoes upstairs, suddenly feeling like an intruder at this party, even though she's been here for nearly four hours. But she knows she's an outsider among the late-night crew still lingering here, especially since she's no longer with Carrie, who's a chameleon among groups of friends. Everyone on campus gives Carrie an upward head nod as they pass her. Then they look at Maya with vague recognition, as if to say, "Oh right. Carrie's friend."

"Carrie?" she says softly, embarrassed, not wanting to appear to anyone as if she's Carrie's keeper, Juliet's freaking nursemaid.

No answer.

She cracks open a bedroom door. Empty, with the lights on, and almost no furniture, except a bed that has a comforter and pillows on top of it, but no sheets or pillowcases.

She walks down the hall and gingerly pushes open another door. The lights are dim, but not so dim that she can't see that Carrie is on the couch, sitting close to someone. Nick from precalc. Each of them is holding an empty shot glass.

Carrie turns when she hears the door open. "There you are," she says, as if she's the one who's been looking for Maya all this time. "Ready to go?"

She gets up, and Nick protests. "You're leaving now?" He casts an irritated look in Maya's direction.

"Gotta get our beauty rest," Carrie says, leaning down and giving him a chaste kiss on the cheek. "Thanks for having us."

"You serious, Colts?" Nick asks. "I thought we were hanging out." His tone is joking, or trying to be, but his face is starting to cloud with something close to genuine anger. He glances disdainfully at Maya again, as if she's to blame for Carrie's unanticipated departure. Maya suddenly feels the urge to get the hell out of there immediately.

"I'm always serious," Carrie says, and it sounds sexy and clever, even though Maya is aware that it doesn't actually mean anything at all. "And we were hanging out. But now we're done. See you around."

The girls trot down the stairs and out the door; Carrie is moving quickly alongside Maya, and Maya wonders if she, too, has sensed Nick's simmering rage at being denied what he felt he was owed. It is a relief to be outside in the cold, their breath coming out in misty puffs; it's March, almost spring, but Vermont stays cold well into May. The girls pull their beanies out of their pockets and put them on their heads in unison. Carrie sways slightly as they walk, but she isn't as bad off as Maya's seen her on plenty of other occasions. She links arms with Maya to steady herself and sighs contentedly. "What a night, huh?" Carrie says, resting her head atop Maya's briefly. She's way too tall to rest her head on Maya's shoulder. "Did you have fun?"

"Yep," *Maya lies. Sometimes she really does have fun at parties, but this party was boring—no conversations whatsoever, just loud, bad music and far too many cigarettes being smoked indoors—the kind of party that could only have been fun for people who were drunk or on drugs.* "What was going on with you and Nick?" *Maya asks quietly. Carrie has seemed smitten with Pete these past few months, and for her part, Maya is over . . . whatever her feelings were. She's also forced herself to accept that Carrie didn't steal Pete away, because even if Carrie didn't exist, he'd never be interested in Maya. Besides, it's been nice for her best friend to date someone Maya likes. It makes it easy for them to all hang out. She should be happy. Some of the guys Carrie seemed interested in freshman year were jerks, and the last thing Maya would want is for guys like that—guys like Nick, in fact—to be hanging around their dorm room all the time.*

Carrie laughs a little. "Yeah, things are great with Pete. Nick and I were just talking. He's hot, though, don't you think? And I kind of like that he isn't a jock and can talk about something other than sports."

Yeah, like himself? *Maya almost asks. She also wants to point out that Nick's gelled hair looks like it takes him an hour to perfect, and that she's never once seen him smile, but she holds back. In any case, she's certain that Nick doesn't find "Megan" attractive, either, so at least they're on the same page about each other.*

"Nothing happened, obviously," *Carrie adds quickly.* "He was coming on to me, but I told him I had a boyfriend. No harm in flirting, though, right? And I don't know. I really like Pete, but do I like him enough to be his girlfriend? How do you know when it's enough?" *Maya assumes Carrie knows she's asking the wrong person, that it's a rhetorical question. Carrie proves her right by continuing before Maya can answer:* "Plus, you know what's annoying? The entire lacrosse team refers to me as 'Pete's girl.' I still have a name," *Carrie says, rolling her eyes.* "I don't want to just be known as someone's girlfriend. Or wife, or mom, in the future, for that matter. I want to be *myself, first and foremost.*

"Thanks for waiting for me," Carrie adds suddenly, squeezing Maya's arm. "Sorry we never made it to the other party. Hopefully Pete won't be too pissed. He's probably so drunk he didn't even notice. Oh well. We'll see him tomorrow. Maybe we could pick up some bagels and bring them to his room in the morning? Find out what we missed?"

Maya nods, already knowing that she'll be the one to go pick up the bagels when Carrie wakes up with a debilitating hangover.

CHAPTER SIXTEEN

Thursday

When I wake up the next day, my mouth is dry and my head is spinning. *Ugh.* Why did I drink so much last night? I'm not even sure I remember going to bed. I'm hungover and irritable. And embarrassed for getting so drunk.

Our conversation comes back to me like a slingshot, and I remember, with a violent grimace, that I told Maya about Kyle. What was I thinking? Why did I tell her? It felt good to unburden in the moment, but it was so much safer when no one knew. I trust Maya, of course; she'd never tell Pete, or anyone else. She's a locked box. She's more than proved that over the course of our friendship. But still, I hate the fact that she knows. Especially since she herself would never make a mistake like the one I have.

I roll over in bed, mentally and physically preparing to get up and go to the bathroom to pee and take some much-needed Tylenol. I'm expecting to see the familiar sight of Pete's shoulder—he always sleeps on his side—but he isn't there. And it's brighter than usual in our room, unwelcome daylight creeping in aggressively through the window.

I grab my phone: 11:00 a.m.

What the hell? It's a Thursday. How did I sleep until 11:00? Kelsey has school.

I practically fall out of bed, put on my glasses instead of taking the time to put in my contacts, and run upstairs to the kitchen without even brushing my teeth. Maya is at the table, drinking coffee and reading a newspaper. She's dressed in jeans and a white turtleneck, hair brushed, mascara in her eyelashes. Four breakfast plates are drying in the rack. I picture her, Pete, Lola, and Kelsey eating breakfast together while I slept off my hangover downstairs, and bile rises in my throat.

"Good morning!" she says brightly. "I took the girls to school. We didn't want to wake you." My brain trips on her use of the word "we." "I convinced Pete to let you sleep. I thought some extra rest might do you good." She gives me a meaningful look, and my feeling of regret over revealing my secret tightens in my chest.

"Thanks," I tell her, unsteadily, my vision slightly blotchy from hangover and disorientation. "I can't believe I slept so late. I have no idea why my alarm didn't go off. I always set it for six thirty." But did I set it last night? I honestly can't remember. Did I really drink that much?

"Well, we certainly made our way through some wine last night," she says, laughing. "It's understandable." And yet, Maya seems completely fine, her skin fresh, voice clear. No trace of a hangover whatsoever detectable on her. So clearly, it was mostly me who made my way through the two empty bottles of wine that sit on the counter.

"Pete's downstairs?" I ask her.

"Yep, he's working," she says. "He's using Lola's room. He was happy to see you getting extra sleep, too. He says you've been tense in Montauk. Now I understand why, of course. It's a lot that you've been dealing with." I wince, especially since Maya is speaking at full volume. It was bad enough when Maya was consoling me about my herbs. Receiving sympathy over my *affair* when her husband is *dead* makes my guilt about ten times worse. I am desperate to get out of this conversation.

"Do you know if Kelsey took lunch to school?" I ask in a small voice, feeling like the worst mother in the world. My memory is a little fuzzy, but I don't think I said good night to her last night. It's the one thing Kelsey and I still have, that good night kiss, even if she tolerates it under duress. I hate knowing that she's at school right now without me having said good night *or* good morning to her. I know she probably doesn't care, but I am suddenly aching to see her; the next four hours will feel excruciatingly long.

"Yup, I made them both TBMs," Maya says, grinning. "Lola's favorite," she adds. *Other than the salmon she didn't touch,* I muse silently. I was surprised Kelsey was okay with eating a TBM; last I checked, she hated tomatoes on her sandwiches. But as long as she's fed, I guess I should be happy. And grateful to Maya, for taking care of everything this morning. For looking after my family.

So why do I feel so—itchy, instead?

"Thank you," I tell her quietly, my shame reaching near-intolerable levels. "Okay, I'm going to bring some coffee into my office and get some work done." *Fat chance,* a discouraging but honest voice in my head responds. I try to dismiss it; my hangover aside, I'm actually excited to get back to work on my manuscript. I made a breakthrough yesterday with a plot hole and wrote about ten decent pages in a flurry of inspired productivity. I'm hoping I can keep the momentum going.

"Let me know if you want to go for a walk later," Maya says. "If you need to unload more about Kyle, I'm here for you." I flinch again. I can't believe she just uttered his name out loud in my kitchen with my husband downstairs. But she doesn't seem to see anything wrong with this, as she looks at me with gracious knowing. I badly wish I could take back ever having told her.

I plod downstairs with my coffee and poke my head into the spare bedroom—"Lola's room," now, apparently—where Pete's working, but he's on the phone, so I can't ask him why the hell he didn't wake me up. I stand there for a second, but he doesn't turn around.

I'm about to leave Pete to his call when something on Lola's bed catches my eye. A piece of paper—no, a photograph—poking out from underneath her pillow. I go over and grab it.

It's the picture of me that Kelsey cut out of the yearbook.

Why would Lola have it? Didn't Kelsey say she needed it for a history project?

I tap Pete on the shoulder, hold the picture up to him, and mouth "What the hell?" He shrugs and waves me away, trying to focus on his call.

Unsure of what to do, I put the picture back under her pillow. There has to be a rational explanation, like that Kelsey was working on the project on Lola's bed while they hung out in here.

But my skin feels even more crawly than it did upstairs, when Maya was telling me that my affair is "a lot to be dealing with."

I shut the door behind me and head into my office. As hungover as I am, I am determined to get some work done today. Some good work, like yesterday. Wasn't it Ken Kesey who used to write while on drugs and then revise while sober? Same idea as me writing with the shakes, right? Granted, I'm not exactly working on the next great canonical novel down here; the chapter that I wrote yesterday involved white jeans, a period, and a feigned ketchup spill to cover it up. Still, it was an entertaining scene. I take a sip of Maya's too-strong coffee and grimace at the taste—though I could certainly use the extra caffeine today.

I open my computer, expecting to see my Word doc pop up on the screen. I never close it out, preferring to just pick up exactly where I left off.

But instead, I'm greeted by the home screen. My nostrils flare with annoyance. Already, I can tell this is not going to be my day. My laptop must have rebooted for some stupid update.

I go through the steps of unlocking the screen and opening my documents, searching for the doc called "Fall work-in-progress." I never choose a title until I'm actually done with the draft.

But I can't find it anywhere. There are other work-in-progress drafts—three that became books, and a few that tried to but didn't. But "Fall work-in-progress" is nowhere to be found.

Dread rises within me, but I know I have the document loaded onto my Google Docs, too, for this exact reason. It's always good to keep a live document, in the event of a laptop crash. Maybe since I left it open when my computer rebooted, it somehow got deleted. Crazier things have happened.

I open my Google Docs, confident that I'll see it right away. It was the last document I opened, without a doubt. It will be there.

But it's not. I scroll down for it. I scroll all the way to Writing Center scheduling documents from years ago when I was still working at Fairley. I'm deep in the trenches of my Google Doc history.

And it's nowhere to be found.

"No. No. No," I start muttering to myself. "No." It's impossible. Impossible that it's gone from both places. I ricochet back and forth from Word documents to Google Docs, looking for it again and again. The definition of insanity. Doing the same thing over and over, expecting different results.

Of course, the document is still not in either place.

I am suddenly a thousand degrees warmer. Red spots form behind my eyes. At my last OB-GYN visit, my doctor told me I could be entering perimenopause soon, and hot flashes would be a normal and expected part of that phase of life. Whether this particular hot flash is from panic, hangover, or because my youth is disappearing, I have no idea, but either way, it's intense, and my pores start to emit sweat that smells like it's 90 percent alcohol.

I slam my laptop shut and stand up. I'm about to run out of my office and enlist Pete's help when something on my desk catches my eye.

A hair tie. But it isn't mine. I only wear scrunchies because hair elastics crease my hair.

This is a thin red elastic. It doesn't look like one of Kelsey's, either. Hers are black, and thicker, because her hair is long and wavy and wouldn't be contained by such a thin hair tie. And Maya doesn't even wear hair ties; her hair is too short to put in a ponytail.

Which means this one has to be Lola's.

CHAPTER SEVENTEEN

What the hell was Lola doing in my office? Could she have—*would* she have—messed around with my manuscript? And if so, *why?*

I fly out of my office. I can hear Pete clacking away at his keyboard, having migrated back to his desk in our bedroom. I fling open the door. He looks up at me, blinking with surprise at my dramatic entrance. "Yes, lovely?" he says cheekily, taking in my appearance with comically wide eyes. I'm still in pajamas, my hair and teeth unbrushed, glasses on. Not that I ever look particularly polished, but this is disheveled even for me.

The words can't tumble out fast enough. "My Word doc—it's gone. My newest manuscript. It's not on my computer or in my Google Docs anymore. It's *nowhere.*" My voice trembles a bit, and tears start forming in my eyes.

Pete shuts his laptop partially and gives me his full attention. He looks genuinely concerned. "Are you serious?"

I start crying. I can't help it. The pages weren't perfect, or anywhere close, but they were *something*. I could have made them better. And they were all I had. All I had to show my agent and editor, all I had to show for the past six months of my life, the only proof that I am an actively working author. Gone.

Pete stands up and wraps me in a hug. "Hon, we'll find it," he says softly. "I'll do a little research, find out how documents can be recovered. We could even go to the Apple Store in East Hampton this weekend, see what the Apple Geniuses have to say about it. We'll find a way to get it back. I know it."

I breathe into his chest and immediately feel better. "Are you sure?"

"Pretty sure, yes," he says.

"I just don't understand how it could have happened," I sob again, aware that I sound like a child. But sometimes it feels good to cry, to be held, to be taken care of.

"It's very frustrating," he agrees, stroking my hair.

"Pete—there's something else. I found Lola's hair tie right next to my computer."

He releases me so that we can be eye to eye and nods in a slow, measured manner. "Okay. Firstly, how do you know it was hers?"

"Well, it wasn't mine or Kelsey's. And Maya doesn't need hair ties."

"Babe, do you really know *all* your own hair ties? And all of Kelsey's?" He looks at me dubiously.

"Well, I'm the one who buys them for her, so yes, I actually do," I retort, though I know Pete doesn't deserve to bear the brunt of my frustration.

"Okay. Just so I'm clear here, you're saying that you think Lola might have been the one to delete your manuscript?" He raises his eyebrows at me. "And why on earth would she have done that?"

I shrug uncertainly. "I'm not saying that she did, necessarily—just that I think she was in there. Maybe she needed to use my computer for something, and then deleted it by mistake. Or—I don't know. I just—something isn't right. First my herbs, now this. And did you notice that my yearbook picture was in her room?"

"What do you mean, first your herbs?"

"Lola *said* she used basil from my garden to make freaking *TBMs* or whatever. She was the last person to pull herbs from it. And then the next morning, no more herbs. Do you not think that's weird?" My tone is more combative than I mean for it to be, but I don't appreciate how dismissive Pete is being of what I think are very legitimate concerns.

Pete shakes his head warily. "Hon, you can't just go around accusing people of destroying your stuff. Especially when they have no known motive whatsoever. She's a *kid*, Carrie. And you have no proof."

I know he's making good points. But am I really so off base? I think of Lola's probing questions. Of her hovering over Pete's chair, laughing, her long hair brushing his cheek. Of how she's made Kelsey her little lap pet. Of the way she calls me Carrie so breezily as if we're peers. How she doesn't seem at all like she's just lost a dad—and the elaborate lie she told about finding his body. How she made me a sandwich. I know it was nice, but it was also *weird*. Right?

Or maybe I'm the weird one, for looking at a kind gesture through a suspicious lens.

Deep down, I know that Pete's right. I have no idea why she'd want to mess with my things. She's just a child. The child of one of my dearest friends.

A friend who knows everything about me.

My stomach drops. Maya and Lola are close, obviously; sometimes they seem almost more like friends than mother and daughter. Could Lola know my darkest secrets, too? Having one person in my house who knows my innermost shadows is bad enough. But two would be intolerable.

Which reminds me of something else important: I'm not the only one who's hidden something big. "Did you know that Maya's husband didn't really die of a heart attack?" I ask Pete. "He was driving drunk. She told me last night."

Pete nods. "I'm not sure what that has to do with Lola's hair tie in your office, but yes, Maya told me this morning. She apologized for lying. And honestly, I get it. People lie to cover up shame all the time. She was embarrassed. She hasn't seen us in years—she didn't want to lead with the fact that her husband was a drunk." Pete is right. People do lie to cover up shame all the time. I know that better than he realizes.

"Look," Pete says with a sigh. "Let's backtrack for a second. Your manuscript. I'm sure there's an explanation. It's probably in some hidden folder." He checks his watch. "I have another call in a minute, but I'll take a look at it later today, okay?" He releases me and then wrinkles his nose. "Babe, is that you? I think you might need a shower," he says with a laugh, and I hit him weakly in protest. "I can smell the booze. You and Maya really got after it last night, huh? Was it good to catch up with her?"

"Yeah," I lie, inwardly shuddering again about the fact that I told her about Kyle. I desperately wish I could snatch the confession back.

"Good," Pete says. "By the way, I'm going to have to go to the city tomorrow," he adds offhandedly. "Just for a day or two. We have some investors coming in from overseas. I need to show face. Shake some hands, make some jokes, check that my guys have their bases covered in what they're presenting."

"Okay," I tell him, my head spinning too quickly to even focus on what he's said. I go into our room to shower, but before I get in, I turn my bathroom upside down looking for red hair ties, emptying bins and the entire contents of our medicine cabinets, already knowing that I won't find any.

CHAPTER EIGHTEEN

I'd hoped the shower would help my hangover, but as soon as I turn the water off, the pounding returns to my head. I force myself to put on a little makeup and some "real" clothes, a pair of jeans and a burgundy sweater, instead of my usual leggings and sweatshirt. Maybe looking presentable will help me feel better, too.

I go back to my office and check my computer again, just to make sure my manuscript is still gone. It is, of course. To make matters worse, I have an incredibly ill-timed text from my agent: We're coming up on 11/25! How's it going? November 25, the day I'm supposed to send her my pages so she can review them and pass them along to my editor by December 1. I wasn't exactly thrilled with what I'd written, but at least I had *something* to show. Now, I literally have nothing. All I can do is pray that Pete's right about there being some obscure way to recover it.

Upstairs in the kitchen, Maya is scrolling through her phone at the table. "Hey!" she says, and then looks up. "Wow, you look nice. Feeling better?" My skin prickles a bit. I know she doesn't mean to, but she's making me feel like a degenerate for being hungover and sleeping late.

"Yes and no," I tell her. "The shower helped"—*barely, though I'm not about to admit that to you*—"but the manuscript I'm working on somehow got deleted. From both my desktop *and* Google Docs. It's really bizarre. So I'm kind of freaking out."

"Oh my God," she says. "That's terrible. I'm so sorry. Technology was never your friend, I guess, huh?"

My eyes narrow. "Hmm?"

She laughs lightly. "Remember in college? Whenever assignments were due, you'd have printer disasters and be running around campus in tears holding a box of floppy disks. Remember, you once had to write an entire paper without using the letter *p* because the key was missing from your laptop and none of the library desktops were available, since you'd left it to the last minute?" She laughs a little louder before stopping herself, remembering the crisis at hand. "That is very distressing about your manuscript, though. And totally not the same thing. I'm sure there's a way to get it back." My skin flushes with annoyance that she's making fun of me for being technologically inept while I'm already at a low moment. Sorry that we all couldn't be like Maya, writing essays before the professor had even assigned them. Besides, I *am* a professional author now (not a hugely successful one, but still), not a teenage girl writing *p*-less essays.

And from what I recall, it was only the conclusion that I had to write without using a *p*. I'd already written most of the essay. It wasn't that big of a deal. It was a funny challenge; we'd laughed about it together at the time.

But the way Maya described it has altered the memory for me. Suddenly, it's like I'm back on campus, panicking about an impending due date.

As if she can read my mind, she quickly says, "You more than make up for your disputes with technology with your creative prowess. It wouldn't be fair for someone to be talented in both areas, anyway!" She grins at me and I smile back, but with effort. "You'll get the manuscript back, I'm sure. I'd be happy to take a look for you if you want me to."

"That's okay," I tell her coolly. "I'll probably take it to the Apple Store."

"Well, let me know. So," she says, changing the subject, "want me to get the girls this afternoon?" I look at the clock and see that it's already nearly two. How the hell did that happen? I haven't even eaten anything yet today. No wonder I'm still feeling so poorly.

"No, I'll do it," I tell her, phrasing it in a way that doesn't exactly leave the door open for her to join. I feel like being alone, if only for a short car ride. God forbid she bring up Kyle again; it's the last thing I feel like discussing.

"Okay, I can organize some things for dinner, then," she says eagerly. "Any requests?"

"Um, I think Pete's making his chili, actually," I say quickly, even though it's not true. He'll do it, though, if I ask him to. We probably have canned beans and corn in the newly organized pantry, and ground beef or Beyond Meat in the freezer. Enough for him to whip something together. I just can't stand the thought of Maya serving another wonderful meal in my kitchen.

"Okay, sounds good. So, anything I can do to be helpful?" *Keeping your daughter out of my office might have been helpful. Stop it, Carrie. Stop it.*

"I don't think so. Thanks, though. Just relax! I'll be back soon." I grab an apple from the bowl and the keys from the key hook and head outside to the deck without a backward glance.

The entire time I'm driving to East Hampton, my mind barely registers the road. All I can think about is my Word document, that hair tie, and how the hell I'm supposed to respond to my agent's text.

As if things could get even more stressful, my phone buzzes with another text from Lara G., Hazel's Mom as I'm passing into Amagansett that simply says, Really?

I delete it immediately. My brain doesn't even have the capacity to worry about him right now.

When I get to school, the girls are already outside on the curb, and they start walking toward the car. Lola is walking slightly ahead of

Kelsey, and they don't look as chummy as they have for the past few days.

When they get into the car, neither of them says a word.

"Hi, girls," I say carefully, treading lightly. "How was school?"

"Fine," mutters Kelsey. Standard.

"Okay," murmurs Lola, and her tone catches me by surprise. I turn around to glance at her. Her face is pale, and her eyes seem downcast. I wonder what happened today.

"You sure?" I ask, trying to make the question sound casual. Teenage girls can sniff out an agenda like airport dogs.

"Yes," they say in unison. I glance in the rearview mirror again and see Kelsey looking at Lola with concern. As usual, I find myself caught in that place of wanting to respect the boundaries set by a teenager and wanting to claw my way into her brain so that I can find out what's going on.

This time, it just happens to be with a girl other than my daughter.

"Okay," I say, deciding to let it go for the moment. "Hey, by the way. Were either of you using my computer, by any chance? My manuscript somehow got deleted."

"I have my own computer," Kelsey says sharply.

"I wouldn't use your computer without asking," Lola says in a hurt voice. I glance in the rearview at her again, and when I see the injury on her face, I wish I could take my question back. She is a kid. If she's anything like Kelsey, a sensitive one. It's easy to forget that, because Lola seems so oddly mature, in many ways.

"No, I know. It's just, I found a hair tie in there that I thought might be yours. So I just wondered."

"So you think I went into your office and deleted your manuscript?" Lola's voice is so small I can barely hear her. *Shit. Shit. Shit.*

"No, of course not. I certainly didn't think it was done intentionally, in any case."

"Well, it wasn't me," Lola says vehemently. Kelsey stares out the window.

"I'm sorry. I wasn't trying to accuse you," I assure her, feeling that I've badly botched this conversation.

"Good, because it wasn't me," Lola mutters again, and as I glance at her in the mirror, I am aghast to see what I think is a tear sliding out of her eye.

CHAPTER NINETEEN

Later that evening, with his chili simmering in the Crock-Pot (he'd raised his eyebrows slightly at the random request), Pete announces that he's going to take the train back to the city before dinner. "It'll be easier if I go tonight," he says with a sigh. "This meeting's at ten a.m. I don't want to leave here first thing in the morning and be stressed about making it on time. I'll sleep better if I'm already where I need to be." Since our apartment is occupied by subletters, he usually gets a room at the New York Athletic Club when he stays in the city.

I get why he wants to leave tonight, but I also really wish he weren't going.

"You sure you have to?" I ask him, sitting on our bed watching him as he packs an overnight bag. "You can't just do the meeting via Zoom?"

"Not this one," he says, leaning down to kiss me on the cheek. "But I'll be back tomorrow. And we'll figure out your manuscript this weekend, I promise. Besides, you have Maya to keep you company." Maya, who has cleaned my countertops more times in the last three days than I have in the last three months. And Lola, who has stayed in her own room all afternoon and evening, rather than in Kelsey's. Something must have happened between them. Doubtful that Kelsey will tell me, but I'm going to try to talk to her about it tonight just the same.

Or, worse, it has nothing to do with Kelsey, and Lola is still upset by what I insinuated about the hair tie. I feel awful about it.

"There's something I want to show you before I go, though," Pete says, clearing his throat. He seems almost nervous, which he never does, and I'm immediately uneasy.

He sits down next to me on the bed and takes his phone out of his pocket. "You know I have this place souped up with the Ring cam, right? I did it a couple of years ago when my mom started complaining about the neighbors." I nod, vaguely remembering. "So we have a camera on the deck. I should have thought to do this right away, but I never look at it, and it only occurred to me when you brought up the herbs again this afternoon. I pulled up the footage from the other night, the night something happened to your herbs. And you were right. Someone *was* on the deck." He holds out his phone for me and presses play.

I see a figure walk out onto the deck from inside the house wearing a hoodie and leggings. The clock on the Ring camera shows that it's 2:04 a.m. The figure moves lithely, and appears to be holding a large pair of kitchen shears. She hovers over each row of herbs briefly and then seems to scatter what she's holding over the edge of the deck before she walks back inside. Her face is completely obscured by the hood of the sweatshirt, and even if it wasn't, the video quality is too grainy to show facial features.

But someone was there, with scissors. That much is clear.

"Oh my God. Okay. So who was that? Is it Lola? Can you tell?" I feel vindicated. I was right. Someone *did* mess with my herbs.

Pete is silent. We watch it again.

"It's impossible to tell," I admit, frustration building inside me.

"Babe, are you serious?" Pete looks at me dubiously. "I think it's you," he says softly.

I gape at him. "Me? No it's not. I didn't do that. Why would I wreck my own herbs?"

"Well, it looks like you, and that's your Middlebury sweatshirt," he points out. In unison, our eyes go to the dark-blue sweatshirt that's hanging over my closet doorknob. I rarely put it away because I wear it so frequently. "Walks like you, too," he adds quietly. "Tall, thin. Like you."

"But—I didn't," I say quietly, feeling tears forming once again at the bottom of my throat. "I wouldn't."

"What if you were sleepwalking?" he asks cautiously. It's not an absurd suggestion. I used to sleepwalk right before my first and second books came out, my nerves doing strange things to my brain. But I haven't done it for a couple of years, except for one other time just after Kelsey's suspension. It's brought on by stress. So it's not the craziest notion that I would have been sleepwalking the night after Maya and Lola arrived. I was definitely a little antsy that day.

But every time I've sleepwalked, I've basically gone from my bed to the couch, or another bedroom. I've never brandished a weapon and destroyed something I care about. It's a terrifying notion, thinking that I could have done that while unconscious. If I really was out there, faculties compromised, it was incredibly unsafe. I could have fallen or cut myself.

Pete folds me into a hug. "Look, I'm not sure what's going on. I think between everything that happened with Kelsey, and my mom dying, and moving out here . . . it's a lot, and it's gotten to us both." *Not to mention my goddamn affair,* I think to myself. "We need a little R&R. When I get back from the city, we'll figure out your manuscript situation. We'll get a few good nights of sleep. Go for some walks. Just try to relax. And then let's make a plan to get away, the three of us. Take a little trip. Somewhere warm. Maybe we could go to that Club Med in Puerto Rico we went to when Kelsey was five."

"Oh, I'm sure she'd love that," I say dryly. But I already feel relieved thinking of the three of us sitting on a beach together somewhere far away. A mojito in one hand, a paperback in another. No stress.

And no Maya and Lola.

$\sim$

2002

"Okay, surprise!" Carrie takes Maya's blindfold off. Seated before her are all their friends: Kaitlin and Ashley and a few other girls from their hall, and Pete, of course, and a couple of his lacrosse buddies, the nice ones. Everyone is dressed up and seated at a big square table with a silver flat-top grill in the middle of it. Maya still doesn't really know where they are, just that it's a restaurant, and they drove about fifteen minutes in Carrie's Jetta to get there. Carrie insisted that Maya stay blindfolded for the drive. It was unlike Carrie to volunteer to be designated driver on a Saturday night, but she said she didn't trust a taxi driver not to blow the surprise by saying out loud where they were going.

"Happy birthday, Maya!" Carrie exclaims, clapping. Their friends already have fruity drinks with umbrellas in front of them, and they raise their glasses to her and repeat after Carrie: "Happy birthday!"

Maya laughs nervously and flushes. "Thanks. Thanks, everyone!" She sits down, smoothing the black lace Forever 21 dress that Carrie gifted her earlier. "Kind of perfect, since you're twenty-one!" Carrie said when she'd handed her the bag, giggling. "Not that you have to wear it tonight, if you don't want to." But Maya loved the dress and agreed that it was the perfect choice for her birthday dinner.

Maya shrieks uncharacteristically with delight when the chef squirts sake into everyone's mouths. She takes some herself and likes its dry flavor. She gasps when the chef makes the surface of the grill go up in flame. She takes her disposable camera out of the Coach wristlet she borrowed from Carrie and snaps a picture of the steaming onion volcano. She eats more shrimp than she can count and sips her tropical punch with a pineapple garnish happily. She beams when all the waiters, along with her friends, sing "Happy Birthday" to her and serve her green tea ice cream with a candle.

After she blows out the candle, she leans into Carrie. "This is so fun," Maya says, meaning it with every ounce of her being. "Thank you."

"I had a feeling you'd like it," Carrie says, squeezing her shoulder.

Maya pulls back and looks at Carrie, who is glowing with pleasure at the success of the surprise. She is so genuinely happy that Maya has enjoyed herself.

In moments like these, it's easy for Maya to forget about the version of Carrie who has thrown parties in their room even though she knows Maya has a huge exam the next morning. To forget the version who begs Maya to stay up late quizzing her on biology terms, only to accidentally sleep through the test the next day after Maya's left for work, bleary eyed. The version who is dating a guy that, despite all her efforts, Maya still finds herself dreaming about at night.

And the fact that Carrie has the ability to make Maya forget about these things is both her favorite and least favorite thing about her.

CHAPTER TWENTY

I drive Pete to the train station reluctantly, and when I get home, I walk up the stairs onto the deck, glancing at my missing herbs as I pass them. Could I really have been the one to destroy them? Something about it feels strangely plausible, familiar, almost. Like my body remembers what it felt like to hold the scissors as I stripped them. It makes me queasy with confusion and disbelief.

I open the sliding door to the kitchen—and practically jump out of my skin when I find that Maya is standing right there. I didn't see her because of the glare from the kitchen light on the glass.

Her arms are crossed and she's frowning. "Sorry for startling you," she says, creasing her brows even more. "But—did you accuse my daughter of deleting your manuscript?" she asks incredulously.

Shit.

"Oh my gosh," I say, holding up my hands surrender-style without meaning to. I put them back down quickly. "No—no, it really wasn't like that. Or at least, that's *so* not what I meant to imply. It's just—I found her red hair tie in my office, so I thought maybe she'd used my computer. I wasn't trying to accuse her of anything, but I thought if she *had* used it, maybe I could figure out where the manuscript went. You know, based on . . . what functions may have been opened or whatnot?" *You sound like an idiot, Carrie.* "Anyway, she said she didn't use it, and of *course* I believe her. No question."

Maya narrows her eyes at me. "Is that why you wanted to pick them up alone this afternoon? So that you could interrogate her without me being able to intervene? Do you have any idea how *inappropriate* that is?" The way she's described it does make it sound pretty bad. But it isn't as if I *plotted* to pick them up by myself for that reason.

Though truthfully, now that she mentions it, I wonder if I would have brought it up if Maya had been in the car with me.

I shake my head vigorously. "Of course not. And honestly, I was asking *both* of them if they'd used my computer—not just Lola."

"Well, next time you have a question like that for my daughter, please keep me in the loop. She just lost her father, Carrie, for heaven's sake. She's under enough stress as it is without you piling onto it." *Dammit.* I know that Maya is right. I have no grounds upon which to suspect Lola of any wrongdoing. Especially since I secretly speculated that she'd mutilated the herbs, too, and apparently, they were destroyed by none other than *me.*

Which makes sense. I have a tendency to wreck things that are important to me.

"Again, Maya," I say softly, pleading, "I'm so sorry, but please know that I was certainly not trying to blame her. I was only asking. And I'll apologize to her, so that she knows that's not what I intended." Maya's face is still stony, but she looks more or less placated. I can feel the heat of embarrassment in my neck and cheeks.

"Thank you," she says curtly, and then adds, "also, I think we're going to head out this weekend."

"Oh, Maya, I hope not because of this. I really didn't mean—"

She waves her hand sharply. "No, I know. It's just time for us to go. I don't want to overstay our welcome. We have to go home and face reality eventually."

"You haven't overstayed at all. It's only been a few days." I don't know why I'm begging her to stay when the thought of them leaving brings me immense relief. But if they leave now, I'll just be left feeling guilty about how I've behaved. And more guilt is the last thing I need in my life.

She looks at me warily. "Okay. Maybe another day or two, then. We'll play it by ear. I don't want Lola to miss too much more school." Her eyes suddenly cloud over, turning from brown to gray in an instant. It's peculiar. I've never seen them do that before.

"Just please know that as far as we're concerned, you're welcome to stay as long as you want. I mean it." I smile at her tentatively.

She smiles back, appearing to soften somewhat. "Thank you, Carrie. I appreciate that."

"Sorry, again, about . . ." I trail off. It's too mortifying to say it out loud again.

"Thanks," she says, saving me from having to find the words to describe my egregious behavior.

I retreat to my room, shaken. I also realize, now, that there's no way in hell I'll ever be able to ask why my yearbook picture was under Lola's pillow. I've done enough damage without insinuating additional allegations.

I pick up my phone, hoping for a distraction from the awkward conversation that I've just emerged from, and instead am greeted by yet another text from Lara G., Hazel's Mom. *Ugh. Please. Not this again.*

I just miss you.

Shit. It was almost better when his texts were hostile, bitter. Knowing that he still has feelings for me, is still holding out hope for the two of us, makes my stomach turn. I'd rather deal with his hatred than with his love.

I delete his text message as usual and am just about to throw my phone on the bed to get it away from me when another message comes through. One that makes my stomach twist even more.

Montauk isn't that far you know.

Jesus Christ. What the hell does that mean? Is he just begging, trying to make the point that we can make it work long distance?

Or is it a threat? A reminder that he could easily drive out here and blow up my life anytime he wants?

He wouldn't. He has a wife and kids, too. Discretion was always our shared top priority.

Until, of course, he started talking about leaving his wife. And I realized that we didn't really view our affair the same way after all.

Montauk isn't that far.

I delete this text, too, but removing his words from my phone won't help me forget them.

CHAPTER TWENTY-ONE

When I go into Kelsey's room that night to say good night, after a rather strained and quick dinner shared between the four of us of Pete's chili (no wine tonight), she's already in bed, her back to me.

It's early, only 9:00 p.m., and I'm a little surprised that she and Lola aren't hanging out. They've seemed off ever since I picked them up. Of course, we all seemed a little off at dinner; I'd apologized to Lola right after I'd spoken to Maya, and she'd accepted readily, again assuring me that she would never do something like that, but there was still some tension in the air.

"Hey," I whisper, perching on the edge of Kelsey's bed and working up the nerve to try to rub her back. She shakes my hand off her, though. I take a deep breath and try to swallow the hurt of rejection. I imagine myself with armor. "Are you okay? You and Lola didn't spend much time together this afternoon."

"Fine," Kelsey spits out, as usual. Her favorite word. *Fine.*

"You can talk to me, you know," I whisper.

"No, I can't," she says, and there's a sadness in her voice that breaks my heart.

"Why do you think that?" I ask her, for what feels like the thousandth time in the past six months.

She's silent for a minute. "Because I just do," she finally replies.

"Well, you can." I vow silently to myself to get Kelsey back into therapy like she was in the city. If she can't talk to me, she needs to talk to someone. I don't want her to be alone with her feelings, the way I often find myself. I've considered going to therapy as well. But I probably couldn't bring myself to be honest with the therapist about everything I've done, and then I'd just be wasting both of our time.

"It was nothing, okay?" Kelsey sighs. "She was upset about something that happened at school. Something some of the kids said in English. It wasn't a big deal. And then you made it ten times worse with the whole computer thing. She was already upset as it was, and then you come along. You can't just go around accusing people of doing things, you know," she hisses, her voice barely audible in the dark. "That really wasn't cool."

"Honey, I really wasn't trying to accuse her."

"Whatever."

Kelsey is silent again and completely still in her bed, like she's playing dead in the hopes that I'll leave. But my hand is on her arm now, and she isn't trying to jerk it away, which is a surprise. If I close my eyes, I can imagine that she's four, her little body safe and warm under the covers as I tuck her in and ask all her stuffed animals one by one to take extra-special care of her while she sleeps, kissing them so that she'd be surrounded by my kisses all night long. When she was little, she used to want me to "tell her her dreams" every night—fun or beautiful things she could dream about, like unicorns taking a swim class, or eating an ice cream cone with twelve scoops of ice cream on it. I know she's the same girl, but sometimes it's hard to believe.

"What was said in class that upset her?" I ask. I know I'm pushing my luck, but I'm curious.

"Forget it," she says with another big sigh, as if talking to me is too taxing a chore to handle.

"No, please. Tell me. Tell me anything. About what happened at school. Or"—*Do better, Carrie*—"about why you're so angry at me. Nothing you say to me will make me love you any less. Please just talk to me. Tell me what's going on."

Kelsey rolls over begrudgingly to face me. "Fine. This girl Olivia was saying that Rose Mary Walls was deplorable for refusing to leave the dad. That she could have saved the kids if she'd wanted to, but she was weak and that it was her fault the family was so messed up." Kelsey pauses. "Lola didn't like that." I think she's about to say more, but she doesn't.

"Why didn't she like that?" I ask.

"How should I know? She just said Olivia had no idea what she was talking about, and that was something that only someone who'd never had to deal with real problems would say. She didn't say it to Olivia or anything—just to me. But most of the kids were agreeing with Olivia; I mean, even I thought Rose Mary was kind of awful, to be honest. But I could tell Lola was mad about what Olivia had said." I mull this over briefly; perhaps Lola felt defensive of Maya standing by Elliot despite his alcoholism. Or maybe there's even more to their story than Maya told me.

"Look, please don't tell Lola I told you, or say anything else to her about your stupid computer. I don't want them to leave. I like having them here," Kelsey says, her voice practically a whisper. A wave of remorse washes over me as I think of how lonely Kelsey must have been these past few months after we'd ripped her away from her life, her friends, with such little warning. I know our intentions were good, but I really am no longer sure if it was the right move.

Add it to the long list of decisions I'm not proud of.

"I'm glad you're enjoying being with Lola," I tell her, and a part of me means it.

Another part of me is still undeniably wary of Lola in a way that I can't explain.

"Why weren't you guys hanging out tonight, then, if what happened at school was no big deal? Was it because—"

"—of my mother blaming her for something she had nothing to do with?" Kelsey finishes bitingly.

I take it and absorb it silently. It hurts, though. Of course it does. Moms are human, too. And no matter how many times Kelsey says it, I will never get used to the pain of hearing "I hate you" from a nearly fully formed person I birthed.

I straighten my armor. "Well, was it because of that?"

"No," Kelsey mutters. "Not everything is about you, you know. And I'm tired. I want to go to bed, okay? I have to go to school a little early tomorrow for extra help in chemistry."

"Sounds good," I say softly. I kiss Kelsey on the forehead as I always do, holding my lips there for a split second longer than normal. She allows the extra second of stillness, which feels like some kind of progress. "I love you, Kels. Always have, always will. No matter what."

"Okay," she responds, and buries her face into her pillow.

CHAPTER
TWENTY-TWO

Friday

It feels like I've only been sleeping for minutes when, having tossed and turned for most of the night, I wake to Kelsey shaking my shoulder. I never sleep all that well when Pete's away. But my guilt over what happened with Lola and bewilderment about the camera footage of the herbs had something to do with my restlessness, too.

I squint at Kelsey and see that she's already dressed for school. "Mom," she whispers, "we have to go."

"What time is it?" I mumble.

"It's six forty-five. We're going early today, remember?" she reminds me grumpily. *We.* So Lola is going, too, despite whatever happened yesterday that got her upset. At least today is Friday, so it'll be her last day accompanying Kelsey. I think that's for the best.

"Okay," I whisper, rubbing my eyes. I force my legs to move from the bed with difficulty. "Let me just put my contacts in." I plod to the bathroom.

I pass Maya's room; still closed. Now I can return the favor of letting her sleep in. Upstairs in the kitchen, Lola is already dressed in black leggings and a red top, fully made up with her signature winged eyeliner. How early must she have risen to complete this look? Kelsey, at least, is back in her usual uniform of joggers and a hoodie, and I'm grateful that she chose extra sleep over a glam session.

We walk to the car in silence, and the girls tumble into the back seat. Driving to school without having had coffee feels like it should be illegal, especially since it's still practically dark out as we cruise slowly along Montauk Highway, but we make it there in one piece, and Kelsey and Lola slide out of the car and onto the curb. "Bye, Carrie," Lola calls pleasantly, and I'm relieved that she seems to have forgiven me for my hair tie gaffe.

I'm about to pull away when Kelsey doubles back. For a second, I think she's coming to kiss me goodbye, and my heart actually starts pounding, as if she's my crush and not my daughter.

"I forgot, Mom. There's a concert tonight at Gosman's. Nancy Atlas. Can we go?"

I'm as shocked as if she really did kiss me. "Of course. That sounds really fun. Great idea."

As I pull away, I'm grinning ear to ear.

When I get home from dropping the girls off, my plan is to make some coffee—my way, this time, half-caff—and bring it into bed with me, maybe watch some morning news and start the day slowly.

But Maya is already in the kitchen, dressed in jeans and a flannel and having brewed coffee already.

"Hi," I say with surprise as I close the sliding door behind me. "I was expecting you to still be sleeping. You *should* still be sleeping. What are you doing up?"

"I heard the car pull away, and the house was so quiet, and I got nervous. I texted you," she adds pointedly. "Why did you leave so early?"

"I'm sorry, I haven't checked my phone," I tell her. I yank it out of my pajama pocket, and sure enough, there's a text from Maya: **Where did you guys go?** I gratuitously show her the text so that she believes me about not having seen it. "Kelsey wanted to go to school early this morning. Think she was meeting with a teacher or something," I say with a shrug.

"You didn't ask her?" Maya says, and the edge in her tone catches me off guard.

"Of course I asked her," I say slowly. "That's what she told me. That she was meeting with her chemistry teacher. I didn't pry—God knows I wouldn't have had any luck if I had," I add with a raise of my eyebrows. But Maya's point hits home. I should be trying harder to talk to my own kid. Why didn't I ask her what she was struggling with in chemistry?

"Sorry," Maya says, shaking her head at herself. "I guess I just got scared when I woke up and everyone was gone." It hits me how insensitive it was for me to whisk her daughter away without telling her—I'd expected that Lola would have told Maya they were going early, but why should I have assumed that, when my own teenager tells me as little as humanly possible? Maya has just lost her husband—she's clearly on edge when it comes to her daughter's well-being and safety. I should have been more communicative.

I start to tell Maya all this, but she cuts me off before I can start.

"It's fine," she says. "I really am happy that Lola's had a good week at school with Kelsey. Honestly, maybe we should move here—she's more enthused about East Hampton High than she ever was about her own school!" She laughs a little before her face drops suddenly. I return her laugh weakly, unnerved at the idea of them moving here, even though I know she's joking.

"So, your manuscript," Maya says, changing the subject abruptly. "You know, I'd be happy to look at your computer. I'm pretty good with technology. I've been an office manager for almost twenty years, so I've had to familiarize myself with this kind of stuff." I momentarily want to contradict her, remind her that we aren't nearly old enough to have been working at a place for twenty years; what she's said sounds absurd to me. But then I remember that she's right. Twenty years since college.

How did that happen? "There are a few places on your computer that I could check," Maya continues. "It must be *somewhere*."

Hope rises in my chest. "That would be great," I concede. "Do you mean right now?"

"I'm free if you are!" she says cheerily, and we walk downstairs to my office, coffees in tow.

She sits at the desk chair, and I stand behind her, feeling large and helpless, just like I did while she was cooking dinner in my kitchen. "What was the file called?" she asks.

"Fall work-in-progress," I tell her. She nods and starts opening folders and functions on my computer I've never seen, let alone used before. She goes to Settings and then is clicking so quickly I can't even keep track of where she is.

About ninety seconds pass silently before she triumphantly declares, "Found it!"

"What?" I shriek.

Maya looks up at me, amused. "Well, you already had this recovery software installed to your computer, so it was easy. I just opened the software, and then it enabled me to scan deleted items from your recycling bin. Has this happened before?"

I try to remember. Accidentally deleting documents does sound like me, but I don't specifically remember having downloaded whatever recovery software she's referring to. "I don't think so," I say, perplexed.

She shrugs. "In any case, it's back. There you go, Fall work-in-progress, right here, safely with your other Word docs. You should add it to your Google Docs, too, while we're at it. It's always good to save a live document, in case—"

"I always do that," I interrupt pathetically, feeling defensive. I'm not an idiot. I know the rule about saving a live document in case a computer crashes. "It got deleted from Google Docs, too. I'm not sure how."

I can't help it—my mind flashes to the red hair tie. *Stop it, Carrie.* That ship has sailed. Enough already.

"I can't thank you enough," I tell her effusively.

"It was no problem," she says. She claps her hands to her legs and stands up. "I think I'm going to go for a long walk. Want to join me?"

"No, you go," I say, shaking my head. "I'm going to get back to work, I suppose, now that I can, thanks to you!"

"Glad I could help," she murmurs modestly, and leaves the room.

I stare at the Word document, wishing it could tell me its secrets about where it has been and with whom. Because I really don't think I accidentally deleted my own work from two separate places.

~

2003

"You have *to come to the city with me after we graduate! It's going to be amazing." Carrie is buzzing, gleaming, holding her offer letter from* People *magazine. Her dream job, as she's said probably about a hundred times over the past couple of months. The offer is modest—25k a year—and she doesn't seem to have acknowledged the fact that the position is clearly an administrative assistant role, instead acting as if she'll be writing exposés about Winona Ryder's shoplifting and visiting film sets and rubbing elbows with Reese and Gwyneth. But Maya isn't going to be the one to burst her bubble.*

"I want to," Maya says, "but there's no way I can afford the city. It's so expensive there, and I have some savings, but not much. And, unlike you, I still don't have a job lined up."

"You'll find a job," Carrie assures her. Maya knows that she probably could find a job like Carrie's—an assistant position somewhere, a receptionist, customer service—but she also knows that, unlike Carrie, she's not going to have a parent paying her rent and covering other expenses to make the paltry salary livable. She either needs to find a job that actually pays or live somewhere less expensive. Or both. As much as Maya loved her classes, she

somewhat regrets majoring in English—something like accounting might have been much more practical.

"*Our own apartment in Manhattan. Just think of it! We should try for West Village, but Murray Hill is okay for our first year, too, if necessary. I hope we can find something with a little outdoor space. And maybe your office will be close to mine, and we can meet for lunch and happy hour after work. It's going to be* incredible," *Carrie says, undeterred. She sighs dreamily and flops onto Maya's crisply made bed.*

"*Pete's going to the city, too, right?*"

"*Ugh, yes. I wish he was moving somewhere else. It would make it so much less awkward.*"

Maya furrows her eyebrows. "*Why is that?*"

Carrie looks at her like the answer is obvious. "*I'm breaking up with Pete when we graduate. I want to be single when we move to the city.*" *Maya looks at her blankly, and Carrie rolls her eyes.* "*We've talked about this before, Maya!*"

Maya is sure they have not.

Carrie shrugs casually. "*Pete's great. But this was a college relationship. I have no idea who I'm going to be after I graduate. And I need some space to figure that out for myself. I don't want to deprive myself of the chance to be on my own. And to meet other people, too. You know?*"

Maya nods slowly. "*Does Pete know that?*"

Carrie bobs her head from side to side, considering. "*Well, we haven't talked about it explicitly. And graduation is still a few months away, so there's no need to hurt him right now. But I think he knows it's coming. I've told him that I don't want to get married for a long time, if ever. I want to be independent. I mean, my parents got married when they were twenty-three, and my mom was clueless about stuff like taxes and oil changes until after my dad died. And I don't want to be like that. Pete and I have discussed all that before. So I really don't think he'll be that surprised that I want to be single for a while.*"

Maya thinks of Pete and the adoring way he looks at Carrie, still, after over two years of dating. She is quite sure that he will, in fact, be surprised.

She is also quite sure that Carrie knows nothing of taxes and oil changes, either.

Carrie twirls a piece of blonde hair between her fingers. "I just don't think people should settle down when they're this young. I barely know who I am yet, or who I want to be. And there are so many people in the world, you know? Middlebury's pretty homogeneous. I owe it to myself to have more romantic experiences than just Pete. I owe it to him, too." Maya is amazed at Carrie's ability to make dumping Pete sound like an act of service.

"Anyways, you're coming with me, one way or the other. My mom will pay our rent, so you won't even have to worry about that." Carrie's mom is already paying for Maya's share of their off-campus apartment. Maya felt wildly uncomfortable about it, but Carrie was insistent, telling Maya that only weirdos stayed on campus during their senior year, and that her mom didn't want Carrie living alone in any case ("She doesn't trust me," Carrie said matter-of-factly with a shrug), so in a way, it was really Maya who was doing her mom a favor, according to Carrie. Maya doesn't like being indebted to other people, but after three years of living with Carrie in a tiny room, the idea of having her own bedroom did appeal to her, and she reluctantly acquiesced. But she isn't going to let Carrie's mom pay her rent forever. Especially not in the "real world." It's time for her to fend for herself.

"I can't let her do that again," Maya says firmly, shaking her head.

"You're not going to make me go to the city alone," Carrie admonishes.

"We'll see where I get a job, I guess," Maya counters.

"Plenty of jobs in N-Y-C," Carrie declares firmly. "I need you."

CHAPTER TWENTY-THREE

I spend the next thirty minutes puttering around in my office, unable to settle back into working on my manuscript. For some reason, it now feels unfamiliar, like it was written by someone else. I can't really grasp where I was going with any of it.

I get up from my desk chair to collect the laundry: Kelsey's room first, ours next. I pause outside Maya's door, which is ajar. I hesitate for a second, wanting to respect her privacy. But I'm also pretty sure she hasn't done laundry yet, and maybe she'll appreciate the gesture. It's the least I can do to repay her for getting my manuscript back.

Plus, I know Maya thinks I'm useless when it comes to chores. She's already done more cooking and cleaning in the past few days than I have in the past month. The feminist in me hates that I feel shame about slacking on tasks like these. And yet, the guilt remains.

I walk into her room and immediately see her small pile of dirty clothes in the hamper at the foot of the bed. Easy. I dump it into the hamper that I'm holding.

And now, I know I should leave. I know that.

But instead, I glance around the room casually. A pad of paper sits on the desk. Without knowing why, I walk over to the desk and flip through it gingerly. On one sheet it says, "Pharmacy and grocery." On another it says, "Estate modifications." She mentioned having to sort out some finances related to Elliot's death.

I flip through more pages. I feel my brows furrow when I get to the end of the pad. On one page, she's scrawled "I'm so sorry," and then crossed it out. On another, she's written "I just can't" and then crossed that out, too.

At first, I wonder if she meant these notes for me. In college, whenever I could tell she was annoyed with me about something, I'd tape a Post-it apology to her mirror: nothing major, just quick, sincere apologies that immediately cleared the air and made whatever had passed between us water under the bridge. But what on earth would Maya be apologizing for? Reorganizing my kitchen without permission? I think I concealed my feelings about that well enough that she shouldn't even know I was annoyed. How she came down on me for implying that Lola might be responsible for my missing document? But I deserved that, and I think Maya would agree. So whatever she's sorry for probably has nothing to do with me. What is it, then?

I look around the room again, and something in Maya's suitcase catches my eye. A small orange bottle. I bend down quietly, aware that I've shifted now from innocent favor to snooping. I pick up the pill bottle. Valium.

I look at the bottle more closely. The prescription was just filled here in Montauk, at Whites pharmacy. Which means it's not a "just in case" prescription, but something she's relying on.

I take a deep breath, thinking about what this means. As usual, Maya is pretending that everything's okay when it isn't. She's just lost her husband, and no matter how "fine" she seems, she is low enough to have been prescribed medication to deal with anxiety and sleeplessness. So she isn't fine at all. And maybe the notes have to do with the fact that she blames herself for Elliot's death. Maybe writing down how she feels is therapeutic for her.

I should have known she was hurting more than she was letting on. And I need to be a better friend. To be her rock. It's the least I can do for her, after all that she's done for me.

My phone rings and I yelp quietly, feeling as if I've been caught. It's Pete. I take the hamper and slide out of Maya's room, shutting the door behind me, and answer the phone once I'm safely out.

"How's the city?" I ask him eagerly. I can picture the fruit vendor by our apartment, my favorite flower shop, the commuters pouring into and out of the subway stations. I miss everything about it.

Well. Almost everything.

"City's the same as it always was," Pete says wryly. "Loud and smelly." He doesn't necessarily share my twisted affection for the incessant sirens and the dog-poop-infested sidewalks. "Hey, so I'm calling because you've got a dermatologist appointment in East Hampton on the twenty-first, and a call with your agent on the twenty-fifth. And you already made reservations at Harvest for my birthday, so thanks for that. Good choice, by the way. Know how I know all of this?"

My left eye starts pulsing. "Uh, no? How?"

Pete laughs. "Somehow our phone wires have gotten crossed. Our calendars are synced. Notice anything weird on your end?" I put Pete on speaker so that I can look at my phone screen and open my calendar. Sure enough, all his calls and meetings are there, filling up blank spaces on my usually sparse calendar.

"What the hell?" I murmur. My head is starting to spin.

"Yeah, very weird. Luckily, I still have all my own stuff, too, so I can work." I don't want to tell Pete that his ability to keep up with his conference calls wasn't exactly at the top of my list of concerns here.

"That's good, but how did this happen? And how are we going to fix this?"

"I'm sure there's an easy solution," Pete says breezily. "Just a glitch in the matrix or something. Maybe it has to do with the family plan? I don't really have time to dig into it right now, but if you're able to figure it out, that would be great."

"You know I'm not really good with technology."

"You could probably just google it or call Apple if you wanted to. But look, it's not like it's urgent. Though I can't promise I'm not going to look back and find out if you were secretly sneaking off to a day spa when you claimed to be working!"

Pete thinks he's being hilarious, but his comment fills me with a sick dread.

As careful as I've been about deleting all my text exchanges with Kyle, I've been considerably less careful about my calendar.

All our hotel mornings are noted in my calendar. They aren't labeled in any way, but the times are blocked off so that I could remember not to book anything else on those mornings. Kyle and I would figure out the next time we were meeting when we were together, and I'd mark it in my calendar.

The entries aren't explicitly revealing. But still. They're certainly enough to make Pete curious, if he were to come across them—especially since they occurred multiple times. I could delete them all right now, but what if Pete gets some sort of a notification that I'm deleting calendar entries? That would make him even more suspicious.

If he does see them and asks, I can lie. I'll have to. I can say I blocked off the time to be strict with myself about work, or something.

But how many more lies can I tell this man before my nose grows so long and heavy that it simply falls off?

My vision goes blotchy.

"Okay, well, let me go, so I can try to fix it." My tone is more urgent than I'd intended for it to sound.

"Yes, ma'am. Thanks. Hey, by the way, I'm probably going to come back tomorrow morning instead of tonight. I'm supposed to go to a dinner, and there's no point in coming back so late."

"Sure, okay." I'm a little disappointed that Pete is staying another night in the city, but I'm also eager to end our call so that I can go figure out how the hell to get my calendar off his phone.

As soon as we hang up, I race upstairs to the kitchen, but Maya isn't there—right. She went for a walk. *Shit.* I'm sure she'll be back soon, but I'd rather deal with this now.

She was *just* fiddling with my computer to recover my document before this happened. One possible explanation is that she did *something* that *somehow* caused Pete's and my accounts to merge, on the cloud, or whatever. Hopefully, she'll realize what must have happened and be easily able to undo it. This is not how I want Pete to find out about what I did. I don't want him to find out, period. But especially not through something so dumb. And preventable.

I put on my sneakers, trot down the deck stairs, and walk briskly in the direction of the ocean, the wind slapping me with every step, as if trying to punish me for what I've done.

I shuffle down the steps to the beach and am relieved beyond measure when I recognize Maya's wool peacoat on a figure in front of me. But she isn't walking. She's sitting in the sand, staring out at the ocean.

As I get closer to Maya, I notice that her shoulders are shaking. Her head is buried in her hands.

She is crying.

Not just crying. Sobbing. Howling, almost, like a hungry newborn. With total abandon.

I stop in my tracks. My calendar problem suddenly feels embarrassingly selfish and trivial. Maya's mourning her husband. And all I care about right now is that mine doesn't find out about my horrifically ill-advised, selfish affair.

First the Valium, now this. I feel awful that I haven't realized how badly off she really is. That she's been taking trips down to the beach so that she can weep privately.

I slow my stride and approach her quietly, respectfully. "Hey," I say softly, putting my hand on her shoulder.

She looks up with surprise. "Oh hey," she says, taking big gulps of air to even her breath, sniffling loudly, and wiping her eyes.

"Are you okay?" I ask needlessly. She so clearly isn't.

"Yeah, just having a moment," she says. She's gripping something in her hand—a photo of Elliot, maybe. She sees me looking at it and shoves it into her pocket. Whatever it is, she wants to keep it to herself.

"I am so sorry to interrupt you," I say lightly, truly meaning it. "Do you want me to leave, or stay with you?"

"Were you looking for me? Is everything okay?"

"Everything's fine. I was going to ask you to help me with something, but it can totally wait, and it's not important anyway."

The tears start to fade from Maya's eyes. "No, tell me. It's okay."

"Are you sure?" I ask her. I really feel like a jerk pushing on with this request given the state she's in.

Maya wipes her eyes with the backs of her wrists. "Yes. What's going on?"

I breathe deeply. "Pete just called, and apparently, our iPhone calendars have synced."

Maya looks at me blankly, seeming not to understand what I'm talking about and why it's a problem.

I continue hesitantly. "Is there any way that whatever you were just doing on my computer could have caused it? I'm kind of freaking out, because—"

"Ah. I gotcha. Because there's evidence of your lover in your calendar, and you don't want him to see."

I recoil as if I've been struck. "I mean, he's not my 'lover' anymore, but yes. I am worried about what Pete could see, to be honest." Once again, a wave of regret about confessing to Maya rolls through me.

Maya looks back at me closely, not speaking for a second, before taking a measured breath. "Carrie, what I was doing on your computer was literally in your folders and your recycling bin. It had nothing *whatsoever* to do with your phone, your Apple ID, your cloud, your calendar, *anything* like that."

"But my calendar is loaded onto my Google account, and I was logged in to move the document back there, so—"

I try to protest, to explain what I've been thinking, but Maya cuts me off. "So something goes wrong with your phone, and you think it's my fault because I helped you recover a lost document? Plus, you were right behind me watching what I was doing the entire time. Do you hear how nonsensical you're being?"

I do hear it. Why was I so sure that it was such a logical explanation the whole time I was hustling down here?

Maya sighs heavily. "Sorry, but I can't help. I don't even have an iPhone. I'm sure it's a common issue, though, with an easy solution. One that you should look up. I'm going to keep walking." She turns her back and starts heading away from me.

"Sorry, Maya," I call after her. "Sorry. I'm not sure what I was thinking."

"It's cool," she calls back, and I hear the words even though she doesn't say them: *I'm used to it from you.* My eyes sting violently.

CHAPTER
TWENTY-FOUR

About an hour later, I've sorted it out by logging in to my cloud and changing my sharing settings. I instruct Pete to do the same. Then I go ahead and delete all the blank time blocks from my calendar. There were nine of them. Nine. God. I'm disgusting. But, as disgusting as I am, I appear to be out of the woods.

For now, at least. On this. But now I am suddenly aware that there are any number of ways Pete could find out about Kyle and me. I always used my real name for the Arthouse Hotel reservations; it was a decent hotel that required ID, after all. It wasn't a motel in the middle of nowhere that rented rooms by the hour. What if, I don't know, a crime took place at the hotel while we were there, and the police contact me as a witness? What if Kyle wasn't as careful as I was about deleting texts, and his wife finds out, and she takes vengeance by telling Pete? What if Kyle himself gets fed up with my zero contact and blows me up to retaliate? What if one of Pete's friends or work colleagues saw me going into the hotel one day, and they mention it to Pete, ever so casually and innocently? "Hey, I think I saw your wife at the Arthouse last spring!" I've been stupid to think that Kyle and I were careful. We really weren't.

There's no way to completely cover up something that did, in fact, take place. The blood always shows, sometime or other.

When Maya gets home from her walk, I am waiting for her at the kitchen table. Waiting to apologize. Yet again.

"I've figured it out," I tell her, feeling dumber and more ashamed than ever. "And sorry for thinking that you'd somehow caused that to happen. I'm so embarrassed."

"Sorry for reacting rather rudely," she says. "I get why you might have assumed that, honestly. You just caught me at a bad moment."

I nod understandingly. "You know, you seem so fine that sometimes I forget what you're going through. But I guess you've always been that way. Able to cope with anything and everything."

She shakes her head. "I'm really not, as it turns out."

"Well, it's okay to not be okay. I'm here for you." She nods lightly, but I think I see her scoff ever so slightly, though I hope I'm imagining it. "So, anyway, I forgot to tell you. Kelsey mentioned that there's a concert over at Gosman's Dock tonight she wants to go to. Nancy Atlas. She's a local favorite. It's a little cold, but we could bring a picnic and some blankets. What do you think?"

She rubs her hands under warm water from the sink. "That sounds perfect. What a fun idea. Want me to pick up some stuff in town for us to take with us?"

"I'll go with you," I tell her, desperate for a chance to redeem myself. "I'm craving a juice from Naturally Good. We can pick up the girls after." I'm trying to be better. The kind of person who drinks juice, accompanies her friend places when she's having a bad day, and cheerily suggests concert picnics.

Naturally Good is crowded, and Maya and I try to stand out of the way as we wait for our juices and sandwiches. My phone buzzes in my pocket, and I take it out. Pete. I consider letting him go to voice mail and calling him back when we're in the car, but I'm a little paranoid that he's calling to tell me that he can still see my calendar. "I'm going to step outside for a minute," I tell Maya, gesturing to my ringing phone. She gives me a thumbs-up.

"Hey!" I exclaim to Pete chipperly. Too much so. It's uncharacteristic. The phone fire drill kicked my guilty conscience into high gear.

"Hey," he says. "How's it going over there? Thanks for sorting out the phone thing."

"No problem." I gulp. As if I had a choice but to get it fixed as soon as possible. "All good over here. Maya and I are at Naturally Good. Hey, I forgot to tell you that she got my manuscript back for me." In the midst of the calendar fiasco, I didn't even mention this to Pete.

"That's awesome," he tells me. "Wow, Maya is a tech wizard, huh? How'd she do it?"

"I'm really not sure," I say softly, suddenly feeling like the *p*-less essay girl again. *That Maya. A "tech wizard."*

"So what's your plan for today? Sorry again that this is turning into an overnight, but these clients are mostly single guys without families to rush back to, so I feel obligated to show them a good time." I hate the idea of Pete out at trendy restaurants and clubs with a bunch of young finance players, though I realize how hypocritical that is. Because he's never done anything to make me question his trust; it's me and me alone who's broken promises.

"We're going to see Nancy Atlas at Gosman's. It's a little cold, but it should be fun. It was Kelsey's idea, believe it or not."

"Oh man! Bummed to be missing that. That'll be great. Way to go, Kels."

Suddenly, my breath catches in my throat: across the street, someone is getting out of his car, a black Jeep Cherokee, and walking into the Gig Shack.

Not just someone.

Kyle.

I'm sure of it. I recognize his black baseball cap, his green jacket, his walk—everything. I've spent enough time with the guy to recognize the back of his neck, the slope of his shoulders.

What the *hell* is Kyle doing in Montauk? It seems his text about Montauk not being that far really was a threat. One that he's making good on.

"Sorry, babe, I have to run," I tell Pete hurriedly. "Our food is ready. Call you back in a bit."

"Later, Car," he says, hanging up before I do.

Sending me menacing texts is one thing. But showing up here out of the blue, to what, *hunt me down*, is quite another. Thank God I'm in town with Maya, and not Kelsey or Pete. I can't believe Kyle would do this. We always promised each other our privacy.

Then again, how well *do* I really know him? It was only a few months, after all. So maybe his promises don't mean that much. And it's becoming clear that he was much more invested in us than I ever was.

But whatever he's thinking, my avoidance strategy obviously isn't working. And now that he's here, it's time for me to put a stop to this. Right now.

I run across the street, barely looking to see if cars are coming, which they are. A man in a Bronco honks at me with irritation, and I wave at him awkwardly before continuing to scurry across the street. I trot over to the Gig Shack without a plan, without knowing the words that I'll say, only knowing that I need to confront Kyle and tell him to *leave me the hell alone*, to get out of my town.

But the Gig Shack is nearly empty, save for one couple sitting at a table, one server, and the bartender, who's cutting oranges and limes.

"Help you?" he asks halfheartedly. He is tan and weathered and looks like he would much rather be surfing than working behind the bar.

"Sorry—did someone just come in here? A guy, early forties?"

He looks around the restaurant pointedly. "Um, what you see is what you get," he says with a small laugh.

"Right. Sorry, I just—I thought I saw someone I know come in here."

He looks back at his limes. "Maybe he went into Herb's Market next door?" He shrugs with disinterest.

"Thanks," I mumble. I walk out in a daze, and Maya is standing in front of Naturally Good holding our bags, looking confused. She spots me and nods, her hands too full to wave. I walk back across the street to her, remembering to check for cars first this time.

"Where'd you run off to?" she asks. I think I can detect slight irritation in her voice.

"Sorry," I tell her, my ears burning. "I thought . . ." I trail off as I try to process it. Was it Kyle that I saw? If I wasn't even correct about which store the person walked into, then how well could I really see him? I saw the back of someone's head, and essentially flipped out. My dad always used to say, "The simplest explanation is the best." The simplest explanation here is not that Kyle is in Montauk stalking me; it's that I saw someone who looks like Kyle, from a distance, from the back, who wasn't actually him and who probably doesn't even look like him up close. And I ran across the street like a lunatic to chase after him.

The simplest explanation is that my guilt and paranoia are causing me to imagine things. The simplest explanation is that people aren't made to keep secrets this big. That cracks will start to form.

And mine are growing at a dangerous pace.

Maya is looking at me expectantly. "You saw what?" she asks, eyebrows raised with interest and a little bit of concern.

"I thought I saw someone I knew from the city," I finish hurriedly. "Kelsey's old soccer coach," I add, just in case she's started to guess at who it *really* was. "I wanted to say hi, but I was too slow. It might not have been him, anyway." I shrug in what I hope is a casual, offhand manner.

She nods slowly. I realize that she's still holding two heavy bags all by herself, sandwiches for all of us to eat at the concert and some miscellaneous groceries, while I stand there uselessly. "Let me take one of those," I say, embarrassment flooding my face. But when I reach out to grab the bag, the handle rips off, and the bag drops to the ground between us and topples over, avocados rolling out of it onto the sidewalk.

CHAPTER TWENTY-FIVE

When we pick the girls up from school, I am still badly shaken from seeing . . . whoever it was that I was so sure was Kyle. The rational part of me knows it wasn't really him, that it's my anxiety causing my mind to do strange things. No doubt these were the contributing factors to my apparent sleepwalking and inexplicable herb mutilation the other night, too.

But it really looked like him.

Kelsey and Lola, at least, seem back to their old selves. They spill off the sidewalk laughing and pile into the car. Lola, especially, seems to be practically buzzing. Maya turns back to them and grins. "Good day at school?" she asks. "Lola, I didn't even get to say goodbye to you this morning! You're quite the committed student, going in early on a Friday." She laughs. "Of course it would help if it was actually at your own school."

Lola gives her a funny look. "I'll take that under advisement," she says, and for a second, a nebulous wave of weirdness passes through the car.

The girls are wedged in the back seat with our Naturally Good haul, and I can see in the rearview mirror that Kelsey is poking through the bags to see what we got.

"Yes, I got your favorite tuna," I tell her.

"Thank you, Mother dearest," she says, but this time, her sarcasm is gentle, teasing. We almost feel like us again.

"I'm excited for this concert," Lola says. "I've never been to a—" She pauses. "Nancy Atlas show." I thought she was going to say she'd never been to a concert, but that would be crazy for a teenager.

"Yeah, Nancy is well known in this area, but I don't know that you would have heard of her if you weren't from around here," I tell her. "But she plays in Montauk frequently. She's great."

When we turn onto our street, I see immediately that Ida's son is standing in our driveway wearing mesh shorts and a T-shirt.

"Um," Maya says, gesturing toward him with her head.

"What the hell?" I mutter.

At least he doesn't have a beer this time. And he's fully dressed. He moves to the side of the driveway so that we can pull in, but he seems to be waiting for us rather than venturing back over to his own property.

"Hang tight for a second," I tell the three of them, suddenly feeling fiercely protective. I turn the car off and step out of it, shutting the door behind me.

"Hi?" I say in a tone that I hope isn't completely unfriendly, but that also communicates that I'm not thrilled to find him loitering by our house.

He skips a greeting entirely. "Your sprinklers are going onto our lawn," he says flatly. "My mom wanted me to tell you. She doesn't want her flowers overwatered."

"Oh, I'm so sorry. We'll reposition them, no problem. Thanks for letting us know."

"Yeah. She doesn't want her garden to end up looking like . . ." His eyes go up to our deck, where the skinny, bare stems of my herb garden are on display for all to see. He then glances back into the car.

"Oh, that was—well, we're not sure how that happened. Some sort of accident. Anyway, sorry about the sprinklers. We'll fix it." I narrow my eyes at him. It's weird to me that he would have noticed the herb garden. It's only partially visible from the driveway. "What's your name, by the way?" I ask suddenly. It feels like I should at least know the name of the person trespassing.

"Ryan," he mutters.

"Ryan. I'm Carrie. Sorry we haven't properly met before."

"Got a lot of company, huh?" he asks, ignoring my attempt at niceties as he peers into the car again.

"Not really. Just my friend and her daughter."

"They'll be here for a while?"

"I'm not sure," I reply vaguely, but the subtext in my tone says *none of your business.*

He seems to catch my drift because he replies, by way of explanation, "I like to know what's going on in the neighborhood, you know? Help keep it safe. It's not like the city, where you folks are from; there aren't that many of us here in the winter, and we have to look out for each other." His eyes zero in on Kelsey, who's still in the back seat. He lets his eyes linger for a second too long, and I have to suppress the urge to leap into the back seat and cover her with my body, shielding her from his view. *What the hell is this guy's problem?* My stomach roils at the idea of him fancying himself as some kind of neighborhood watch. I want to tell him that we don't need him looking out for us, but I don't want to confirm what he already thinks about me by being rude.

"Okay, well," I say, clearing my throat, "we need to head inside, but we'll address the sprinkler issue right away. Sorry again."

"Uh-huh," he says, with one more glance into the car. He turns around, saunters back over to his own lawn, and walks through his front door.

The girls and Maya get out of the car, finally.

"That was odd," Maya says quietly.

"It was, right? He really gives me the creeps," I whisper. I glance at Kelsey slouched in her seat and hope she remained oblivious to the look he gave her. She's fifteen, for God's sake. And already, adult men are leering at her? My fists clench and I feel my veins fill with fire and I am reminded of what I've always known: that I would kill for this girl.

"Let's go relax before we head to the concert," I suggest, trying to shake off the discomfort of this encounter.

We walk to the front door and I open it, silently deciding that we should no longer leave it so casually unlocked.

CHAPTER TWENTY-SIX

When we arrive at the lawn of Gosman's Dock, where the concert is, we all help smooth out our oversize blanket before we sit down on it. I take out the sandwiches, as well as some brie and bread and chips and olives, and wine for Maya and me. Though I'm going to be very careful not to drink nearly as much as I did the other night.

It's chilly but bearable, and it feels good to be out doing something fun. All around us, people are sitting in beach chairs, sipping wine from thermoses, unpacking picnics of their own. Couples holding hands, watching little kids run around, relishing a Friday night after a long week of work. Nancy Atlas is joking around with some fans and friends up by the stage while her band sets up. It's times like these, when I can really see Montauk's heart, that I love it the most and find myself grateful for the pause that we took from city life. Especially since Kelsey, who at this moment is chatting with Lola and popping olives into her mouth, appears happier than I've seen her in months.

Maya seems content, too; she borrowed one of Pete's gray fleeces, which is way too big for her, and she's got it wrapped around herself like a cocoon. She's looking at the girls contentedly as they laugh together, although not joining in. She seems to have forgiven me for my several blunders, and I've promised myself that there will not be another one.

I'll be the perfect host for the remainder of their visit, however long that is. I won't accuse her or her daughter of messing with my stuff in any way. It doesn't seem like it should be so hard to do.

I feel around the picnic basket for a wine opener, and then realize I left a separate bag with cups and the opener in the car. "I'll be right back," I tell everyone.

"Want me to come with you?" Maya asks.

"No, you relax. I'll be two minutes." Kelsey glances up at me from the card game that she and Lola have started, and the expression she gives me is halfway amiable. It's a good night already.

I trot across the street to where we parked. The parking lot for Gosman's is huge and not that full; even though this event is well attended, it's almost winter, so there aren't the crowds that summer would bring. I open our trunk and grab the canvas tote bag with the rest of the picnic supplies, slam it shut, and whirl around, ready to return to my evening.

But I'm blocked.

By Kyle.

Kyle. In Montauk.

So it really was him I saw in town earlier today. *I knew it.*

I gasp and try to take a step back, but the back of my car is preventing me from getting any more distance between us. He's close. Too close. He's in khakis and a collared shirt and is freshly shaved, as if he's dressed for a date.

"What the hell are you doing here?" I manage.

He looks confused. He'd been smiling, I realize, which seems bizarre to me. He knits his brow. "Uh, hello to you, too?"

"Seriously. Are you insane? Why are you here?"

He looks at me incredulously. "What? Carrie, I'm here because you *told* me to come."

"*What?*" My mouth drops open. "Kyle—" I stop myself and glance over toward the lawn, realizing that, though we're at a distance and it's almost dark out, we are in a direct sight line to where Kelsey, Lola, and Maya are sitting. I grab Kyle's wrist and pull him around the other side of my car to change that immediately.

"I did *not* tell you to come here. I haven't responded to any of your texts. I want this to be *done*. I thought that was pretty obvious. Why would you think that I—"

He cuts me off. "That's right, you didn't respond to any of my texts—until early this morning, when you told me to meet you here. At this concert. I drove out this morning, got a hotel, and here I am. As instructed."

I shake my head vehemently. "No, Kyle. No. That didn't happen." Is he crazy? Is it possible that I was having an affair with someone who is completely unstable? Suddenly, I feel unsafe being alone in this parking lot with him. No wonder he hasn't stopped texting me; he's unhinged. How could I not see that? I glance around me, hoping to see other people, but I don't. I can hear the opening chords of one of Nancy Atlas's better-known songs from the stage. The concert is beginning.

"Yes, you did," he says, his tone frighteningly calm. He reaches into his pocket. Instinctively, I cower. He looks at me agape again, seemingly unable to believe that I would think he was about to hurt me. He was only getting his phone. He swipes a few times and then hands it over to me.

I squint at it. His font size is smaller than what I have my phone set to. Once my eyes adjust, I can see that what I'm looking at is a screenshot of a text thread between me and him. I'm in his phone as "Gary Contractor," something we once laughed about together, I recall with revulsion. We were so callous.

I read the thread slowly, not comprehending.

Lara G., Hazel's Mom: I just miss you.
Lara G., Hazel's Mom: Montauk isn't that far, you know.
Lara G., Hazel's Mom: Really, Carrie. I miss you. I want to see you.

Gary Contractor: Would you come here?
Lara G., Hazel's Mom: Of course. When?
Gary Contractor: Tonight. There's a concert. Meet me at Gosman's Dock at 6?
Lara G., Hazel's Mom: I'll be there. We can talk?
Gary Contractor: Yes. We can talk.

When it's clear that I'm finished reading, he takes his phone out of my hands, puts it back in his pocket, and then looks at me expectantly.

"I didn't write that," I tell him plainly.

"Sure," he says with a sneer. "Look, if you regret inviting me here, that's one thing. But you're really going to deny it outright?"

"I didn't write those messages. I really didn't. I think I'd remember." Though a trickle of self-doubt creeps into my head. I apparently wrecked my own garden. I drank way too much the other night and told Maya about Kyle. There is a chance I deleted my own manuscript. Is there any way I could have texted him without remembering?

I dismiss the thought. I know I wouldn't have texted him because I genuinely don't want him here. It's not like there's some subconscious part of myself that still has feelings for him. I really am over him. I'm actually a little repulsed by him. Because when I look at him, I see a version of myself that I hate.

And I didn't even see that last text of his come through: Really, Carrie. I miss you. I want to see you. I don't remember ever getting that.

Which means someone must have deleted it from my phone before I saw it.

And responded to Kyle from my phone.

Maya's face floats through my head, along with my dad's words: *The simplest explanation.* And I'd be lying if I didn't admit that what feels like the simplest explanation to me is that Maya has something to do with all of this.

Everything started happening when she showed up. That has to mean something, doesn't it?

But as complicated as our relationship is, I can't imagine that Maya would want to hurt me and wreck my marriage. And besides, I can't very well go making another accusation with no evidence or basis—surely, that would be the straw that breaks the camel's back. And I don't want our friendship to be over.

I don't think I do, anyway. Assuming I'm wrong about my inklings. Which I must be.

Something else is rubbing me the wrong way—Kyle showed me a screenshot, not an actual conversation. Could he have doctored it somehow? Made the whole thing up as an excuse to come? Guessed at where I was, which wouldn't have been too hard, because practically everyone in town is at this concert?

And even if he really did receive those texts from my phone—why did he screenshot them? Is he gathering evidence to use against me?

"Look," I tell him, trying to sound firm and confident, even though my voice is shaking, "I don't really know what happened here, or how to explain what you showed me, but I didn't write that to you. And don't want you here. You need to go. This is over."

"You can't just do this to me," he says, his voice suddenly low and gravelly. Horrifyingly, I think he's fighting tears. "You ghosted me, after all those amazing months together. I was ready to leave Jessica, to start over with you, and then you just disappeared. And then you open a door, finally, and now you're just slamming it shut on me again?"

"I'm sorry, Kyle," I tell him, glancing toward the concert, praying that Kelsey doesn't come to the car for another jacket or something. What would I say? How would I explain who Kyle is? "I shouldn't have handled it like that. The guilt just caught up with me, I guess, and I thought it best to end it quickly and quietly. It wasn't right. You deserved a conversation, at least." I am trying to make my voice gentle, hoping that he'll be more agreeable if he feels that he's been heard. "But truly, I don't know who sent those texts."

Kyle looks at me icily. "Look, I'll leave you alone. If you'd have just been honest with me, I'd have stopped texting long ago. Consider me gone. But Carrie . . ." He gives me a long, loaded look. "If someone is really writing messages from your phone, as you claim, then it sure as hell sounds like someone already knows about us."

I know he's right. But I don't have too much time to think about it, because I feel a squeeze on the back of my shoulders. And I don't have to turn around to see who it is, because there's only one person who touches me like that.

Pete.

CHAPTER TWENTY-SEVEN

"Hey, babe," Pete says, the slightest hint of trepidation in his voice, no doubt due to finding me in the parking lot with a stranger. "Surprise!"

"Hey!" I say, way too enthusiastically. My voice is so shrill it's practically a shriek. Kyle is staring at Pete, and Pete is looking at me expectantly, waiting for me to explain who I'm talking to in the dark parking lot by our car. "What are you doing here? I thought you were staying in the city tonight!"

"Yeah, I was going to, but I decided to bail on dinner tonight. They don't really need me for it, anyway," he says with a shrug. "I hopped on the train and grabbed a cab over here from the station. Wanted to surprise you guys." And then he turns to look at Kyle, apparently accepting the fact that I'm not going to be making an introduction. "Hey, man. How's it going. I'm Pete."

"Kyle," he says, and they shake hands. I can see that it's a firm handshake, both showcasing their masculinity by trying to squeeze the other's hand harder.

In this moment, the moment where my husband is shaking hands with the man I slept with repeatedly, I wish I could make myself evaporate.

"I know Kyle from the city," I explain hurriedly. It's vague. Too vague. I try to recover by adding a little bit of color. "He used to work with my agent. We met a handful of times, back in the day." *What day, Carrie?* It still sounds thin, but it's the lie we'd always planned to tell if anyone we knew ever saw us together: that he was somehow connected to my literary agent. Hearing it deployed in real life makes me realize how weak the story is. Kyle is a sports agent. If Pete asks any follow-up questions about his job or, God forbid, finds a way to google him later, immediate red flags will be raised.

"Nice. Are you on vacation here in Montauk?" Pete asks congenially. He keeps glancing at me, and I wonder if it's because he can tell how spiked my blood pressure is, how rattled I am. I can feel hives forming on my chest and neck. Thank God I'm wearing a turtleneck. Kelsey used to call turtlenecks "penguin necks" when she was little. *Shit. I don't deserve her. Or Pete.*

"Uh, yep. Quick getaway. I have family in the area," Kyle says, and I am silently grateful to him for his effort, and for being a better liar than I am. He looks calm and collected, given the circumstances. "Anyway, I don't want to hold you two up," he says, and offers a smile that miraculously looks charming and genuine. He is playing this much more smoothly than I am. "Good seeing you, Carrie. Nice to meet you, Pete." He takes a few steps backward while giving us a wave, then turns around and walks through the parking lot toward his black Jeep, gaining speed with each step. Finally, he gets in his car and slams the door behind him.

My breath returns, somewhat.

Pete gives me a longer, tighter hug than the one he gave me when he first appeared. "That was random, huh?"

I nod. "Yeah. I'm surprised he even recognized me. We met years ago." *Liar. Liar. Liar.*

Pete nods. "I wonder what he was doing here if he isn't staying for the concert. The shops at Gosman's are closed."

I shrug. "Yeah, I don't know. Maybe picking up from one of the restaurants over there or something." I jerk my neck roughly in the direction of Salivar's and Sammy's.

Pete bobs his head from side to side, considering my suggestion. "Maybe. But he didn't have food with him."

"Yeah, I have no idea," I say, trying to sound as disinterested as possible in continuing on this line of speculation. "Anyway, it's so nice to have you back! This is a great surprise!" Minus the horror of Kyle being here and Pete *actually meeting him*, it really was. "Why didn't you tell us you were coming? And what made you change your mind?"

"Well, I was so jealous when you said you guys were doing a concert and picnic! And besides, the investors are younger guys, looking for a good time. Clubs and whatnot. In the words of Danny Glover, 'I'm too old for that shit.' I figured they'd be in better hands with the guys on my team than with an old fogy like me."

"You aren't an old fogy," I assure him, leaning into him and breathing him in. He smells like pine. He always has, ever since we were nineteen. He squeezes my shoulders again, and I hug him even tighter.

"Thanks, but I feel like one. I think I pulled a muscle sitting on the train for too long. Might need you to massage my glutes later." He gives me a wink, and I laugh as we walk toward our blanket, but I can't help glancing behind me uneasily, wondering if Kyle is on his way out of Montauk yet, and if he will finally leave me alone.

And more importantly, wondering who the hell texted him from my phone and asked him here.

CHAPTER
TWENTY-EIGHT

The rest of the evening proceeds uneventfully, thank God, though I'm still shaken from the encounter in the parking lot. Kelsey looks completely shocked to see Pete when I walk back to our blanket with him, calling, "Look who I found!" Pete teases Maya about borrowing his fleece without asking. We tease him about having to drink wine from the bottle since we didn't bring a cup for him. Nancy Atlas is energetic and soulful as always. Lola bobs her head along to the music with a big grin on her face. And, coincidentally, as we are leaving the concert, Pete runs into someone he knows from the city, an old work colleague, which I think makes my encounter with "Kyle, my agent's colleague" seem a lot more plausible.

It all goes as well as it possibly could, given that my husband and my . . . whatever Kyle was . . . stood face to face in a parking lot and shook hands earlier this evening. And that Kyle was invited here by someone using my phone. It's all I'm thinking about as I watch Nancy Atlas rock out on her guitar. I keep glancing at Maya, wondering if somehow she's behind all of this. But as I watch her gaze up at the band—and once, she closes her eyes and tilts her head up toward the sky—it's just hard to imagine that she'd hurt me like that. She's one of the best people I know. Always has been. A whole lot better than me, that's for sure.

When we get home, the landline is ringing for the first time since Maya called me telling me she was ten minutes away. God, that feels like a month ago, even though it was only four days. I run up the stairs to the kitchen ahead of everyone to answer it.

"Hello?" Despite the horror of the earlier part of the evening, my voice is bright from good wine and music.

"Hi, Ms. Colts? Agnes Curry with the school."

I gulp audibly. She isn't just *with* the school. She's the *principal* of the school.

Calling our home. On a Friday night.

I immediately feel the ground shift beneath me. I'm transported back to the spring, when the school called and told us what Kelsey and her friends had done with the fire alarm. It's never a good sign when the principal calls your home at night.

"Hi!" I say cheerfully, as if I'm excited to hear from her, when excitement is the absolute last emotion I'm feeling.

"Hi there," she says, in a decidedly more muted and somber tone. Professional. Cold. My feet grow even more unsteady. "Sorry to call so late—I've tried you a few times this evening, and figured I'd give it one more shot before calling it a night. Glad I finally caught you."

"Sorry about that," I tell her, my voice already shaking. "We were at a concert. The one over at Gosman's."

"Fun," she says, her voice clipped. Pete comes into the kitchen and looks at me quizzically. I raise a finger at him, and then grip my hand tightly around his forearm, as a way of bracing myself for whatever Principal Curry is going to say. He stands next to me, studying my face with concern.

"So, I'm calling about an incident that took place at school today," she says. *Shit. No. Please.* "A fire alarm was tripped by a student during last period." *No. No. Not again.* "There wasn't a drill planned, so there was quite a panic at school, and the East Hampton Fire Department arrived in a hurry, thinking it was a real emergency. They had to sweep the whole building, which took quite a while. That kind of thing costs the township a lot of money, as you can probably imagine. And the students missed an entire period. Lessons were unfinished and tests were compromised, which will result in extra work for many teachers this weekend."

"That's very frustrating," I tell her, my voice tight.

"Yes, it is," Principal Curry says crisply.

She clears her throat to start talking again. I dread whatever she's going to say. "So, Kelsey's English class was meeting that period, and Ms. Fulton remembered that Kelsey and her visitor had gone to the bathroom during the time that the fire alarm was triggered." She pauses, and the silence is crushing. I say nothing. I'm unable to speak, and I have no idea what I'm supposed to say, anyway. "Look, we aren't accusing Kelsey of anything, but we did glance at her academic record, and saw the suspension from last year. We called the Trewell School to find out what had happened—something we should have done when she enrolled, honestly, and we're culpable for not doing so—and—" *Shit.* "Well, obviously, this appears to be . . . quite similar to the incident there."

"Yes. I can see that." *Shit. Shit. Shit.*

"Again, we aren't trying to make accusations. But we also need to be realistic about the evidence. Unfortunately, unlike Trewell, we don't have surveillance in the hallways. Only at the entrances to the building." I can hear what she's really saying—*East Hampton High is not your rich, snooty New York City private school. You don't belong here, especially if you're going to abuse our resources.*

"Okay," I respond, taking a deep breath, trying to slow my racing heart. "So where does that leave us?"

"Well, we're going to interview some students on Monday, see if they saw anything suspicious. Of course, we will not disclose that Kelsey is—" *Our prime and only suspect.* It's what she wants to say but doesn't. "We won't say Kelsey's name," she clarifies gracefully. "In the meantime, tonight or tomorrow, I'd simply like for you to talk to Kelsey. Tell her that you know what happened and ask her if she wants to share anything. We believe that parents know their kids best. If she was involved, perhaps she'll come clean. And we also trust that you'll be honest with us about your conversation."

"Of course we'll talk to her." *Right. Like it's so easy. Like we've had any success trying to these past months.*

"Thank you," Principal Curry says. "And lastly"—*Here it is,* I think—"I do want to let you know that regardless of the outcome of your conversation with her, we can't have Kelsey return to school on Monday until we have a little more clarity on our end as to what may have happened here. So we're respectfully requesting that you keep her home on Monday, and until we give her the green light to return. I hope you understand."

"So she's suspended?" My heart sinks.

"No, not exactly," Principal Curry says; she's trying to sound reassuring, but I can hear the impatience creeping into her voice. "We just can't have her in the building until we have a better understanding of this incident, which hopefully we'll get from our interviews with other students, and your family, too. Our next step will most likely be a meeting with the four of us: you, your husband, Kelsey, and me. If Kelsey *is* responsible for tripping the alarm, we'll need to determine whether it's prudent for Kelsey to continue here at East Hampton High, or if we should come up with another plan for her." *We. As if we're a team. As if she's on our side. As if I don't already know that she's quite certain my daughter is a bad seed.* "We trust students here to do what's best for the entire community. And Kelsey may be demonstrating that she needs more supervision than we're able to provide. Our classes are large, and our teachers can't babysit individual students."

I flinch at her words. Then again, how can I blame her for thinking it was Kelsey? It's the *exact* same thing she did at Trewell, and she happened to be out of her classroom at the exact moment the alarm was tampered with? No one with a logical bone in their body would think it a coincidence.

"We'll talk to her," I promise, hoping I sound more confident than I feel. "And we'll call you back."

"Thank you," she says once more, and then she rattles off her home number without first asking if I have a pen handy. I scramble to enter it into my cell phone. She sounds tired. This is clearly not how she wanted to spend her Friday night. "Have a good evening," she adds. *Right.* As if that's possible.

I hang up, and, in a whisper, I briefly fill Pete in on the half of the conversation that he didn't hear. "Jesus Christ," he says with a big exhale, rubbing his temples, suddenly looking exhausted and years older. We stare at each other for a moment, silently acknowledging the weight of uncertainty that all parents must feel sometimes: that we aren't at all sure how to handle this. That we may very well screw it up royally.

Finally, Pete shrugs, his shoulders sagging wearily. "Let's go talk to her," he says bleakly, and we walk downstairs slowly, holding hands.

~

2003

"I just don't understand how this happened," Carrie wails. She is flopped on her bed facedown, as she's been so many times during the four years that Maya has known her. "How is this my life?" she moans, the pillow muffling her words.

For the moment, Maya is silent. She isn't sure what to say, because this time, it's not just a failed quiz or a tiff with another friend or an expensive missing earring that Carrie borrowed from her mother without asking. When Maya got back to their apartment from work that afternoon, Carrie was sobbing on the bathroom floor, a pregnancy test with two bright lines on the tiles beside her. Maya sank down next to her and put her arm around her, resting her head against Carrie's and letting her cry for nearly half an hour before coaxing her out of the bathroom and to her room.

"I just don't get it," Carrie whimpers.

Though she's not about to say this to Carrie, Maya knows that the answer to that is simple—it probably happened because Carrie and Pete had unprotected sex. Carrie often joked with their friends about being on a method of birth control called "pull and pray." So it really isn't such a mystery at all. Maya knows she's being judgmental, but after four years, her patience for Carrie's catastrophes (even the real ones, like this) is wearing a little thin. And how hard can it really be to use a condom? (Though Maya doesn't know the answer to this personally since, to both her relief and frustration, her virginity is still very much intact.)

"We'll figure it out," Maya says, sitting beside her on the bed and rubbing her back. "This happens." To people who have unprotected sex, *Maya adds silently. "We can go to Planned Parenthood. I can help you tell Pete. Whatever you need."*

"You don't get it," Carrie says. "I already went *to Planned Parenthood. That's where I got the test, and that's why I was MIA all morning." Carrie didn't show up to the Italian architecture class that she'd insisted they take together in their final semester, but Maya didn't think much of it; it is May of senior year, after all. Carrie misses a lot of classes these days. Most of their friends do.*

"Why didn't you tell me? I'd have gone with you." Maya is surprised that Carrie went to Planned Parenthood by herself; it's just in the next town over, but it's unlike her to keep something big like that from Maya, even for a morning.

"I know you've been stressed out about applying for jobs and saving money, and that you've been working extra shifts at the coffee shop. I didn't want to worry you for no reason." Maya is taken aback for a second. Carrie isn't wrong; Maya is just a little surprised that she's noticed.

"And I was sure it was nothing, anyway," Carrie continues. "I thought I was just being paranoid. But I wasn't."

Maya takes a deep breath. "So what did they say?"

Carrie rolls over and looks at Maya miserably, her eyes dark and flat. "It's bad, Maya. They said—they said I'm almost seven months pregnant."

Maya's jaw drops. She's sure she's misheard. "Seven? Are you serious? That's not possible." She immediately looks at Carrie's belly. It is a bit rounder, sure, and Maya has noticed that Carrie's gained a little weight, but Maya assumed it was because of all the boxed merlot and late-night pizzas that Carrie regularly indulges in. In fact, many of the senior girls have put on a few pounds, now that they're at the top of the social hierarchy and no longer feel the crushing need to impress people all the time. It's the good kind of weight gain: power being reclaimed, space being occupied, a collective admission that salads are gross and the StairMaster is boring. (Unfortunately, the salads and six a.m. workouts will return next year, when they all start their first jobs and go back to trying to win everyone's approval.)

"Did you miss any periods?" Maya asks, still in disbelief.

Carrie buries her face in her pillow again. "I guess, but I didn't really think anything of it. I'm always irregular, and my periods are kind of light." Of course they are, *Maya thinks with an inward eye roll, before reminding herself that Carrie's position is nothing to envy right now. "And I haven't felt any different. Other than some gas recently, which the Planned Parenthood people told me was actually kicking. I just didn't really think anything like this could happen to me," Carrie finishes lamely, and Maya understands how the charmed life that Carrie has led up to now would engender this kind of thinking. Things have always worked out for her. Always.*

Carrie rolls over onto her side. "Seven months, Maya. Seven freaking months. It's too late for an abortion. There's, like, a real baby in there. What the hell am I supposed to do? My mom is going to absolutely kill me." Maya wouldn't want to have to deliver this news to Carrie's mom, either; while she's always been kind to Maya, every time she visits, wearing her blazer and pearls, she's had some choice comments for Carrie about the length of her nails, her unmade bed, her B-minus in British literature. Carrie once told Maya that ever since her dad died, her mom had felt the need to be twice as critical as she usually was, so as to cover his bases, too. So disclosing an advanced-stage pregnancy to her would be a considerable hurdle to clear.

"She already thinks I'm a screwup, after seeing my first-semester report card. You're so lucky you don't have anyone riding you, attacking everything

you do." Maya raises her eyebrows in disbelief. Did Carrie really just tell her she's lucky that her parents abandoned her and the grandmother who raised her is dead? That she is completely on her own?

Oblivious, Carrie continues: "Like anyone even cares about college GPAs? All they care about is which college you went to. Besides, I already have a job. So what do I need straight As for?" Ah, yes, the Job, *the entry-level position at* People *magazine, Carrie's ticket into the world of entertainment journalism and celebrities. Carrie is determined to be the next Kelly Ripa or, at the very least, the next Giuliana Rancic. "My job," Carrie moans, remembering. "How am I supposed to work with a newborn? What the hell am I going to tell them?"*

"You could give the baby up for adoption," Maya says gently. "You still have options."

"Yeah, that's exactly what Planned Parenthood said, too," Carrie whispers hopelessly. "They gave me some stupid pamphlets and a million forms to fill out. But if I do that, not only will everyone find out I'm an idiot who got pregnant; they'll also think I'm a terrible person for giving the baby away."

Maya is quiet for a moment. "What do you think Pete will want to do?"

Carrie looks at Maya sharply. "I can't tell Pete," she says. "He'll want me to have the baby and for us to get married. I wasn't even planning on staying with him after graduation. You know that. He can't find out. He'll propose to me, like, that minute, and then my entire life will be planned out. Married to Pete, living in the suburbs, pumping out kids. No. That's not what I want. I don't want him or anyone else to know." Carrie lets out a sob.

Maya takes a measured breath. "But, Carrie—do you really think you shouldn't tell Pete, or your mom? You're going to need support. Regardless of what you choose to do, you can't do this all on your own."

Carrie sits up suddenly and drapes herself over Maya, roping her clammy arms around her neck. "That's why I'm so glad I have you," she says, tucking her wet cheek into Maya's cardigan.

CHAPTER
TWENTY-NINE

We knock on Kelsey's door together, and even though all she says is "What?" rather than "Come in," Pete pushes open the door slowly. She and Lola are lying on Kelsey's twin bed side by side, each with one headphone in her ear, listening to a song from Kelsey's phone. Mr. Sparkles is lying between Lola's legs.

"Can I help you?" Kelsey says. What she's really saying is *Get out*.

"Lola, do you mind giving us a few minutes with Kelsey?" Pete asks, his voice far calmer and gentler than I'd be able to manage.

"Sure," Lola says, and slides off the bed. She and Kelsey exchange a brief look, or perhaps I imagine it. "Let me know when it's safe to come back," Lola calls softly to Kelsey as she exits. Mr. Sparkles scampers after her.

Pete and I sit down on the bed without asking Kelsey if we can. "Kels," Pete begins. "We got a call from the school. About what happened this afternoon." Kelsey's eyes immediately darken. She looks down at her legs. "Kelsey? Do you already know what we're going to say?"

She's silent.

"The fire alarm," I say quietly. "The school is pissed, and rightfully so. They think it may have been you. Was it?"

She looks up at both of us, tears in her eyes.

"I'll only talk to Mom," she emits finally with a small sob.

Pete and I look at each other. He looks as surprised as I feel. I haven't been Kelsey's preferred parent in some time.

I shrug at him, unsure of what to do. I want to be a united front, but we also need Kelsey to talk, and if she wants to only talk to me, then so be it.

Pete nods. "Okay, Kels. Whatever you want. Please know that I'm here for you, too, though. And I love you."

"Thanks, Dad," she whispers, another choked cry escaping her throat.

As soon as he shuts the door, she collapses on her bed, her body shaking with convulsive sobs. I go over and sit beside her, rubbing her back, her feet, her legs. She lets me.

Finally, I speak up. "Kelsey, what happened? You can tell me. Did you pull the alarm?"

She rolls onto her back so that she can look at me. Her eyes are hurt and angry. "No, Mom. I didn't." She sighs. "But I need to talk to you about some stuff. I'm so tired of pretending. I'm really, really tired." And I can see that she is. The circles under her eyes. Her pale cheeks. The heaviness around her mouth; how much effort it would take for her to smile right now. My poor girl. "I didn't pull the alarm, but it *is* my fault."

"What do you mean, it's your fault?" I put my hand on hers. It's been so long since we've sat side by side like this on the bed. And yet, it still feels like the most natural thing in the world. She lived inside me for nine months. Flesh of my flesh, blood of my blood.

She pauses, takes another deep breath. "Mom, you know how I got so mad that you accused Lola of deleting your manuscript?"

"Yes?"

"It was because I did that." She pauses. "I wrecked your herb garden, too."

My heart stills. I am silent for a moment as I register what Kelsey has said. *Tread lightly, Carrie,* I tell myself. *Keep the lines of communication open.* I nod slowly and wait for Kelsey to continue.

"I almost told you about the herbs right away, because our weird neighbor was outside smoking at the time and saw me do it. I thought he was going to rat me out this afternoon. But he didn't." Kelsey takes another shuddery breath.

No wonder Ryan was looking at Kelsey so intently this afternoon. He was wondering what kind of a person destroyed their family's herbs in the middle of the night.

"Okay," I say, keeping my expression neutral. "So why'd you do it?"

"Because I want to go back to the city. I'm sick of being here. I know I messed up at Trewell, but that doesn't mean that you can just take me away from my life, from my friends. Even if you didn't like them." I nod at her, slowly trying to process. "And I know you don't like it here, either. You're miserable in Montauk. So I thought that, maybe, if bad stuff kept happening—that you'd blame it on being here in Montauk, and say you'd had enough, and we could all go home."

"Okay," I say again, slowly. "Kelsey, I get that you're not happy about being here. We can definitely talk about going back. And the herb garden is one thing. But deleting my manuscript—that's my work. That's a big deal." My heart races as I try to grapple with what Kelsey's revealed. It makes sense why it looked like me on the grainy Ring camera footage from the deck; Kelsey and I are both tall and thin and have a comically identical gait. If she was wearing my Middlebury sweatshirt, it's no wonder why Pete thought she was me. Neither Pete nor I considered that Kelsey could be responsible. Even after what she'd done at Trewell. We're both guilty of having a sizable parental blind spot, apparently.

A stab of shame pings my stomach. I'd suspected Lola. And why? Because she asks odd questions and makes unsolicited sandwiches and dresses provocatively? No wonder she was so hurt when I asked if she'd been in my office. She had nothing to do with it.

"I know it's a big deal," Kelsey says, her eyes narrowing. Suddenly she seems angry again, and I worry that I'm losing her in this conversation. I need to soften myself again.

"Nothing you say or do will ever make me love you any less," I breathe, an incantation. I've been saying this to her since she was a toddler. I meant it then, and I mean it now.

"It wasn't just about wanting to go back to the city. I *wanted* to hurt you, to punish you. I'm—I'm so—*mad at you*, Mom."

"I've gotten that impression, yes," I tell her. "And I'll totally concede that keeping you out here after everything that happened was perhaps not the right thing to do. Especially since Dad and I just sort of made the decision without you. It must have seemed terribly unfair to you. I get that. I really do. And I'm sorry."

"It isn't that," Kelsey says, and another sob comes out of her throat. "I *know*."

"You know what?"

"I know about your stupid *affair*!" she says, and the way she hisses the word feels like it is being branded onto my very soul with a hot iron.

I am momentarily speechless. But it doesn't really matter what I say. What matters is that she knows.

"How?" I ask her simply, quietly.

"I *saw* you," she chokes out. "My art class was walking to the park one morning to gather materials from nature for a project. I saw you walking into a hotel with him. You were laughing. And I just—I knew." Our hotel. We always met there in the morning. We thought it was so much safer, so much less suspicious, than meeting at night. It looked like we were walking in for a work meeting, we told ourselves.

But it wouldn't have looked that way to people who really knew us. Who loved us. Who trusted us. And clearly, it didn't look that way to Kelsey.

Kelsey is gaining momentum as she talks, and I can tell what a relief it is for her to have finally admitted out loud what she's been holding inside for all these months. "I was walking next to Hannah, and she said, 'Isn't that your mom?' and I told her no, it wasn't," she says, her eyes clouding over with anger as she looks at me, until she can bear the sight of me no more and breaks my gaze, looking down at her lap instead. Hannah, one of Kelsey's oldest friends, whom she'd suddenly dropped like a hot potato in favor of hanging out with new ones instead. New friends who smoked pot and cut classes and were *never* actually at the movie they claimed to be seeing.

But they were new friends who didn't know her parents and who hadn't seen her mom going into a hotel with some guy.

Suddenly, it all makes sense. Kelsey's changes in behavior. Her anger, more directed at me than at Pete. Her unwillingness to talk about it. Of course she couldn't talk about it because she was keeping my secret hidden from Pete. To protect me. To preserve our family.

All of it was my fault. All because I wanted to feel new again, to feel wanted and seen for someone other than just a wife and mom, to feel like the future was yet to be written and that I wasn't living the very life I'd been trying to avoid when I'd broken up with Pete at the age of twenty-two.

And perhaps, too, maybe I had an affair because on some level I *wanted* to be caught, to be punished. I knew I deserved a reckoning and had eluded it for far too long. So I had to commit a new crime, to finally get what was coming to me, for Pete to learn at long last that I am not a good person, and that he'd have been better off refusing to take me back when I'd begged him to at twenty-three.

But I certainly didn't mean to drag Kelsey into the flames I'd created. Ever.

Tears fill my eyes and I grab Kelsey's hands. "Kelsey, I am so, so sorry," I tell her, meaning it in the depths and crevices of my bones. "I cannot imagine how awful it was to see that, and how terrible it must have felt to keep it to yourself for all these months. I completely understand how angry you must be with me. I've let you down. I've let our family down. I made a mistake. A big one. And I'm so ashamed. Please know how much I regret it. If I could take it back, I would."

"But you can't," she says, shrugging her shoulders with sad, matter-of-fact defeat. "And the worst part is that you haven't even broken things off with him. When I went to wake you up this morning, I saw that you had a text from him. It was obvious that someone named 'Lara G., Hazel's Mom' doesn't miss you. There's no Hazel. It was him. Why won't you just end it?"

My heart sinks again. "I *have* ended it, believe me . . . I haven't responded to him in months. He just kept reaching out."

"And your strategy was, what, to ignore him? Mom, do you realize how immature that is? Even teenagers are more direct when they dump someone."

I close my eyes. "You're right. I know. But it is very, very over now."

"Yeah, well, I would hope so."

I pause, slowly putting the pieces together. "Kelsey, when you saw that text from him . . . did you text him and ask him to come here?"

Kelsey shrugs her shoulders. "It was an impulse. I thought maybe if you were forced to confront him face to face, you would finally end things once and for all. I didn't think that Dad was coming back tonight." So that's why I didn't even see the text from Kyle this morning. Kelsey had circumvented it. It's also why Kelsey looked momentarily alarmed when Pete showed up at the concert. *And here I thought Maya was to blame for luring Kyle to Montauk. What is wrong with me?*

Another light bulb goes off. "And did you somehow put my calendar on Dad's phone?"

Kelsey's forehead creases. "Huh? No. I have no idea how to do that."

I feel my brow crease, too, mirroring Kelsey's. "Well, the good news is that I think he got the message loud and clear that it's over. Kels, I can promise you that nothing like that will ever happen again. I love your father deeply, and I've loved him since I was nineteen years old. I screwed up big-time." *Again.* "But I'm going to try to make it right. I'll tell Dad, and apologize, and try to earn his forgiveness. I don't want you to keep this secret for me for a second longer."

"But what if he can't forgive you?" Kelsey sniffles. "I don't want you to get divorced. That was the whole point of me not saying anything."

"No, I don't want that, either." I put my arm around her shoulders and hug her close to me. "But I trust that your dad knows my heart well enough to know that what I did isn't who I am. And I'll remind him every day from now on that you and he are the only things in my life that matter to me." I pause when I hear a creak outside the door, thinking that someone's about to knock. But no one does, fortunately; this conversation is too important to interrupt. "Thank you for finally telling me the truth about why you've been so mad." I press my head against hers lightly. Her soft hair against my cheek reminds me of when she was a baby and she'd fall asleep on my chest, her fuzzy downy head tucked up under my chin, tickling it. I can remember the exact weight of her in that position.

I snap to, suddenly remembering how we got into this conversation in the first place. "So, Kelsey, hang on—the fire alarm today. If you didn't do it, why do you think you're still to blame?"

She breathes a shaky breath. "I told Lola," she says. "Not about the affair, but about my plan. To try to get you to hate Montauk and bring me back to the city," she whispers. She glances at the door herself, seemingly afraid that Lola might hear what she's saying, though she's speaking so quietly she's nearly inaudible. "I also told her about what I did with the fire alarm at Trewell, and she said if we did that again, you'd have no choice but to take me out of school here and bring me back. So I think she was trying to help me, kind of? Plus, she didn't like Ms. Fulton's class. Remember how I told you that she was upset because of what Olivia had said about Jeannette Walls's mom being weak for not leaving the dad?" Kelsey's eyes fill with fresh tears. "Anyway, I told

Lola no. I told her it wasn't a good idea. But she said she'd never done a prank, and she wanted to have a 'teenage experience.' Like me. I have no idea what she meant."

I nod, holding my breath. "Okay. Let's take a beat. Did you actually see Lola pull the alarm while you two went to the bathroom together?"

Kelsey shakes her head. "No. I really went to the bathroom. She said she'd wait outside in the hallway for me. And the alarm is right there. Mom, it wasn't me. I swear it wasn't me."

"I believe you," I say firmly, meaning it. I try to take a deep breath. My mind is racing. But I know that, right now, my only job is to take this burden off my daughter. To make sure she knows that this isn't for her to worry about anymore. I'm far too late in doing so, I know.

"I'll talk to Maya," I tell her, thinking to myself, *That's gonna be a fun conversation.* "We'll get to the bottom of this. I promise. And you did the right thing by telling me. All of it," I add meaningfully, hoping she can feel the genuine remorse that will live forever in my body.

She breathes a sigh of relief, and as messed up as everything is right now, I am comforted that this weight is off Kelsey's shoulders, finally.

And I feel horrible that I was the one to put it there. I'm supposed to protect her. Make her life easier, better. Not inflict her with secrets to keep on my behalf.

"I'll check on you before you fall asleep," I whisper to her, and get up to leave. She surprises me by pulling me back in for a hug, and I allow myself to savor the sweetness of the short moment before walking out of her room to face my reckoning.

CHAPTER THIRTY

When I leave Kelsey's room, the house is dead quiet.

Maya's and Lola's respective doors are shut. It's late, so maybe they've already gone to bed. I don't think this can wait until the morning, though.

I pop up into the kitchen to see if Pete is there, but he isn't. He's not in our room, either. I'll have to tackle this discussion with Maya on my own.

I knock lightly at her door, almost hoping that she won't answer. But she does. "Hey," she says, looking surprised but not displeased to see me. "What's going on? Everything okay? You guys sort of disappeared as soon as we got home."

I take a deep breath. "Can I come in?" She nods and lets me into her room but keeps the door open. We sit on the bed next to each other, and for a moment, I'm transported to our freshman year dorm room. Sitting on one of our beds, dipping pretzel rods in peanut butter, laughing about nothing.

The spell breaks, though, when I remember what I need to tell her. "It was the school that called. They said that a student pulled the fire alarm today. That fire trucks had to come, and it was a whole mess."

Maya sucks in air. "Shit. The same thing Kelsey did at Trewell, right?"

"Yes, which is why they thought it might have been her. But Maya . . . Kelsey says it wasn't her. She says . . ." I falter, knowing that what I'm about to say next will likely be the nail in our friendship's coffin. "She thinks it was Lola."

Maya's eyes narrow. She says nothing. I have no choice but to continue.

"See, apparently, Kelsey's been trying to devise ways to get me fed up enough with Montauk to bring her back to the city. The herbs, my manuscript . . . it was all her." I can't bear to tell Maya that Kelsey knew about my affair the whole time. Saying the words out loud might kill me. In spite of everything, I still care so much about what Maya thinks of me. "And . . . ," I continue with a gulp, "she thinks that Lola may have done this to sort of . . . help her cause. Also, I guess they were in English at the time, and Lola had been having some issues with the content of the discussion?"

Maya nods very, very slowly, never breaking her gaze with me.

"Maya, I'm so sorry, but I'm going to have to tell the school. Look, they'll probably still blame Kelsey either way, since Lola was our guest. But I'm obligated to tell them what Kelsey told me."

She nods again.

Then she smiles at me, but it isn't a real smile. It's the smile that a lawyer would give a defendant whom they knew they were about to crush.

"So let me get this straight," she says, her frightening smile growing even wider. "Your daughter admitted to the things that you've been suspecting and accusing mine of for the entire time we've been here. And now there's another transgression, one that your daughter is literally already known to have committed prior. But you think that the most likely explanation, still, is that *my* child is the guilty one."

I hear how illogical it sounds coming out of her mouth. And yet.

"I trust my daughter," I tell her quietly.

"What about mine?" she spits back, venom in her voice. "You are so chronically incapable of taking any responsibility for your actions. Do you even know that? It would be funny if it weren't so . . . disgusting." She stands up from the bed, and for once, she towers over me, since I'm still sitting. She grabs her bag from the floor by the foot of her bed. "We are leaving. Now. Coming here was a mistake. And, Carrie, don't even *think* about saying one word to Lola. Don't even look at her. You don't deserve to. Understand?"

My eyes fill with tears. I knew this would go poorly, but it still stings to lose Maya like this. Especially after I only just got her back. "I'm sorry, Maya. I understand why you're so mad. I just needed to be honest about what Kelsey said, that's all. Maybe we could try talking to the girls together, to really get to the bottom of it."

"Like I said, you're never to talk to Lola. You are not worthy of her time." I blink dumbly, my eyelids heavy with hurt. "You don't deserve any of this. All the second and third and goddamn millionth chances you've been granted. You don't even know." She stuffs her bag with clothes and pushes past me into the hall. She knocks on Lola's door. Lola answers, wearing boxers and a T-shirt, ready for bed but looking wide awake. "Get dressed," Maya says roughly. "We're leaving."

For a split second, Lola looks at me with something like longing. "Okay," she says quietly, and they both retreat to their rooms to pack, shutting the doors tightly behind them.

CHAPTER THIRTY-ONE

I stand awkwardly at the front door as they leave. Pete is still nowhere to be found, and Kelsey hasn't come out of her room, which is probably for the best. I'm sure she feels terrible for telling on Lola, but what choice did she have? "Maya, please. It doesn't have to be like this. We can figure this out together. Let's just talk through it a bit more," I plead.

Maya laughs almost maniacally. "Carrie, there's nothing to talk through. We're done here."

"Lola—" I start, about to apologize, but Maya cuts me off.

"I told you not to fucking talk to her," Maya hisses. "We're leaving. Thanks so much for having us!" she adds with facetious scorn.

She lets the door slam behind them, leaving me standing there with my mouth open and hands shaking. Mr. Sparkles, who'd been trailing Lola, turns to look at me accusingly.

A few minutes later, I hear Pete come into the kitchen from the deck, and I walk upstairs.

"Where were you?" I ask him. It was such an odd time for him to disappear, and I really could have used his help mitigating the situation with Maya.

"I needed to go for a walk," Pete says. His voice is husky. "Where are Maya and Lola? Their car is gone."

"They left," I tell him quietly. "Kelsey said that Lola is the one who pulled the alarm. When I told Maya that, she got furious, and they're gone."

"Wow," Pete murmurs, sitting down at the table and putting his head in his hands.

"But that's not it," I whisper, terrified for what I know I need to tell him. "I have to talk to you about something else, too."

Pete puts one hand up to stop me without raising his head to look at me. "I already heard."

I gape at him. "You were listening?"

"Yeah, Carrie, as if my eavesdropping is the issue here. I wanted to know what was going on with our daughter. *Unlike you.*"

"What does that mean?"

"An affair is one thing, Carrie. It's not good, but it's not necessarily unforgivable, either. What I can't make my peace with is that something's been off with Kelsey for *months*, and you never once considered that perhaps she'd seen something she shouldn't have? That maybe she was carrying the load of a secret she couldn't bear? You should have dug deeper. You should have *cared* more. She's our *daughter*, for Chrissake. And she's just been living with this—this—" His face turns red as he struggles to find a word big enough to encapsulate what I've done and how badly I've injured everyone.

And I know he's right. I should have tried harder to talk to Kelsey. It never even occurred to me that she might know. But how could this possibility not have crossed my mind? In retrospect, her rage was clearly directed at me. I should have been more willing to look inward and consider why. But I suppose I was terrified of what I might see.

"Can we talk about it?" I beg. "I'll answer any questions you have. I can try to explain—"

"Not right now," he says, closing his eyes and shaking his head abruptly. "I can't deal with it right now. I do have one question, though."

"Okay. Anything."

"Was that him?"

"What do you mean?"

Pete glares at me. "Was that *him*, Carrie? Tonight in Gosman's parking lot. Was that him?"

Shit. My chest grows hot and my eyes fill with tears.

"I knew it," Pete says. "I had a feeling about that guy. So you had him here, in Montauk? It's still going on? Are you fucking kidding me?"

"It wasn't like that, Pete. It's been over for months; he just showed up and—"

"I don't believe anything you say."

I am silent, and the space between us seems to grow and grow.

"So what happens now?" I ask in a small voice.

"I'm taking Kelsey back to the city first thing in the morning," he says. "It's what she wants, and we both need a break."

"A break—"

"A break from *you*, Carrie. Besides," Pete says bitterly, "it's not like Kelsey has school on Monday, right? We're going to take a few days. I'm going to give her the attention and love she deserves. Let her see her friends. Take her to lunch. Bring her to a goddamn Broadway show, maybe. *Talk* to her. And then we'll figure out what to do next." He looks at me with an abhorrence I've never seen from him, let alone been on the receiving end of. "I'm sleeping on the couch tonight," he adds gruffly.

"It's okay. You can have our bed. I'll take the—"

"I don't want it," he snaps.

I go downstairs and tiptoe into Kelsey's room. She is fast asleep, her hair splayed across the pillow, no doubt worn out from her long-awaited unburdening. She looks so young and so peaceful and my regret is so deep that I feel like I am drowning in it. I kiss her forehead and remember how when she was a baby she used to sleep with her butt in the air and her thumb in her mouth. All I cared about back then was keeping her safe and warm and fed and happy, protecting her from harm. I never could have imagined then that I'd hurt her the way I know I have.

I lie in bed awake for hours, stewing in the putrid muck of my shame. I finally doze off around three, and when I wake up with the morning light, the house is quiet, and I know they're already gone, and that I'm alone.

CHAPTER THIRTY-TWO

Saturday

It takes me hours to drag myself out of bed, because I know that as soon as my feet hit the carpet, it will be real.

I am caught. My husband and daughter have left me. My daughter suffered for months keeping my disgraceful secret. My husband might never forgive me. My marriage could be over. And on top of that, my oldest friend never wants to see me again. I'm all alone. And I have only myself to blame. I don't want to get out of bed, because if I'm still in bed, I can pretend it's all a bad dream. I have to use the bathroom, but I hold it for hours so that I can continue to avoid reality.

When I finally have no choice but to get up and go to the bathroom, I look in the mirror and see that I've aged twenty years overnight. I look like a haggard old woman. Which is exactly how I feel.

I send Pete a text. I love you, and I'm so, so sorry. I text Kelsey, too. I'm so sorry, honey. I love you forever. I don't expect responses, and I don't get any.

I decide to take a shower—a long shower, where I scrub and shampoo and shave, as if I could wash it all away, everything that's happened. Everything that I've done. I sigh heavily when I find that my razor isn't even in the shower. Not like I could shave off an affair, anyway. Kelsey probably borrowed it and didn't return it. But right now, something that would normally annoy me only makes me miss her more.

I put on a robe and plod around the house aimlessly for a while. I go into Kelsey's room and pick up books and knickknacks and framed photos of her and her New York friends. I return to our room and open Pete's dresser and refold a couple of pairs of boxer shorts. I go into the rooms where Maya and Lola were sleeping. Their stuff is gone and the beds are stripped, dirty sheets on the floor. Very unlike Maya to be discourteous and leave dirty linens behind, but their departure was so hurried that even Maya couldn't maintain her usual perfect level of decorum. Besides, I'm sure she no longer gives a shit what I think of her. It's for the better, too, that I'll have some extra laundry today to distract myself from the tatters of my life.

Eventually, I force myself to get dressed and, zombielike, walk to the car to go into town for some food. I can't wallow in the house alone forever. I'll likely start drinking wine if I do, and that's the last thing I need right now. I need to think, to walk, to eat, and try to get some clarity about what to do next. What I can do to make all this better.

At Naturally Good, I order a juice and a sandwich, barely registering my surroundings or the words exchanged between me and Kova, one of the women who works the register. I snap to life, though, when she says, "Just missed your buddy, by the way."

Kova has a gift for remembering everything about everyone—their regular orders and personal details. *So sorry about your mother-in-law,* she said the first time I came in after Pete's mom had passed, even though I'd only been to Naturally Good with Helen once, almost a year earlier.

"Hmm?" I ask her, eyebrows raised. *My buddy?*

"The woman you were here with the other day. She was just here, too. Got the same sandwich as you," Kova notes.

"Oh," I say, feeling my face twist with puzzlement and surprise, hoping Kova doesn't notice that my reaction is off. "Too bad I missed her."

My skin prickles. What is Maya still doing in Montauk? If she was so eager to get as far from me as possible, and haul Lola away from this mess at school, why are they lingering? It's midday already. They've had plenty of time to head home.

"Just out of curiosity," I venture, "was she with her daughter?"

"Her daughter?" Kova makes a confused face. "Oh, I guess that could have been her daughter, yeah. I don't know. She was with a young woman. They didn't look alike." She hands me a bag containing my sandwich and juice. "Have a great one!"

"You too," I murmur, taking the bag from her and glancing around as if Maya is about to jump out at me from one of the grocery aisles.

A young woman.

She is right. Maya and Lola look nothing alike. Nothing at all.

~

2003

When Maya gets home from class, Carrie is sitting on their Target couch, eyes vacant. Maya notices that her stomach is pooched out over her jeans, but it still doesn't look like a baby bump, and part of Maya understands how Carrie could have gone this long without realizing she was pregnant.

Another part of her can't fathom how someone could miss seven periods and never give it a second thought.

Then again, it's Carrie. Things always work out for her. So of course she assumed it was nothing to worry about.

"Hey," Maya says gently. "How are you doing?"

"I'm—okay, I think," Carrie says. Her eyes are still settled on the wall in front of her, and her voice sounds strangely sedated. "Something kind of amazing happened. Or could happen. I don't know yet."

Oh God, here we go, Maya thinks grimly. Usually when something "kind of amazing" happens to Carrie, it inevitably involves Maya—from

186

going with her to Rutland to get a fake ID their freshman year to driving to New York with her and waiting outside at a coffee shop while Carrie had a job interview. Yes, Maya could have said no to any of these requests, but at this point, Carrie is the closest thing Maya has to family. "Chosen family," like they've always said. She is Maya's only tether. And as much as Carrie aggravates her sometimes, Maya doesn't think she'd like the feeling of floating out in space all by herself.

"What happened?" Maya asks hesitantly.

Carrie turns to face Maya. She takes a deep breath. "So I went to health services to get some free melatonin. I haven't slept a wink since I found out about . . ." She makes a whistling motion with her mouth and points to her stomach. It's too comedic a gesture for the gravity of the situation, and Maya almost laughs. "Anyway, I ended up telling the nurse I was pregnant, to make sure I was even allowed to take melatonin. And it all just came out—about how it was all a surprise, and I have no idea what I'm going to do about it. And you won't believe this, but the nurse at health services—she thinks she knows someone that will do a private adoption. Off the books, so to speak?" Carrie shrugs uncertainly.

Maya's mouth drops open. "Are you serious? What exactly did she say?"

Carrie nods. "I know, I couldn't believe it, either. I mean, how lucky, right? Apparently, she has a cousin who is desperate for a baby but can't have kids of her own, and she and her husband can't afford to go through the adoption process. Or there was some reason they wouldn't be eligible for it—I'm not really sure." Carrie waves her hand dismissively, as if those details aren't important. "Anyway, they live right here in Vermont, in Pittsford. And Debbie—that's the nurse at health services—said maybe they'd be willing to host me for the summer and help me deliver. Her cousin is a nurse, too, and they live in a farmhouse and have plenty of room. So I could stay with them, deliver the baby, and then head to New York as planned. She said my name wouldn't even have to be on any paperwork. They'd file it as a home birth and put the cousin down as the birth mother. I mean, wouldn't that be perfect? Graduation is next week, and I could go straight from here. I wouldn't even have to tell anyone I'd ever been preg-nant. Thank God graduation gowns are enormous. And I'm not starting at People *until September anyway, so it could really all work out. You and I will still have time to find an apartment in the city by the end of the sum-mer, too." Carrie's eyes are shining with hope and excitement.*

Maya's head is swimming with questions she isn't sure she even wants to ask. "But what will your mom say about you going off to live in Pittsford for the summer instead of going home to Connecticut?"

Carrie shrugs. "Yeah, I thought about that. I'll tell her it's, like, a writing retreat, or an 'agricultural internship,' or something like that. She'll be fine with it. She'll probably be relieved not to have me at home for the summer. My sister's living there while she finishes law school, and she and I do not belong under the same roof, trust me. Anyway, all of this will be done before you know it." Again, she gestures vaguely to her stomach when she says "this," but it's not funny like it was a minute ago.

*"Plus," Carrie says, clearing her throat, "my mom will be much more okay with the whole 'me going to live on a farm' thing if she knows"—*here we go, *thinks Maya—"that we're doing it together."*

"I can't," Maya says quickly—too quickly. Carrie flinches, stung. Maya softens her tone. "I'm sorry," she says, "but I have the internship with Professor DeLisle. It starts right after graduation." Maya has been hired by her philosophy professor to help with some clerical and administrative work this summer. He's having surgery in June and won't be completely mobile, so in addition to being sort of an office assistant, she'll also do some errands for him, help him to and from his car, and so forth. She is excited about it. She loved Professor DeLisle's class junior year, and this job will be way more interesting than working at the coffee shop. He runs a summer honors class and he said he'd let her grade some papers. It pays more than the coffee shop, too. A little more, anyway.

Carrie scoffs. "That's not really an internship. You're basically babysit-ting an invalid. I'm sure he can find someone else to bring him extra toilet paper."

Maya's eyes darken. "He's not an invalid. *He's in his fifties! He's just having bunion surgery. And I'm going to be helping him with other more academic things, too." Why does she even feel the need to justify her internship to Carrie? Maybe it isn't* People *magazine, but it's a great summer job, and a good addition to her résumé. "And I'm going to need the money if I'm really going to try to live in New York with you." Maya still hasn't agreed to Carrie's New York plan, but she hasn't shut it down, either, and she's been applying to jobs there, somewhat to her own surprise. While she doesn't want to move to New York just because Carrie wants her to, she loves the idea of moving to a city where she could feel so anonymous. If she was in New York, she could finally say goodbye to the Maya who was unceremoniously left on her grandma's front steps when she was four. She could be brand new— anyone she wanted. And she's had a few good leads, some phone interviews set up. One in particular at an education nonprofit in Brooklyn that she's really excited about.*

"Please, Maya. I need *you to do this with me. I can't go live with these people by myself. It'd be so awkward. And then I'll be all alone when I deliver the baby? Come on. I would do this for you."*

Maya searches Carrie's eyes carefully. "You could still tell Pete, you know. I know he'd be there for you."

"Ugh. Enough with that already. I know what he'd say, and it's absolutely not what I have in mind, so I'm not going to tell him. It's for his own good, anyway. Spare him the messy emotions, you know? What he doesn't know can't hurt him. We're practically officially broken up as is, besides." Maya wonders if Pete is aware of that, or if their new relationship status is known only to Carrie.

Maya takes a measured breath. "Okay, look. Let's see how this all shakes out with these people first," she says. "The health-services lady probably still needs to talk to her cousin, right? Let's just see what she says, and get some details; then, if it's really happening, I'll think about coming with you."

"It had better *really happen," Carrie says impetuously. "I don't know what the hell I'm going to do otherwise."*

"Don't you need to learn more about these people before you commit to anything?" Maya presses. "Do you know anything else about them, other than that she's a nurse?"

"I'm sure they're great. They live on a farm and want a baby. Vermonters are salt of the earth. We know this. I just hope they're on board with it." Carrie looks at Maya imploringly. "And you, too. Seriously. I can't do this by myself. We can spend the whole summer finding you a kick-ass job for when we get to New York. And we can put on your résumé that this was a sustainable-farming intensive or something, like I said."

"But I won't make any money!" Maya reminds her.

"I'll give you my confirmation money. Seriously, I'll do anything. How much were you going to earn with DeLisle, like, eight bucks an hour?"

Fifteen, *Maya corrects silently. But she says nothing.*

"I need *you, Maya. Please."*

Maya looks at Carrie. She thinks about their rule. Never leave a party without telling the other one. Never walk home alone. For all her faults, Carrie has never once abandoned Maya. Even if she was wasted, she always found her. Always. And Carrie has gone out of her way to make sure Maya is included in literally everything she was invited to, from the first day of freshman year. These things might not sound like much, but to Maya, whose own parents didn't even want to be with her, being chosen and having a friend who sticks around no matter what is everything.

And if the situation were reversed—which it never, ever, ever would be, *Maya can't help but note silently—Maya knows that Carrie really would go with her, as she claims. Of this, Maya has no doubt. She wishes she did. It might enable her to say no.*

Maya takes a shaky breath. "Okay. If this really happens, I'll go with you." She knows even now that she'll come to regret this, though she could never imagine how much. But when Carrie hugs her fiercely with gratitude, Maya closes her eyes and hugs her back tightly.

CHAPTER THIRTY-THREE

When I get home, I sit at my office desk and eat my sandwich, unable to think of anything but Maya, maybe not too far away, eating the very same sandwich. Why is she still in town?

I also think of how I owe Agnes Curry from the school a call, but I'm going to put that off for as long as possible. What is there to say, anyway? That it wasn't Kelsey who pulled the alarm, but the girl we were responsible for sending to school with her, who was essentially doing it on Kelsey's behalf? We're still to blame, either way.

Besides, Kelsey is gone, for at least a few days. It's not like we're trying to convince them to allow her back to school on Monday.

I send Kelsey another text. I hope you're doing okay. I hope you can forgive me, eventually. Having you as my daughter is the greatest joy of my life.

The text turns green. Her phone is off.

Her phone is never off.

But maybe Pete took her to a Broadway matinee, like he said he was going to. Or maybe she's taking a nap. The idea of her getting some rest brings me peace. I decide not to text Pete again, for the moment. He probably would prefer I give him some space. Understandably.

I stare at my computer. I contemplate trying to work, but I know I wouldn't accomplish anything. I consider watching a show, but I know I would never be able to focus on it.

Mr. Sparkles meows from my doorway. Shit. I forgot to feed him. Add him to the long list of those whom I've wronged. He's obviously mad that Lola is gone, too, in addition to being hungry.

As I look at him, an odd recollection pings into my brain. I shut my eyes tightly, trying to grasp it more firmly so that I can make sense of it.

An orange cat, weaving in and out of two stone pillars. *What am I remembering?*

But the memory isn't about the cat. Not really.

It's about Lola.

She was allergic to cats.

That weekend we spent with them at a bed-and-breakfast in the Hudson Valley when the girls were eight—there was a cat who lived on the property. It belonged to the owners. Maya asked that they do their best to keep the cat out of the common areas while we were having meals, because Lola was very allergic.

Very allergic, she said.

It's been hard to trust myself lately, what with my inexcusable actions and decisions, but of this recollection, I'm sure.

People outgrow allergies all the time, I suppose. It might not mean anything.

But it might.

A compulsion comes over me: an itch that needs immediate scratching.

I type "Lola Callahan" into my Google search bar. I scroll down through a few irrelevant items until I find a link from an upstate New York NBC affiliate news site that grabs my attention. When I open it, my blood freezes in my veins.

Father and Daughter Killed in Alleged DWI Crash

A Catskills community is mourning the loss of a fifteen-year-old girl and her father who died tragically late Tuesday night when their car hit a tree.

Louisa (Lola) Callahan was a rising sophomore at Stone Ridge High School who loved punk rock music and skiing. Elliot Callahan was a local real estate agent who did carpentry in his spare time and, according to neighbors, had recently begun treatment for alcohol addiction. They are survived by wife and mother Maya Matthews.

A private service will be held at Humiston Funeral Home. In lieu of flowers, a request has been made for donations to Mothers Against Drunk Driving.

The article includes a picture of Maya, Elliot, and a girl smiling widely in front of a firepit. I squint at the photo and realize that I'm looking at her teeth, none of which are chipped. They are wearing down jackets, holding mugs with what look like marshmallows peeking out above the tops. They look warm and happy. The girl has that sheepishly resistant but secretly pleased expression that only teenagers who've been coerced into taking a photograph with their parents can wear so perfectly. Elliot has a long arm wrapped around both Maya and—well, Lola, I guess, except it isn't the Lola I know.

And Maya said Elliot died just a few days before she arrived in Montauk, but the article is from late August, almost three months ago.

My head spins.

I look at the picture more closely. And I see that the face of the girl is undeniably the same face as the child we spent a weekend with seven years ago in the Hudson Valley.

So *this* is Lola.

It's just not the Lola who stayed in our home for the past week.

I grip my desk, trying to steady myself; even though I'm sitting down, I feel as if I might fall over.

Lola is dead?

Maya's daughter, Lola, is dead? I immediately put myself in Maya's shoes, and my body sags with the weight of this news. Maya's daughter is dead.

But also: If Lola is dead, who was the girl with Maya? And why did she tell us it was Lola? *What the hell is Maya doing?* It doesn't make sense. None of it makes sense.

I think of Lola—or who I thought was Lola until a few seconds ago. Of her pointy chin, her gangly limbs, her height, her dimple. The loaded looks that occasionally passed between her and Maya.

My yearbook photo under her pillow. The sandwich she made me. Her strange questions about my past. Her hurt when I asked her if she'd messed with my computer.

And suddenly, I know exactly who she is. The answer, as impossible as it seems, is inevitable. The truth lives within me, trapped underneath layers of bone. It has for the past twenty years.

Maybe a small part of me always knew who she really was.

After all, how could I not?

And then I hear the door open.

~

2003

Maya breathes deeply, trying to calm herself enough to go to sleep. But her heart is pounding, and the creaking from the bed above as Carrie tosses and turns is difficult to ignore. Maya hasn't slept in a bunk bed since their sophomore year, and she's reminded of how much she hated it. She probably should have offered Carrie the bottom bunk, since she's nearly eight months pregnant and gets up to pee all the time, but they'd both just assumed their old bunk positions. Force of habit.

"Are you awake?" Maya whispers needlessly, already knowing she is.

"Yeah," Carrie whispers back.

"What do you think so far?" Maya asks.

"Well, this bed isn't that comfortable. But the house is big and the yard is pretty," Carrie says.

"Not about the house, you lunatic. I mean about Julia and Dan."

Carrie laughs briefly. "Oh. Um, they're fine, I guess? Julia seems nice," she responds quietly.

Nice enough to give your baby to? *Maya wants to ask. Julia is sweet, but she and Dan are weird. For one thing, being in their house feels like stepping back in time; they have one small TV in the kitchen and a rotary phone, but otherwise, there is almost no technology around (and no Wi-Fi, so Maya's chances to job hunt while she's here, as Carrie promised, aren't looking good). There's Jesus paraphernalia everywhere; they're some sort of hard-core evangelical Christians—Seventh Day Adventists maybe. Dan prayed over Carrie's stomach when they first arrived and made several mentions of Julia's "failure" to get pregnant, as if it were a sin (which, in his mind, it probably was). Julia looked so downcast every time he brought it up.*

By dinnertime, it was obvious that Julia does all the cooking and cleaning in their house; Dan hadn't lifted a finger to help and then held court over the table as if he were king. He made sure to thank Jesus for the meatloaf, but not Julia, which irked Maya, since Julia was the one who made it, not Jesus. Dan drank whole milk, which Maya found mildly repulsive, and Julia refilled it for him anytime it was almost empty. Dan read them a Bible passage about how children are a reward from God and looked at Carrie pointedly as he said it, though he refrained from actually chastising her for her immoral behavior and refusal to accept God's gift; she was giving it to him, after all. He couldn't come down on her too hard, at least not out loud, even though it was clearly what he was thinking. Maya felt like she'd stumbled into a chapter from The Handmaid's Tale.

At one point, Maya got up the nerve to ask about what the schools around here were like, and Dan looked at her disdainfully. "Not good, and I should know. I used to be a teacher, before I realized that schools aren't interested in actually educating children. This child will be homeschooled," he said firmly, and Julia glanced up at Maya and Carrie from her mashed potatoes, nodding in what Maya thought might have been reluctant agreement. It was then, too, that Maya spotted the worrying, hand-shaped bruise on her forearm, and Maya understood that disagreeing with Dan probably wasn't an option for her.

Julia really did seem elated about the baby, though. Her eyes glowed when she looked at Carrie's belly, and she'd doted on both Carrie and Maya since the second they'd shown up at the ramshackle farmhouse that had apparently belonged to Julia's parents before they'd passed away. Like her cousin Debbie from Middlebury's health services, Julia was also a nurse, and she had some equipment on hand to listen to the baby's heartbeat. Her eyes filled with tears when she heard it. "And you're really going to give us this gift," she marveled, gazing at Carrie with disbelief and wondrous gratitude. She told them they were going to name the baby Shauna if it was a girl, and Ian if it was a boy, because both of those names meant "God is gracious." Dan was standing in the doorway when she said it, and Maya saw him nod approvingly. Maya doesn't have to wonder who chose the names. She can't believe that this is the home that Carrie's baby will grow up in. That these people are the adoptive parents.

And that so far, Carrie seems fine with it.

"Adopt" isn't the right word, anyway—there isn't going to be any kind of formal adoption. As Carrie explained to Maya before they arrived here, Julia and Dan will claim to be the biological parents on the forms and have Debbie sign off as the midwife on their home birth. Julia assured them that they don't see a lot of people, just their church group, who will all be thrilled with the new blessing and not ask a lot of questions about how it came to

be, and the elderly lady she cares for at night, who is completely senile. So no one will contest that she was pregnant (and to be honest, she is sort of on the big side, anyway).

Maya and Carrie will leave after the baby is born, as if they were never there at all, a puff of smoke disappearing into the air.

"And Dan? What do you think of him?" Maya presses, wanting to confirm that Carrie was as put off by him as she was. *Julia told them that it was just as well that Dan wasn't teaching anymore, anyway, because the church really needs him, and also he is very busy with projects at home (the main one being, from what Maya can tell, building and organizing a sort of bunker in their garage, preparation for the end of days). Maya can only imagine what came to pass that concluded his teaching career.*

Carrie sighs. "Look, he's a bit eccentric, and his whole religious vibe is definitely not my cup of tea, but at least we know they're good people, right? People of God, or whatever. It'll be loved. Cared for."

Maya cringes at Carrie's use of the word "it," but Carrie doesn't see.

If the baby is a girl, she'll be taught that a woman's job is to serve men, *Maya wants to retort.* And being religious does not make someone good. Are you really that stupid? This is your child! *Maya wants to scream.* How can you not care?

As if Carrie can read her thoughts, she says flatly, "Don't get emotionally invested, Maya. It won't do either of us any good." And then, in a softer tone: "Thank you for coming with me. Really. I couldn't do this without you." And that's exactly what Maya fears most: that she is partly responsible for what will happen to this child, to the Ian or the Shauna who grows up here in this dark, creaky house, with Dan at its helm. It's a responsibility that she wants no part of.

CHAPTER THIRTY-FOUR

"Hello?" I call out, hoping I imagined the sound of the door opening but knowing that I didn't.

"It's me," Maya calls in a singsong voice, as if she's just back from a grocery run. As if she didn't storm out of my house last night, seemingly for good.

Shaking, I get up from my desk chair and walk to the front door. She's standing there holding a bottle of wine, swaying slightly. *Is she drunk?* She closes the door behind her. I glance outside, but her car isn't out front. "I thought we could talk," she says, her eyes darting in front of her, not meeting mine. "I didn't like the way we left things. Sorry to sneak up on you like this, but I was worried that if I asked to come back, you'd say no."

"Exactly how you showed up in the first place," I murmur, bewildered.

"I guess," Maya says. She takes off her coat and tries to toss it on the bench, but it slips to the floor instead. She doesn't bother picking it up.

"You're here alone?" I ask her, glancing outside.

"Yes," Maya says. "Lola is—"

"I know that wasn't Lola," I blurt out. "I don't know what you think you're doing, or why you brought her here, but—"

"Carrie, can we please go upstairs and talk about this?" She gestures toward the wine. "I can explain everything. Let's just hash this out like civilized people, okay?" Except she looks anything but civilized; there's a sheen on her face, and the circles under her eyes are so dark they look like bruises. Her hair is wild.

Part of me knows I should just kick her out. She lied to me. And with her vacant eyes and swaying shoulders, I'm a little afraid of her right now.

But I'm also worried about her. If what I read is true—that Maya's lost her daughter—I can't imagine anything worse.

And I can't just turn my back on her. *Never leave the other one alone at a party. Never make the other one walk home alone.* These were our most sacred rules.

"Fine," I say. "Let's go up. Pete and Kelsey aren't here."

"I know. Pete texted me to say goodbye," she says softly. "He really is a great guy, you know," she adds admonishingly. I narrow my eyes at her.

We walk upstairs single file. Maya takes out two stemless glasses from the cupboard that she organized and pours wine into them at the sink, her back to me. She brings them over to the table and we sit. Civilized, just like she wanted. She pushes my glass over to me, and I take a sip from it tentatively. It's an Oregon pinot, and I can tell from the bottle that it's expensive, but I can barely taste it.

"So where is she?" I ask her, not needing to clarify who I mean.

"I dropped her off at the train station," Maya says. "She's heading home. She lives in the city now. In Kew Gardens. She's lived there for a few years."

I try to focus my eyes on the table, feeling like I might pass out. The words coming out of Maya's mouth are dizzying. "I just don't understand. When did you get in touch with her? Why did you bring her here? And Lola—I mean the real Lola, your Lola—she . . . ?" I can't bring myself to say the word out loud.

Maya shuts her eyes tightly. "Lola," she says slowly, deliberately, as if conjuring her. "You know, when I sleep, I can literally feel the skin of her back under my hand like I'm scratching it, which I did almost every night. And I'm so sure that she's really there, that it was all a mistake, a bad dream. But of course, then I wake up and realize that she's not there and never will be again." Maya's face twists and she moves her hands to her ears, unable to endure the sound of her own agonizing words.

I swallow hard. As angry as I am at Maya right now, I can see the depth of her pain. Feel it, too. Without thinking, I reach out and touch her hand, gently removing it from her face, and she doesn't stop me. "So she was with your husband, in the car?" I ask quietly.

Maya's eyes are still closed tightly. She nods. "Yes. Everything I told you was true—he went to the dump to drop off our armoire, and then to a bar. Lola was supposed to be sleeping at a friend's house, but she didn't feel well and wanted to come home. She called me, but I was asleep and missed the call. We'd already texted each other good night, so I thought she was okay. If only I'd—if I had just—" Sobs rack Maya's body. "But I didn't. So she called him, and he picked her up when he was drunk. And now they're both gone."

I tighten my grip on her hand. "I'm sorry, Maya. So, so sorry. Truly."

She opens her eyes, finally, and wipes a tear away.

And then she snatches her hand back, and her expression hardens again.

I clear my throat. "How did you find Shauna? Why did you bring her here? What were you trying to do?"

She takes a sip of wine and swishes it around her mouth. "I never really stopped thinking about her. Worrying about her. How could I not, knowing who we'd left her with? She always occupied this little space in the back corner of my head. Especially after I had a daughter of my own, and I saw how precious she was, how much love she needed

200

and deserved." Maya looks at me carefully. "Did that not happen to you?"

It did, of course. After I had Kelsey, Shauna came back into my mind like a flood. Kelsey came so quickly—I labored for only a few hours, and then it was time to push—three big pushes and she was out. "Surprising, for a first birth to be so fast," the nurses said. "You're lucky!" I shrugged at them uncomfortably, remembering my *real* first birth, which hadn't been nearly as quick. And when I took Kelsey home and marveled over her tiny fingers and toes as I nursed her, of *course* I thought about Shauna. Of course I did. What kind of monster wouldn't?

But I also knew I had to focus on the baby in front of me, not the one I'd left behind. So I gently placed Shauna back in the compartment of my mind she'd always been in, one that occupied considerable space but remained firmly bolted shut. It was easier that way. No. It was the *only* way. Especially because, if I'd known then, when I gave her up, that I'd end up married to Pete with a baby five years later anyway, maybe I would have made a different choice. But I was a delusional twenty-two-year-old who cared way too much what other people thought and who was sure my life was going to be different, exciting, special. I didn't realize then it was going to be exactly like everyone else's.

In hindsight—

But that's way too big a mistake to admit, even silently, even to oneself. So I never have.

"I did think about her," I manage, clearing my throat. "All the time. Always."

Maya nods with exaggerated skepticism, knowing me too well to believe me. "Sure. Well, I used to google her and her family every now and then, and one day my search came up with an obituary. Julia died when Shauna was fourteen. Ovarian cancer. So she was left all alone with *him*." She looks at me carefully. "You never looked them up? You weren't curious?"

I shake my head. "I couldn't. I didn't want to know. It would have made it impossible to function." I shudder. "That's terrible about Julia."

Maya is looking past me. "I was even more worried about her when I saw that, but I always held back from reaching out. It didn't feel like my place. She was never mine, after all. And yet, I always felt culpable. If I'd refused to go with you that summer like I should have, you might have been forced to figure out something better for her. To tell your mom, probably. You always hated doing anything alone. I enabled you." She shakes her head, angry at herself.

"After Lola died," she continues, choking a little on the word, "I couldn't get Shauna off my mind. Maybe it was because I needed someone else to think about. Or maybe it was because I was able to sort of . . . reevaluate life, in some way. Because you never know when your last day will come and it will be too late to right wrongs or explore things that mattered to you. And Shauna . . ." Maya trails off and looks at me finally, a pensive, dreamy expression on her face.

"What?" I prompt her to go on.

"I realized Shauna was my unfinished business. Something I had to make good on before my time came. I knew she was twenty by this point, so I was too late to save her in any kind of a meaningful way. But I had to know where she was, whether she was okay. And if she wasn't, I wanted to help her. I owed her that."

Maya takes a huge gulp of her wine. It's unusual for her to be drinking so eagerly. "How did you find her?" I ask, my voice almost inaudible.

Maya lets out a too-loud laugh. "Believe it or not, on social media. She's very into TikTok. She told me she never had a phone until she left home, so she's sort of making up for lost time, I suppose. She's living in Kew Gardens, like I said, with two roommates. Sort of like our dorm-room days, right? Crazy, that she was only, like, ten miles from you all this time. You may have even passed her on the street sometime. She works at a Biscuits and Bath on the East Side."

I look at her blankly.

"It's a pet day care," she tells me. *A pet day care.* Hence her ease with Mr. Sparkles. "Anyway, I sent her a message. I told her I was a friend of her mother, which was true even though she thought I was talking about Julia, and asked her if she wanted to meet. We had lunch, and I told her everything. She was shocked, of course. She'd always thought Julia and Dan were her biological parents. Just like everyone else did. But as soon as I showed her a picture of you . . . it was like she recognized you." Maya closes her eyes again, recalling this encounter. "When I gave her your picture, she reached out and touched your face, and it was clear to me that I didn't have to convince her I was telling the truth; she already knew."

I am scared to ask what I want to. "And was she—is she—all right? Growing up with Dan, was it . . . ?"

Maya opens her eyes and looks at me sharply. "It wasn't good, Carrie. You knew it wouldn't be. Please don't pretend to be surprised." She shakes her head coldly. "Her mom was loving, but they had to walk on eggshells together, and then after Julia passed, she had to walk on eggshells by herself." Maya takes another gulp of wine and shudders. "She said he went off the deep end after Julia died. Julia had always taken care of everything around the house, and he just couldn't function. He became even more radical in his beliefs, convinced the end of the world was coming, spending all his time at the church. He had Shauna get a job at the local diner to help support them, and that was the first time she learned that not everyone lived like they did, thought like Dan did." My heart races with fear and shame when I think of Shauna in that house all alone with him. I look at Maya, silently imploring her to continue, even though her words feel like hundreds of tiny cuts on my skin.

"Dan failed to file any homeschool paperwork, as Julia had always done, so Child Protective Services came, and when they saw that she was basically taking care of herself, they took her away. But she was already sixteen by then, so they told her she had the option to emancipate herself instead of going into foster care, which is what she did. She got her GED, too. She's really smart," Maya says, looking at me pointedly, her expression softening for just a second. How many times in college had she assured me that I was smart while I was crying about an impending test? Hundreds, probably.

Then her face hardens again. "And that's when she moved to New York. CPS connected her with another emancipated teen they'd worked with, so that's how she found her apartment. She wants to be a veterinarian. She's taking classes; she was eligible for some scholarships and financial aid because of her emancipation status."

"And he . . . ? He never . . . ?" My heart is pounding so loudly I'm sure Maya can hear it. I'm terrified to ask the question, and even more so to hear the answer.

Maya looks at me, evidently deciding if I deserve to hear what she's going to say next. After what feels like a weeklong silence, she says, "She told me he never hurt her. Not physically, anyway. Guess he saved all that for Julia. He sure as hell wasn't a great dad, but neglect is better than what we both know it could have been." She purses her lips tightly and then adds, "By the way, she told me she really did chip her tooth on a bunk bed."

A relief so profound I've never known it fills my bones. I breathe a sigh so deep it fills my whole heart.

Maya continues to glare at me. "And she really wanted to meet you. She asked me right away if I could take her to you. So I came up with this plan because I knew you'd never agree to see her otherwise. You wouldn't have wanted her messing up your perfect little life, exposing your dirty, inconvenient secrets."

"That's not true. I would have—"

"No, Carrie. You wouldn't have," she cuts me off. I say nothing, knowing that she's right. "So I told her I'd bring her, and that she could pretend to be Lola, and then she could decide what came next—whether she wanted to tell you the truth. My part would be over. My—everything would be over."

"Meaning what?"

Maya pauses, takes a breath. "Meaning that this, reuniting Shauna with her biological mother after the hell she went through as a child, was going to be the last thing I'd ever do. Because . . ." Maya clears her throat carefully. "I was going to kill myself when it was done."

"Maya." I let out a gasp and then choke on it, tears immediately forming in my eyes.

"What, Carrie? What?" she snaps. "My daughter and husband are gone, and if there was even a chance that I could see Lola again in some kind of afterlife, or whatever, well, I was very willing to take that chance. I don't believe in that, anyway, but honestly, it would be heaven simply not to wake up every day and remember that my girl is gone." I remember the notes that I found in Maya's room—"I'm so sorry"—and in hindsight, they were probably attempts at drafting her suicide note.

She straightens her posture, composes herself. "But being with you—everything came back to me. Your selfishness. Your inability to accept responsibility for *anything*. Like what Dan did to me."

I shudder, quaking under the weight of Maya's stony gaze.

"And then you told me about your affair, and I saw that you were still the same self-centered girl you were when you were twenty-two. And I didn't want you to get away with it this time. Treating Pete like that." She clicks her tongue. "You really haven't changed." She pauses for a second again, musing. "And Pete hasn't changed, either, but in a good way. He's as sweet and funny and wonderful as he always was. So I was *going* to commit suicide, but then . . ." She trails off.

My hands are shaking and my vision is starting to speckle. "Then what?" I manage. Barely.

Maya glowers at me and shrugs. "Then I changed my mind."

~

2003

When Maya gets upstairs to their bedroom, her whole body is trembling. It feels like chills, but they're sharper, more pronounced—convulsions, almost.

Carrie is unsurprisingly already in bed; she's been exhausted lately, days away from giving birth, and she spends as much time horizontal as possible. She still sleeps in the top bunk, but during the day, she maroons herself in Maya's bed, since it's easier for her to get in and out of. She spends much of the day reading, napping, and eating the meals that Julia brings to her on a tray, along with tea, and ginger ale in glasses filled with ice. Plenty of snacks. Julia says she wants her baby nice and plump. And Carrie seems content to be waited on. She is treating this like some kind of bizarre vacation.

Staying up here also means Carrie doesn't have to interact with Dan at all, be subjected to his lectures on how the government is planning to destroy all the roads and vaccines have microchips and the internet will cause the end of the human race. And Maya has to assume that the avoidance is intentional on her part—the less she learns about Dan, the easier it will be for her to leave her baby in his care, when the time comes.

But Maya needs her to know what just happened. She has to hear it. Whether she wants to or not.

Carrie rolls over when she hears Maya come in. "Hey," she murmurs. "Where were you?"

"I was helping clean up after dinner," she says, and the memory of it comes over her like an avalanche—Dan pressing up against her from behind as he reached around her to fill his water glass.

Maya froze and tried to pull away, but there wasn't anywhere to go; she was stuck in between his body and the sink.

"Excuse me," she whispered. But he didn't budge. In fact, the pressure he was putting on her increased slightly, his groin against the back of her shorts.

"No," she mustered.

And then his glass was full, and he backed away.

"Not a lot of elbow room in here," he said by way of explanation. "I'll leave you to the rest of these dishes," he added. "And you know, you should find some more appropriate clothes to wear. Is that how you want to present yourself to God and the world?"

Maya is wearing cutoffs and a T-shirt. They aren't even short cutoffs. But why is she reflecting on her outfit? Her clothes aren't the fucking problem. Intellectually, she knows that. And yet, it's hard work washing off the training that she and all girls have received about looking at themselves first when trying to figure out why a boy or man took something from them that they didn't want to give.

"Be careful with that gravy boat," Dan called as he walked out of the kitchen. "It's a family heirloom."

Julia walked back into the kitchen as Dan exited it, having come back down from making sure Carrie had enough ice water in her room. Maya stayed at the sink, unable to move, her hands gripping it so tightly her knuckles were white. "Everything all right?" Julia asked quietly. But Maya knew that she didn't want the answer, and that she likely already knew it, anyway. That Julia's keen ability to turn a blind eye to Dan's behavior is probably her biggest asset in this marriage. And her biggest detriment. That Dan could yell at her in the scary way he did, and she would bring him tea, or fucking milk, two minutes later. That Dan could grab Julia's arm, squeezing her flesh until it turned red, all because his favorite shirt was still hanging wet on the clothesline, and she'd apologize for not hanging it earlier in the day.

The worst part is that Maya is fairly certain that Julia actually loves Dan, somehow. They've been together since high school, Julia told them proudly, and she unfailingly speaks highly of him.

If this is love, Maya never wants it. Ever.

Back in their room, Maya's body shakes as she moves toward her bed, the one that Carrie is lying on, and she perches on the end of it. Carrie puts her hand on her friend's leg, and Maya flinches. "Are you okay?" Carrie asks.

Maya turns to her. "Carrie," she breathes. "You can't give your baby to these people. You just can't." She's been wanting to say it ever since they arrived. Now, she can no longer hold it in.

"What are you talking about?" Carrie whispers, agitation creeping into her tone.

It spills out of Maya, what happened in the kitchen.

Carrie looks at her wide eyed. "Are you sure he wasn't just standing a little too close to you? It was really on purpose?"

Maya feels, again, like she's been assaulted. "Yes, Carrie, I'm sure."

Carrie sits up in bed with some difficulty. Her bump is much, much bigger now than it was when they first arrived, and even than it was a week ago. There really is a baby in there.

"Shit." She sighs. "Shit. Shit." She looks at Maya imploringly. "Look, I know he isn't the best guy. But . . . he stopped when you said no, right? It's not like he . . . ?"

Maya's brain feels as if it is being twisted and wrung out like a wet paper towel. "No, Carrie, he didn't rape me. But is that really the standard we're holding men to? Men that are going to be raising your baby? He's not a good person," Maya says, trying to be as plain and simple in her language as possible. "This isn't going to be a good place for your baby to grow up."

"Dammit, Maya!" Carrie yells. It might be the first time Carrie has ever yelled at her. "Don't you think I know that! I'm not blind, okay? I'm not an idiot. But it's too late! It's too fucking late." Tears stream down Carrie's face. "I said they could have the baby, and that's what I have to do. Do you think I don't see how absurdly fucked up this is? How badly I screwed up, as usual? But I have to see this through. I am leaving here without a baby. That's what's happening. And you're making it so much harder by—"

"By pointing out the truth? That this is a huge mistake?" Maya yells back. Carrie motions pleadingly for Maya to lower her voice, and she does. "The baby's going to be taught that women are basically servants and the world's gonna end any day now and it's okay to hurt your wife and gay people are going to hell. The baby won't be safe here. Not with him."

"It will be okay," Carrie insists. "He's not going to hurt a baby, for God's sake! Besides, Julia will be a great mom. It will all work out."

And Maya sees that she must actually believe this, because it has always been true for her. Her privilege has allowed her to believe that things just have a way of sorting themselves out, that problems get solved, that luck prevails. She doesn't see that for most people, this isn't the case. That terrible things happen to good people every day. And the baby inside her could easily be among the unfortunate ones.

Not giving up yet, Maya shakes her head sadly. "But babies grow up, Carrie. And yours will be growing up here. In this place. With him."

Carrie's eyes flash with anger. "Maya, you aren't getting it. It's not my baby. Not anymore. I already said they could have it, okay? What's done is done. I can't think of it as my baby anymore, because if I did, then yes, I would be running out of here and never looking back. And I can't do that, because then not only would I have to tell my mom and everyone else that I was pregnant, I would also have to tell them about . . ." She gestures around her. "This insanity. What I did. It's just a royal fuckup all around, okay? And the only way to erase it, to make all of it go away, is to give them the baby, like I said I would. And you"—Carrie looks at Maya with a bizarre combination of sheer love and total resentment—"you're making it impossible for me to do the thing that I need to do. Okay? This is my only option. Is it a great option? No. Do I feel sick about it? Yes. More than I can even describe. But you aren't helping."

Maya is silent, stunned, and Carrie presses her fingers over her eyelids, trying to stop the tears from coming. "These people are getting this baby. I'm moving to New York childless to start work and resume my life. That's what's happening. It's too late to change course. This is my decision, okay? I really appreciate you being here with me, and I'm so sorry about what happened tonight, with Dan. Truly. I mean, that's fucking awful. But when it comes to the baby, you aren't in charge here."

Maya blinks at Carrie incredulously and stands up. She knows that Carrie's right; what happens to the baby is not Maya's decision.

But it is her decision whether she stays here with Carrie. And she's had enough. More than enough. "Understood," *she says tightly.* "You go ahead. But I'm out of here."

Carrie sits up straighter, panic overtaking her face. "What? You can't leave me here. Come on, are you serious? Look, again, I'm sorry! I know how bad this is, but—" *Carrie gets up with difficulty to start walking toward Maya, who has grabbed her bag from underneath the bed and started stuffing clothes from the dresser inside it.*

But Carrie stops suddenly, eyes widening with fear and confusion as a puddle forms at her feet. "Holy shit," *she says.*

Maya turns to look at her and comprehends with dread what's happening. "Oh my God. I'll get Julia. Stay here."

CHAPTER THIRTY-FIVE

"You . . . changed your mind?" I whisper, struggling to process. "Good. You can't kill yourself, Maya. I'm glad you aren't thinking that way anymore."

Maya says nothing but gets up and pours herself a glass of water. She downs it and then remains standing by the sink. I realize I'm very thirsty, too, but I am too timid to ask Maya for a glass, or even to walk over to the sink and get it myself. The house suddenly feels, unequivocally, like Maya's territory.

When Maya turns around to speak again, the light has left her eyes; she looks like a different person entirely. "You know, my whole life, I've always been the one to step aside, to make room. I molded myself, made myself as small as possible to try to make my parents stay, and when that didn't work, I made myself even smaller for my grandma. I did the same thing for you, in our friendship. Honestly, it's probably what you liked about me, isn't it? That I was your sidekick, your supporting role." *No. I just liked you,* I want to scream in protest. *I liked everything about you and I couldn't believe how lucky I was that we got assigned as roommates. And you were so smart, and I thought that if you liked me, maybe it meant that I was smart, too. That I belonged. And you were funny and kind, and you wanted to go see that stupid poodle in the library on the first freaking day, which was basically the coolest thing I'd ever heard, that you cared that little about doing what everyone else was doing and what they thought of you.*

But Maya's eyes are still glazed, and I know she wouldn't hear me if I said any of this, anyway.

I gulp air as quickly as I can. "If you hated being friends with me so much, why were you? Why didn't you just stop hanging out with me?"

Maya's eyes snap back to life. "I've thought about that so many times. And I'm embarrassed to admit that being in your orbit made me feel special. It made me feel safe. There's something about you that . . . gleams. And I liked being part of that. I liked *you*. I *loved* you. 'Chosen family,' right? That's what you always said. And that meant something to me. No. It meant *everything* to me." She shrugs. "But in retrospect, I think our friendship was always more your choice than mine." She slams her water glass down, startling me. "And that changes now. It's time for me to be an active participant in my own life, instead of always stepping aside. Like I did when you and Pete met, too, even though I had feelings for him." She sees my shocked expression and scoffs. "Don't pretend you didn't know! You must have."

"I didn't," I manage, my tongue thick. And it's true. I had no idea. But that might make it even worse, not better. Because how could I have been so oblivious to my best friend's feelings?

She shakes her head, dismissing my protest. "And then I just sort of . . . disappeared after you gave Shauna to those people. And you never even *tried* to get me back. You just . . . let me go. Just like you did Shauna. Because it made your life simpler to have her gone, and then to have me gone, too, so you didn't have to be reminded of what you'd done."

"Maya, I've always felt terrible about what I did . . . especially knowing what Dan did to you." I blink hard to try to bring the room back into focus.

"Sometimes I still think about him when I wash dishes," she says. "To this day. I'll be scrubbing a plate, and I'll turn around to make sure I'm alone. But I bet you never gave it another thought. It wasn't a big deal to you," she says, her voice monotone and her eyes vacant.

I have thought about it. It was a big deal. But you're right, in that I couldn't think about it too much because every time I thought about what Dan did to you, I thought about the fact that I still let them have her. And it felt like being stabbed.

"Maya," I plead. "I was a kid. I was a scared, pregnant, stupid, self-ish kid. I regret what I did to you, and I regret giving Shauna to them, but once I got past a certain point, I felt like there was no turning back. I had tunnel vision. I'm not trying to justify any of it, but I just . . . it was the only way out that I could see, at the time. And now, I can see how wrong, how awful, all of it was."

But it's obvious from her stoic face that she isn't registering my words. And I wouldn't, either, if I were her. Even I can hear how cheap they sound, even though I mean them. She shakes her head slightly in apparent disbelief as she mulls it all over, reliving it. "And I just disappeared, rather than call you on any of it. I swallowed what had happened to me, and I kept your secret. To make *your* life easier. Just like I'd always done." She sighs with frustration. "It was like that in my marriage, too. I loved Elliot, and I know he loved me, but I was always bending myself to accommodate his wants and needs. To make sure he was happy and would stay. Because I didn't think I would survive being left again by someone who was supposed to love me." Maya glances around the room maniacally, like she's distracted, before she looks back at me. "So yes. I was *going* to kill myself, but after spending the week here, I decided, why should *I* be the one to go?"

My stomach twists. *What the hell does that mean?*

My phone buzzes, and I look down. A text from Kelsey. I desperately want to open my phone to read it, but I don't want to further enrage Maya.

Maya, who, when I look back up from my phone, is holding the razor that was missing from my shower this morning. My stainless-steel, triple-blade razor, the sharpest one I could find online, because I hate shaving and try to do it as infrequently as possible.

I start to stand up as I struggle to process what's going on. But my limbs feel heavy, and I have to steady myself on the table.

"What are you doing?" I ask. My voice sounds strange and foreign in my own ears. My tongue is thick and soggy like an overly saturated sponge.

Maya's eerie smile has returned. "It would be easy enough, I think," she says, a sort of tenderness in her voice. "Look at you. You've been caught in your affair. Your husband and daughter have left you. You're all alone here. You've been drinking wine and mixed it with Valium. You aren't yourself."

"I didn't . . . ," I try to say, and then I realize. Maya's Valium. That's why I feel so outside my own body right now, why it feels like the room is spinning and I can't quite keep up with it. Maya's put Valium in my wine.

"When I took this razor last night, I wasn't even sure why I was doing it, honestly." She laughs. "I just thought, 'Hmm. Maybe I'll take this. Just in case.' And the more I think about it, you know, it really wouldn't be so difficult for anyone to believe, that at this lowest of low moments in your life, you chose to end it instead of facing the music. It's very much like you. Avoid consequences. Skirt unpleasantness. Slink off instead."

Even in my brain fog, I recall the texts I sent to Pete and Kelsey. *I love you, and I'm so, so sorry.* And *I'm so sorry, honey. I love you forever.* And *Having you as my daughter is the greatest joy of my life.* Those messages could easily be read as goodbyes.

A sob escapes my throat, and for a moment, Maya's face shows something close to pity, though not quite. "Look, I know it's hard. And they'll be sad for a while, sure. But once you're gone, it probably won't take them long to realize what a toxic presence you really were. Besides, you had no problem leaving Shauna behind. What's one more daughter to you, right? At least this time, you know she'll be in better hands."

"Meaning what?" I am gasping, feeling like I can't breathe. The table appears to be moving in front of me, and I grip it tightly to make it stop.

"Meaning me," Maya says slowly, her brows furrowing, eyes focusing, seeking to understand her own words even as she says them, like it's the first time she's realizing what she plans to do. "I'll fill the gaps that you leave behind. I'll be a better mother to Kelsey than you've ever been capable of being. Look at what she went through under your watch. She knew about your affair, didn't she? That's why she messed with your herbs and your manuscript?" She nods at me knowingly; I really can't keep anything from her. Just like in college. "Poor thing. Keeping secrets for people really doesn't feel good. I should know. But I'll make sure she doesn't have to go through that again. I'll love her like she's my own—"

Maya's face darkens, and for a moment she pauses, emotion overtaking her. But, with effort, she masters herself. "Kelsey will be just fine. She'll have a new sister because I'll tell her about Shauna. And Pete should have a wife who appreciates him. Who knows what she has in him. You always thought you could do better. And apparently you still think so. But the truth is that you never deserved Pete. So this time, you're going to be the one making space for *me*. Not vice versa."

"Maya, you're not a killer," I plead. "You're the best person I know."

"You have no idea who I am now," she corrects me, and I see again the frightening depths of loss and pain in her vacant eyes.

"You'll never get away with it," I whisper, trying a different tactic. My voice barely works. I take a few tentative steps back toward the stairs, my legs like jelly, and Maya steps closer to me, maintaining the same distance we had before I managed to move.

She squints as her brain works on calculating the specifics of what it is she's doing. "Sure, there will be evidence that I was here, prints and whatnot, but I've been staying here for a week. So the prints aren't incriminating. And I'm parked at the beach. No one knows I'm here right now." Her eyes brighten slightly, like she can't even believe her own good fortune.

And she doesn't even realize the extent of it. Our Ring camera only works on our deck and in the yard. Her tracks really are covered.

Unless I can somehow get her onto the deck, so that, even if she does manage to hurt me—or worse—she won't get away with it. A neighbor will hear me scream—with any luck, maybe Ryan will be lurking around outside, right below—or at least the Ring camera will capture it. I need to get there. The idea of Kelsey thinking that I killed myself, that I didn't want to stay here on this earth and be in her life, is even worse to me than the threat of dying. I can't allow that to happen. I won't.

I take a huge step toward where Maya is standing to try to trade places with her, but my body is clumsy in its compromised state, and it's not as big of a step as I hoped it would be. I try again, lunging for the deck doors, but Maya intercepts me and takes me down easily. She climbs on top of me, straddling me on the kitchen floor, still holding my razor. I try to push her off me, but for as small as she is, she's strong and able to overpower me, especially since my muscles are weakened from Valium-laced wine. I try desperately to scoot on my back toward the deck door with her still on top of me, even though I have no idea how I'll be able to open the door from my position on the ground.

Maya grabs my wrists and pins my arms to the ground. "Hold still," she hisses through clenched teeth. She grabs my hand and wraps it around the razor and then clutches her hand around mine and starts shoving it toward my other wrist. I pull back with everything I have, but my muscles are like overstretched rubber bands. It feels like one of those dreams where you're trying to run through water.

I close my eyes tightly, unwilling to watch her end my life. Instead, my mind zooms in on a still of Kelsey as a baby, her mouth eagerly finding my breast to nurse, her tiny hand wrapped around my index finger, Pete sitting beside us on the couch, kissing both of our heads.

I remember Shauna, too. How it felt when she kicked inside me, once I realized that those strange flutters I'd been noticing were in fact the movements of a tiny human I was growing. I didn't even hold her after she was born—Julia offered, and I said no. I'm ashamed of that. But I never forgot how it felt to carry her in me, and I think a part of me always has.

Or maybe I never gave her a second thought, and I'm just a selfish, heartless bitch who deserves exactly what I'm getting right now. You decide.

I open my eyes a crack. Maya's expression is wild now, her hand still holding mine with the razor between my fingers, her long arm driving desperately to make the cut. Her short hair is stretched back from her face, making her eyes look slanted. Her neck veins are bulging. Maybe I'm fighting back better than I thought.

And then I realize it isn't me who's making her work so hard. We aren't alone anymore.

Shauna is standing behind Maya, pulling her back by her hair.

I never even heard her come in.

I guess Maya didn't, either.

"Get off her!" Shauna screams. With one jerk of her arm, she succeeds in yanking Maya off me. "Stop it!" She moves her body between mine and Maya's, and then she shoves Maya, hard.

Maya topples all the way back to the staircase and one of her feet catches the second stair, causing her to lose her balance. She falls all the way down and lands with a dull, heavy sound.

CHAPTER THIRTY-SIX

"Maya!" I scream, and scoot down the stairs in a seated position, like a toddler. My legs are still tingling and unsteady, as if I've had an epidural. I'm not sure yet if I can walk properly. But as woozy as I was a minute ago, I feel my mental faculties returning because of being catapulted into crisis mode. *Maya is hurt.*

Maya is splayed out in a heap at the bottom of the stairs. I grab her shoulder with one hand and her cheek with the other. Her eyes are wide open, alert, looking at me. Shauna has followed me down the stairs and is alternating between looking at Maya and looking at me, unsure about what she should be doing.

Carefully, I put my hand on the back of Maya's head to move it off the bottom stair so that she can lie flat.

"Do you think anything's broken?" I ask her frantically. "Is there blood anywhere?" I touch her head, and to my relief, my hand comes back clean.

Maya moves her neck slightly and winces. "I don't think so. I rolled my ankle, that's all. And my back hurts, but that's just being forty-two, right?" To my shock, an almost-smile flashes across her face. Just as quickly, though, it's gone.

"We should get you to a doctor. There's an urgent care in East Hampton."

She shakes her head. "I don't think I need a doctor. Mostly I'm just . . ." She trails off.

"Just what?"

She looks at me squarely, and for the first time since she showed up today, her eyes are no longer glazed, but clear, like she's returned to herself. "Tired. So, so tired."

I look over her limbs once more. "But you're okay?"

Her eyes well with tears. "No, Carrie. I'm not okay. My baby died. She *died*. She just—she died. How did that happen? And why?" She starts sobbing then, and I lie next to her and hug her as tightly as I can, as if I could remove some of her pain by suction force. I hug eighteen-year-old her with her wry half smile and color-coded index cards, and twenty-two-year-old her with her rightful indignation about the grievous mistake I was making, and forty-two-year-old her with her shattered heart, and all the versions of her that I missed the chance to know because I was both too arrogant and too ashamed to face what I'd done and apologize.

I feel Maya's hand reach across my back and pull me even closer. While we lie there, I wish with all my might that there were something I could do to ease her agony. But because I can put myself in her position, I understand perfectly that this wound she has won't ever heal. Some holes can't be filled; they'll stay holes forever.

"Let's get you to bed so you can rest," I say after a long moment has passed. I stand up a little unsteadily, and Shauna helps me get Maya to her feet. I start guiding her into the room that was hers, but then I remember there are no sheets on the bed. "Take my room, instead," I tell her, and I lead her there with Shauna's help.

I tuck her in like she's a little girl and smooth the hair away from her forehead.

"Thanks," Maya says, another sob escaping with the word.

"You can stay here as long as you want," I tell her, hardly able to believe I'm saying it, given everything that's happened, but meaning it entirely.

She locks her eyes with mine for a second, and suddenly, I'm back in our freshman dorm room the first time I met her, when she was sitting on her bed in denim overall shorts, reading *Kindred* and looking at me with a combination of wariness and hope.

Then she closes her eyes, exhausted, and in an instant, decades have passed.

CHAPTER THIRTY-SEVEN

With Maya resting, Shauna and I go upstairs. My heart is still pounding. I put on the kettle, hoping that some strong tea will reinvigorate me and further break down the effects of Maya's Valium.

I look at my phone and finally read Kelsey's text: I know. Thanks. I clutch my phone to my chest and breathe deeply. It may not seem like much, but the fact that she knows how much I love her is everything to me. Kelsey. My amazing girl.

When we're sitting, mugs of tea in front of us, I look at Shauna closely—my other amazing girl, except she isn't mine, not really, not in the way that matters most.

I wonder how I didn't see it earlier. Her eyes, her cheekbones, her height. All the same as mine. And Pete's dimple.

"Thank you," I tell her earnestly. "For saving me. How did you know?"

Shauna shrugs. "I didn't know. I just thought, maybe. She seemed . . . a little off when she dropped me at the train. Manic, sort of. I had a bad feeling."

And you followed your instincts. Like I should have followed mine all those years ago. I clear my throat. "I owe you all the apologies in the world, Shauna, for leaving you the way I did." I want to stop and just end it there, but I owe her more. A lot more. I brace myself to hear my own words, the truth, out loud. "I knew Dan wasn't a good person. I knew it. I just cared more about myself and what people thought of me than I cared about you."

Shauna blinks, and I grab her hand impulsively. She lets me. Our hands are the exact same size and temperature. "It's as terrible as it sounds, and it's the last thing a mother should ever admit, especially given that our role is unfortunately one where self-sacrifice is the highest-possible virtue. But it's the truth. And I apologize. I'll apologize until my dying breath. You deserved better from me."

She blinks quickly, warding off tears that are starting to form. As if he can sense that she's upset, Mr. Sparkles jumps onto her lap and looks at me petulantly, in case I have any doubt about where his allegiance lies. "Thank you," she murmurs. "And I'm not mad at you. Because . . . I don't know. I didn't miss knowing you, since I didn't know there was even a you to miss. And if you'd made a different choice, then I wouldn't be me. I like being me. I'm the me I know." She laughs at herself. "I'm not making sense. But my life is my life. It's my story, and it's the only one I have. It's not all bad, either."

I nod at her gratefully, knowing full well that I don't deserve the grace she's offering me. At the same time, her words are a bitter pill because I realize how right she is—her life really is her story, and hers alone, since I elected not to be part of it.

But I hope it's a story she'll let me hear one day.

"Well, I'm glad you know the truth," I tell her. "I'd love to get to know you better. And I'd like to tell Pete and Kelsey, too, if that's okay with you." I shudder inwardly when I think of having that conversation. Maybe Pete could have eventually forgiven me for the affair, but I know he'll never be able to when he learns what I've concealed from him for all these years, and rightfully so, of course. Regardless of the outcome, though, it's past time for me to be honest. No way out of it but through.

And no matter how angry he is with me, there is no doubt in my mind that he'll still welcome Shauna into his life. That's who he is.

Shauna nods. "I would like that, too. Thanks." She blushes, and even though I now know she's twenty, for a moment she looks twelve, and it's easy for me to imagine her as the little girl I never got to meet. "And I'm sorry about the fire alarm. I think I just got swept up in wanting to feel like Kelsey's sister. Like a real teenager. I don't know. It was stupid. I didn't mean to get Kelsey in trouble."

"I get it. I really do. Besides, you kind of saved her, by giving her a reason to finally tell me the truth about something she's been keeping inside for way too long."

Shauna looks at me inquisitively, and I study her sloped brow line and imagine that within some hidden crevice of the moon, or a parallel dimension, I was always her mother. That I gave her back rubs before bed and wrangled her little fingers into her gloves and took her out to celebratory lunches after science fairs and argued over curfews with her and drove her to look at colleges.

Imagining it will have to be enough. For both of us. It's one of many of my unlived lives. Because as Shauna pointed out, you just get the one.

She glances toward the stairs warily, gesturing lightly toward where Maya is sleeping. "You're really going to let her stay here? She was going to kill you. Why are you taking care of her?"

I pause for a moment, unsure of how to answer. "Because she's my best friend," I finally say simply. "And she's been through hell. I would do anything for her."

Epilogue

Maya stretches her toes in her bed. Her legs are tired; they ended up staying at the freshman barbecue for hours, and mostly she was standing. But it's the good kind of tired, and her calves are tingling pleasurably now that she's lying down.

It's nearly one in the morning, and she and Carrie have just turned off their light. Carrie is breathing deeply, perhaps already asleep; she got slightly drunk, having met a couple of other girls who'd come with flasks and offered to share. Maya had sort of assumed that she and Carrie would part ways when Carrie met people who were cooler than Maya and more like her, but she was wrong; Carrie stayed close to Maya all night, presenting the two of them as a package deal to everyone they met. Every time Maya said she was going to the bathroom, Carrie replied, "Perfect timing. I need to go, too."

Maya, for her part, had fun—more fun than she'd expected to, and probably more fun than she'd have had if she'd slunk off to the library by herself to check out the poodle. The food at the barbecue was good: trays of cheeseburgers and sweet potato fries and mozzarella sticks and greek salads in little cups. Her grandma made the same rotation of casseroles throughout Maya's entire childhood, tuna noodle and chop suey and pot pie bake, and they never went out to eat, except to a diner for Maya's birthday every year. At one point tonight, Maya spilled a little ketchup on Carrie's orange dress and started apologizing profusely, but Carrie put a reassuring hand on her shoulder. "It's your dress now, remember? You can spill whatever you want on it!"

In her unfamiliar but cozy new bed, Maya takes a deep breath and tries to will her brain to fall asleep. They have another orientation event tomorrow at 9:00 a.m.; the school probably intentionally scheduled it that way to deter students from staying up too late partying on the first night, and to get them used to waking up for early classes.

"That was a fun night," Carrie murmurs from the other side of the room, startling Maya. Not asleep yet after all.

"It was," Maya whispers back.

"Should we try to grab a coffee before the thing tomorrow?"

"Sounds good. I'll set my alarm for eight fifteen?"

"Perfect," Carrie says with a yawn. "So glad we got put together," she adds, her words running together with tiredness and tipsiness.

"Me too," Maya replies, and she's surprised by how much she means it. Carrie is snoring softly within seconds, this time certainly asleep. Oh well; as roommates go, some light snoring isn't the worst offense. Maya makes a mental note to pick up earplugs from the campus convenience store tomorrow. She rolls toward the wall and closes her eyes, the glow of a promising first night and a brand-new friendship warming her even more than the comforter that once belonged to her mother, before she was gone.

ACKNOWLEDGMENTS

I am indescribably grateful to everyone who has chosen to read this book—it's a surreal gift that I will never take for granted. Thank you from the bottom of my heart!

Thank you to my agent, Kathy Green, for being a wonderful partner and advocate. I'm so lucky to be working with you.

An enormous thank-you to Erin Adair-Hodges for giving this book a home and a path. Your and Kristen Weber's vision and insight elevated it immeasurably, and you both made the revision process gratifying and genuinely fun. (Also, occasionally I still think about how many times the characters smiled in the first draft. Seriously, what were they smiling about? I am sorry that I can't repay you the time you lost wading through all those inexplicable smiles.)

An infinite thanks to Jodi Warshaw for bringing *Mother of All Secrets* and me into the Lake Union family, as well as the world of authoring. You changed my life!

The entire editing team at Lake Union is so lovely and patient and wise and sharp. I'm floored by your skill and grateful to be learning from you. Thank you, Bill, Kellie, Sarah, Malika, Kyra, and everyone else who worked on this book for your keen eyes, careful consideration, and enthusiasm.

I'm constantly telling my daughters how awesome it is to have a sister, and when your sister is also the best twist predictor and beta reader in the world, it doesn't get any better. (Kevin, if you're reading this, having a brother is great, too, LOL!) Thank you, Ellen, for taking the time to read the book halves and wholes that I send you, and helping nudge these stories in the right directions. I couldn't do this without you!

My parents encouraged (and occasionally bribed!) me to read from a young age, and I'm so glad they did because reading has enhanced my life tremendously. Thank you, Mom and Dad, for that, and more so for your unconditional love and belief in me. (By the way, if you see a woman walking around Manhattan offering free copies of my books to strangers, that is almost definitely my mom and you should totally say hi!)

Thank you to the extended Magidson/Frankel/Bennett families for your love and support, and especially to Erica for your committed PR endeavors!

Hi and thanks to my English students for daily making me appreciate that books are so much more than they seem, and for making work not feel like work.

I crowdsourced a problem I was having while editing this book with my beloved Peloton Moms Book Club on Facebook, and unsurprisingly, they had the answer I was looking for. Thanks for being the only drama-free Facebook group in recorded history and for always recommending the exact book I need.

Likewise, the Bookstagram community is a glorious corner of the internet that I'm so happy to be a part of. Thank you for all the creativity you bring to sharing your love for books and authors.

Carrie may have ambivalent feelings about Montauk, but I love it uncomplicatedly, and it was so fun to place this story there. Thank you to the businesses mentioned for being part of what makes Montauk so special.

While this book is not based on a true story (phew!), my friendships with other women have been so special to me and have taught me so much. Thank you to my amazing girlfriends, old, new, near, and far, for inspiring me, commiserating with me, and bolstering me through all of life's seasons.

The books I've written thus far have involved, among other things, killing awful husbands and having affairs, and somehow when my husband reads them, he thinks they're the best books ever written. (Granted, his comparison pool is admittedly limited; know what I mean, Will Hubbard?) Thank you, Eric, for your unwavering support of me in this new chapter (dad joke alert!) of my professional life. It means everything to me.

Zoey and Margo, being your mom is by far my favorite part of everything. "Happy to be with you." Thanks for helping me grow alongside you. I love you forever and always.

ABOUT THE AUTHOR

Kathleen M. Willett is the author of *Mother of All Secrets*. An English teacher who grew up in New Jersey and London, Kathleen lives in New York City with her husband, two daughters, and a cat named Mr. Sparkles. For more information, visit www.kathleenmwillett.com.